Never Just Enough

E.V. Thorne

Thorne & Dagger

Cover art and design by E. V. Thorne

Cover photo by seth0s via Pixabay

First Edition: 2025

ISBN: 979-8-9995206-0-9

Published by Thorne & Dagger

www.thorneanddagger.com | www.evthorne.com

For my husband.

Thank you for being the kind of steady that never asks me to be anything but what I am—even when that means too loud, too late, or too much. You are the calm to my storm and the place I never have to try to belong.

She was too much. He was never enough.

Until they found enough—in each other.

Content Note

This novel features a slow-burn romance, healing arcs, and emotionally intimate, open-door romantic scenes—including mature themes and open conversations about building a life together.

For readers who prefer advance notice, a Spice Guide is included at the end of the book, listing chapters that contain on-page intimacy.

Contents

ACT I

SHIFTED

CHAPTER 1

The Stranger

Rain lashed her face, footsteps pounded behind her—and still, this wasn't the first time she'd run like her life depended on it.

It had started with a drizzle, a mist against her cheeks. But now it poured in sheets, icy and unyielding, soaking her from her cloak to her boots.

Her breath came in sharp gasps as she ran, feet splashing through puddles on the slick gravel path.

She clenched her fists, steadying herself against the rising panic.

The man was still behind her.

There was no need to look back. He was closing the gap.

She'd lost the main road ages ago, and veered left through the trees, past a crumbling gate half-swallowed by ivy.

One wrong turn brought her to the end of a narrow lane. A dead end, hemmed in by stone and shadow. Her heart sank to her stomach.

Then she saw it: a door, dark with age and slightly ajar.

Warm light spilled from within, carrying the faint scent of cloves and rosewater, maybe from a simmering pot tucked just out of view.

Stopping wasn't an option, and she certainly didn't trust the woods. She could have climbed the wall, screamed, fought. But her body moved before her mind could catch up.

The door would have to do.

Inside, she slipped through and pulled it shut behind her. Overhead, wind rattled the windowpanes, distant but insistent.

Rain clung to her lashes as she pushed down the hood that had done little to shield her.

For a moment, she stood there, letting the silence settle around her. Her pulse thudded in her ears, louder than the storm.

Soaked through and cold, but for the first time in half an hour, she wasn't running.

At some point, she'd set her bag down just inside the door, though she barely remembered doing it. The second warmth touched her skin, it vanished from her thoughts.

She should leave. Go back out, climb the fence, find somewhere else to hide. But her legs wouldn't move.

The room unfolded slowly around her: tall, richly furnished, its contours softened by golden firelight. Shadows danced across dark velvet and carved wood, blurring the edges of everything. It was impossibly luxurious, like stepping into someone else's dream.

She brushed the wet hair from her face.

Then she saw him.

He was standing by the fire, one hand resting on the back of a chair. His eyes flicked up at her. Long enough to make her forget she was soaked.

His clothes were dark and well-cut; his posture seemed casual.

She couldn't quite make out his expression, save for the faintest lift at the corner of his mouth.

He was striking, the kind of handsome that didn't seem aware of itself.

"I—I'm sorry," she said, breathless and shaking. "I didn't mean to intrude. I just... I didn't know where else to go. I just... needed to be somewhere else. Anywhere else. And now I'm ruining your floors."

A low chuckle answered her.

She froze, halfway between apology and retreat. For a heartbeat, she thought she might have to run again.

But he didn't move. He watched her like he expected her to disappear.

"I invited you in." His voice was smooth and far too calm for the moment. "No need to apologize."

Before she could say anything more, he stepped forward and extended a thick towel.

"Here," he said.

She took it, fingers trembling.

"Thank you," she murmured, already blotting at her soaked sleeves.

He didn't stare. He simply backed away, leaving her space.

He moved with the quiet precision of someone who'd practiced being unshakable.

And he was looking at her like she was the only thing in the room worth seeing.

By the time she slipped off her wet cloak and draped it across a nearby chair, he had returned with a heavy blanket. It was plush and finely woven.

"For the chill," he said.

The offer stalled her. Taking it felt more intimate than expected. She reached out. Their fingers brushed, barely, but it jolted her more than the cold rain had.

She wrapped the blanket around her shoulders, its weight settling deep into her bones.

He gestured toward the fire. "Please. Warm yourself."

The hearth drew her in before hesitation could catch up. Her hip clipped the edge of the chair as she sat—hard enough to sting. She winced but said nothing, sinking into the warmth like it might erase the ache.

The flames crackled, the scent of smoke mixing with a subtle floral note. A clock ticked faintly nearby.

He moved to pour something from a crystal decanter into two glasses—one for himself, the other set on the table beside her.

Then he sat across from her in a chair upholstered in deep blue velvet, his arm draped over the armrest like he had nowhere better to be.

She studied him, now that her breath had slowed. She guessed he was a few years older, but carried himself like someone who'd been tired for a long time.

His hair was dark and neatly swept back; his beard soft enough to blur the sharpness of his jaw.

The silence deepened. The fire popped sharply, and she jumped.

"I wasn't supposed to be in town long. Just passing through, really." She tightened the blanket around herself.

"I have an aunt—well, she says she's my aunt. More of a distant cousin, really. She lives not quite a day from here." She paused.

"I wasn't planning on stopping, but the carriage broke a wheel near the market, and I..." she faltered. "Well. Things got... complicated."

She laughed, short and uncertain. "It's just... this time of year is..." She swallowed, eyes flicking toward the fire. "...*hard* for me."

"And I didn't feel like spending it being pestered by my neighbor's overly attentive grandson, Mason." She rolled her eyes, but something flickered behind them.

"He means well... I think. But he doesn't hear no." She sighed. "Not once. Not the twentieth time."

She waved a hand. "Anyway. I'm rambling."

"You're not from here, then," he said at last.

"No." She kept her gaze on the hearth. "Small village southeast of here. You wouldn't know it."

"I might."

She searched his face for something: surprise, recognition, even a frown. Anything to prove she'd disrupted his evening.

But all she found was genuine interest. Which only confused her more.

"And you?" she asked, too quickly. "Do you live here? I mean... obviously, you do, but..." She waved vaguely toward the door. "This place, it's... it's beautiful. I didn't know there were homes like this tucked back here."

"There aren't many," he said simply.

"...Well," she fumbled for something else, "were you born here?"

He smiled. "Do you always interrogate strangers, or is tonight a special occasion?"

Her cheeks flushed. "I'm sorry. I tend to talk when I'm nervous."

"Are you nervous?"

"A little," she admitted. "You're very calm. And... well. You're... rather..."

"...Rather what?"

She'd nearly said *attractive*. Out loud. She blinked like the word had ambushed her.

He let the pause linger, then tilted his head, voice low and smooth. "I don't mind your talking. You can fill the silence if it makes you feel safer."

"I didn't say I felt unsafe."

"You didn't have to."

She hadn't planned on unraveling, but the quiet kept tugging until something gave.

"I'm making a mess of your chair," she blurted.

"Everything's still soaked. I—" She glanced down and immediately regretted it.

Her dress had plastered itself to her skin, heavy and damp. "I must look like a half-drowned scarecrow."

She gave a small, awkward laugh. "I'll get out of your way as soon as the rain lets up," she added quickly. "If you could point me back toward town, I'd appreciate it."

He stayed perfectly still.

"There's no rush," he said softly. "You can leave whenever you wish. You need only ask."

Then, almost amused, he remarked, "Though the rain doesn't look like it's letting up any time soon."

She tried to focus on anything except the way her hem was dripping onto the rug. "Still, I shouldn't be taking up your time."

"You're not."

For the briefest moment, he seemed to want to say more. But then he rose, silent again, like he'd thought better of it.

"Would you like something dry to wear?"

Dry clothes shouldn't be a complicated decision, but accepting help felt like surrender.

"Oh... I mean, yes, if you don't mind. Something simple. Anything, really."

He disappeared down the hall without another word.

A moment later, he returned with a folded garment in his hands—a shirt, large and soft, black as ink, with sleeves that looked like they'd swallow her whole. The fabric shimmered faintly in the firelight, elegant in a way that felt out of place.

He held it out to her.

"There's a screen behind you," he said, gesturing toward an ornate folding divider near the hearth. "Feel free to change there."

Clutching the shirt to her chest, she stood quickly. The blanket slid off her shoulders. Her heel snagged the hem of her dress—nearly tripping her. She caught herself, cheeks burning.

She hurried behind the screen before she could feel the weight of his gaze. He didn't seem the type to peek. But she wasn't about to risk it.

Out of sight, she peeled away layers of wet fabric with fumbling fingers. Her skin prickled in the open air.

She slipped the shirt on—it draped over her body, brushing her thighs. Warm, and carrying a scent she couldn't quite place.

Tugging the collar closed, she was self-conscious but not quite exposed.

When she finally stepped back out, his eyes met hers, then dropped—once—to take her in.

Something in his posture shifted, like he hadn't decided whether he was meant to look away.

She sank back into the chair, pulling the hem of the oversized shirt down over her thighs. The fire had dulled the chill from her limbs, but something about his presence kept her sharp.

He sat opposite her once more, his glass untouched.

"You said you were passing through," he said. "But you don't strike me as someone who travels alone."

She almost smiled. "Is it that obvious?"

"Only a little."

"I'm not, really. Used to it, I mean. But I needed the change of scenery. I was starting to feel... stuck."

Nodding like he understood, he said, "Sometimes stuck turns into suffocating. And so, you ran."

She blinked. "That's not what I said."

"But you didn't deny it." His voice was calm and certain.

Her reply caught in her throat as her fingers tightened around the blanket in her lap.

"...Who are you?" she asked finally.

He raised an eyebrow.

"I mean—" She shifted in her seat. "You clearly live here. And you're being incredibly kind to a complete stranger, which I appreciate, but it feels weird not even knowing your name."

He leaned forward. "Valen."

She repeated it softly, the first syllable long and smooth. "Vay-len."

Narrowing her eyes, she caught the way he smiled, amused.

"And you?" he asked. "Or should I keep calling you *you*?"

She hesitated. Then, without thinking, "Annabelle."

He said nothing, letting it hang in the space between them.

Unease prickled. The name wasn't a lie, but it belonged to someone she used to be.

And yet, saying it aloud made her feel newly visible—and somehow more exposed than the shirt ever could.

Then, with the faintest tilt of his head, he said, "A lovely name. It suits you."

It landed gently, yet her shoulders reacted anyway—like a bruise brushed by mistake.

She glanced away, unsure what to say.

"Would you like to stay for dinner, Annabelle?"

She blinked. "Oh—I couldn't impose—"

"You're not imposing," he said. "I'm sure you've had a long day."

"I—" The word faltered, caught somewhere between pride and hunger. "Well... I suppose I have. So yes, I'll stay."

His shoulders relaxed. "Perfect."

She didn't know him well enough to trust. But he didn't flinch when she was herself.

It was disarming. She wasn't used to being herself without consequence.

That alone felt rare enough to make her stay.

CHAPTER 2

The Draw

The corridor was hushed, carpet swallowing footsteps. Shapes flickered along the curtains as candlelight danced in the gilt-edged frames.

Valen opened the tall, carved doors.

The dining room unfolded: vaulted ceiling, stone columns, a polished table that could seat a dozen. Light spilled from the chandelier. Candelabras burned on the sideboard, shadows stretching into the corners.

Bread, still faintly steaming. A pot of something rich and savory, its scent curling in slow tendrils. Roast vegetables.

"Were you expecting company?" Annabelle motioned to the set table.

Valen moved to a seat, glancing back—unreadable, like surprise hadn't occurred to him. "I didn't know I was."

She sat opposite him, eagerly filling her plate.

He poured her wine, his focus on her. "You were hungry."

To her left, a candle flared, wax popping in the quiet.

"I've... barely eaten today."

"I imagine not."

"I sort of... left on a whim this morning," she said, then tensed, as if the words had slipped out. "Wasn't exactly prepared."

Valen hadn't touched his plate.

"You're not eating," she said.

"I don't need to."

"And you avoid answering plainly."

"Keeps things interesting," he said, swirling his glass.

She let out a quiet huff, tempered by amusement.

"You're more relaxed now."

"I'm warmer," she replied, lifting her wineglass. "And I've had just enough of this to make me forget I ran for my life through the rain."

She fiddled with her napkin, searching for something to say.

"So. Do you live here alone?"

"Yes."

"How long have you lived here?"

"As long as I can remember."

"And what is it you do here, exactly?" she asked, masking her unease with curiosity.

"Nothing currently."

"Do you... host guests often?" Her leg bounced beneath the table. She pressed a hand to her knee, trying to still it.

"Not often, no."

"Then... why me?"

That earned the barest ghost of a smile. "Why not? You looked like someone searching for safety."

She studied him as she tore off another chunk of bread. She couldn't tell if his stillness was habit or instinct.

The wine warmed her throat as she eased back in her chair. "You look like you haven't flinched in years."

"I suppose I haven't needed to."

"Do you always throw elaborate dinners for unexpected guests?" She lowered her glass, the base pulling slightly on the tablecloth.

Valen smirked. "Only the charming ones."

Her eyes flicked upward in theatrical suffering, but her tone was light. "So you just... throw dinner parties for your furniture?"

He let out a hearty chuckle. "The candelabras are excellent company."

She smiled, then quickly pressed her lips together, hiding it. "I'm beginning to see that."

Her fork drifted through the remains of her meal. "I still don't understand why you let me in."

"I saw you coming through the trees. You looked like you'd run out of road."

She wondered if she'd truly stopped—or if this was only a pause.

"And that makes me what?" she asked, voice sharp. "A charity case?"

"No," he said simply. "Just someone who needed a place to stop running."

It took her a moment to realize he wasn't asking anything of her. She wasn't used to kindness without a price.

"Well," she said, reaching for her wine, "thank you. For the shelter. And the food."

"My pleasure."

"To your candelabras."

He raised his own. "To my favorite company."

Their glasses met with a quiet clink. He sipped, gaze steady on hers.

"Come with me." Valen stood and turned toward the doorway, certain she'd follow.

With a final sip, she set her glass aside, then trailed after him.

They stepped back into the same hallway and continued down its length.

Tall doors loomed at the corridor's end. Blackened wood, carved with patterns too intricate to admire in passing.

The room beyond stole her breath.

A library—larger than any she'd seen, so quiet it hushed even her thoughts.

Bookshelves lined the walls, filled with leather-bound volumes and glimmering spines. The scent of old paper and smoke threaded through the air. Ironwork ladders slid along tracks, the kind she'd only seen in paintings.

To the left, flames glowed in a stone-framed hearth, flanked by two armchairs and a matching sofa upholstered in deep green velvet. Forest-toned rugs softened their steps, each hue dark enough to disappear into.

At the room's heart stood a marble chess table, the pieces arranged and waiting.

Turning in place, she tried to take it all in. "It's beautiful."

She nodded toward the chessboard. "Is that always set up, or were you expecting someone to challenge your ego?"

"I'm always ready for a challenge."

"Well then. Would you like to...?" She sat, the chair cool against her legs.

"...Do you know how to play? I'd be happy to—"

"Oh, I know how to play," she said, nudging a white pawn forward.

They played for a stretch without words, the pieces clicking softly between them. Somewhere above, the rain drummed steadily on the roof.

"Are all these books yours?"

He glanced at the shelves. "They are now."

"What does that mean?"

"Things tend to end up where they belong." He advanced his bishop.

"You're very good at not answering."

"Maybe you're just asking the wrong questions."

She narrowed her eyes, pausing above her knight. "Um... how does the... horse move again?"

He stifled a grin. "Two in one direction, one to the side. And I think you were looking for 'knight.'"

"...Thank you," she replied, then moved it.

He responded without looking at the board, the game progressing steadily.

She could hold her own—she'd played with her brother enough to think a few moves ahead.

But when he took another piece, she sighed. "Of course you're good at this."

"You're too focused on what might happen next," he said. "You're missing what's right in front of you."

"...Like what?"

He nudged her fallen knight aside. "Like how you just lost that to my pawn."

"Okay, point made."

His gaze lingered on the board, then lifted to her. "You plan three moves ahead, but miss the one I'm about to make."

Something caught in her chest, too quick to name. "I'm trying, okay?"

"You are. You just... get in your own way sometimes."

She stared at him. It shouldn't have hit so hard, but it did.

"You shouldn't say things like that," she said under her breath.

"Why not?"

"Because you don't know me." The words came out sharper than she intended, as if pushing him back might steady her.

"I'm learning."

She folded her arms. "Very well."

"What about *you*, Valen? You live in a massive house, set out dinner you don't eat, speak in riddles…"

"What—do you just sit by the window at night, waiting for lost girls to wander in?"

She meant it to sting, but his pause came like a bruise. She hadn't expected to feel it too.

"I don't make a habit of it," he said quietly. "But I'm glad I did tonight."

His answer disarmed her more than she liked. She shifted in her seat, suddenly aware of how still she'd been.

"Can I ask…" he began, carefully. "What were you running from?"

"A man was… chasing me." She let the words out slowly. "I don't know when he started following me. I just… turned and saw a glint—pretty sure it was a knife."

"I picked up my pace. Heard him do the same. And then…" She shook her head, as if she could clear it. "I was running. Full sprint. And I ended up here."

"You were lucky," he said. "I wasn't sure you'd see the door. Or even want to come in."

He shifted back, as if retreating from his own honesty.

"The market roads draw all sorts," he added. "Especially at night."

"I didn't exactly plan to be out after dark." She crossed her legs, bumping the table. The pieces rattled in place.

He rested his elbows on the arms of his chair. "But what were you *really* running from?"

She laughed once, sharp and uncertain. "What kind of question is that?"

"A true one."

She shifted. The shirt—his—felt suddenly thin, like it couldn't cover anything worth hiding.

"That's a little dramatic, don't you think?"

He waited patiently. And somehow, that was worse.

"I was tired," she admitted. "Not just of the village, but of pretending—waking up every day and twisting myself into a shape that didn't fit. And trying to smile anyway."

"Like wearing boots two sizes too small and telling myself I could walk fine." Her jaw tensed. "After a while, you forget how standing tall even feels."

Silence stretched between them again.

"No one can keep that up forever. Not without bleeding somewhere," he said.

"I—" The words faltered. She adjusted a piece, then slid her queen across the board.

He moved a rook, but his attention hadn't left her.

Her fingers skimmed the polished marble edge. A stalling move, if nothing else. Outside, branches scraped at the windows as wind whistled past the trees.

She hovered near a bishop, then dropped to a pawn and nudged it forward without thought.

Only the fire's low crackle and the steady pulse of rain overhead filled the silence. It sounded endless. As if it had nowhere better to be, and neither did she.

She aimed for breezy. Hit somewhere closer to weirdly loud. "It sounds worse than before. The rain, I mean."

Valen advanced a pawn without looking away from her.

She repositioned, the chair's velvet brushing faintly against her back. "I hope it lets up soon. I should really get going once it does."

"Do you?"

Her lips parted—she should've been ready for that. She wasn't.

"I don't want to overstay my welcome," she said finally.

"You haven't."

"Still... it feels like more than I deserve."

"You can stay. If you want to," he said, softer than he intended.

She took his rook like it might bite, knocking over another piece in the process. She fumbled it back into place.

"Better," he murmured, but it hit like a challenge. He smiled, then nudged his queen forward.

She hovered over a piece. Then moved, if only to be done with the second-guessing.

He made his move without hesitation.

Her gaze dropped to the board. She saw no way to win, but she wasn't going to go quietly.

She pushed the same pawn she'd opened with, surprised it had gotten so far.

Valen studied his king for a long moment, then tipped it over. "I concede."

She blinked. The victory landed strangely in her chest—light and heavy all at once. "Wait—really? You had the game. I was losing."

"You were learning," he said. "That's worth more than winning."

CHAPTER 3

The Pull

The fire crackled behind them, its warmth no match for the quiet left in the wake of their game.

Annabelle sat with her hands folded loosely, pretending she didn't feel the weight of the moment—or the words still echoing in her head: *You were learning.*

Before the silence turned heavy, she stood and crossed the room. Valen watched her from the chess table.

Drifting to the nearest shelf, her fingertips brushed the worn leather spines. Most of the titles were unfamiliar: old, curious, written in languages she couldn't place.

Then her gaze snagged on one that stopped her cold: *Bestiary of the Silent Wood*. She eased it out.

"We had this in our library," she said. "I thought I'd imagined it."

She opened it slowly; the illustrations were exactly as she remembered. Vivid and strange, like a dream she'd almost forgotten.

Turning a page, she took a step, and misjudged the edge of the rug. She caught the book against herself with a quiet curse.

Settling into the velvet cushions, she tucked one leg beneath her, the pages splayed open across her lap.

She didn't look up, already halfway lost in it. "I loved this story as a child. It always felt so... magical."

"What's it about?"

"A rabbit who thinks the moon can grant wishes." She traced the curve of the rabbit's ear.

"Wishes?"

"Mmhmm," she said. "Every night, she makes her way through the forest to the tallest hill she knows, and whispers her wish to the moon."

Valen crossed the room and sat beside her, drawn by the quiet wonder in her voice. "What does she wish for?"

She hesitated, trying to remember the story the way she used to believe it.

"I think she just wanted to be happy. But no matter how many times she wished, it never came true. The seasons changed, the other rabbits grew up and started families... and she just kept wishing."

She lingered at the edge of the page before turning it.

"What happened then?" he asked. His gaze on her now—not the book.

"Well... uh..." She cleared her throat. "One night, she finds another rabbit. He's trapped under a fallen branch, and winter's coming soon. He's hurt—too weak to move it. And she can't lift it alone."

"What does she do?" He leaned closer, his scent settling over her like dusk. Sandalwood, leather, and something darker.

Annabelle turned the page too fast. Valen's smile said he noticed.

"She brings him food every day for the next few weeks... just enough to keep him going. Then the first snow comes, their last chance to try. But he's stronger now, and together, they lift the branch."

"What's she doing here?" He rested an arm behind her on the sofa.

His hand brushed past hers, landing beside the rabbit—ears back, eyes wide—framed by trees stripped bare for winter.

"She's joining him in his burrow—"

She glanced sideways, just in time to catch the look on his face. "Why are you looking at me like that?"

"...Nothing," he said, a little too fast, his smirk impossible to miss. "Go on."

"Well... I mean that was pretty much the end of the story."

"But what about the moon? Did she ever get her wish?"

She flipped back through the pages and paused on the one with the rabbit staring up at the moon.

"I—I don't think she needed it anymore."

She sat with the weight of that realization for a moment.

A smile crept in, uninvited. "I... still make wishes, sometimes. When I see the moon."

She instantly regretted it and gave a short laugh. "I know, it's silly..."

"There's nothing wrong with hope," he said. "When I was young, I used to hide the stories I loved most under my bed. Thought if I kept them close, they might take me with them."

She couldn't bear to face him. Not with his arm around her and that look in his eyes.

"You're trembling," he murmured. "Are you cold?"

"No, I—I'm fine."

"...Do I make you uncomfortable?" he asked.

She gave a small shrug. "You know you do."

"I'm not trying to."

"I... didn't think you were."

He shifted slightly, giving her space. "If I'm too close, you just have to—"

"No, it—I mean..." Her cheeks betrayed her.

He studied her. "Did you… want me closer?"

She stared at the page like she could disappear into it.

Then she turned and found his eyes, firelight catching and turning them to warm amber. "I—I don't know."

Across the room, a log jostled with a soft crackle.

Her eyes dropped to the book. The words blurred, meaningless now.

"Anyway," she blurted. "Have you read any of these before?"

She began flipping through, faster than necessary.

Before he could respond, she stopped mid-turn. "Hah. This badger looks just like you."

A smile tugged at her lips as she pointed.

The badger sat on a mossy throne, arms crossed, a crooked crown on his head and a solitary raincloud hovering stubbornly above.

Valen leaned in, shoulder brushing hers as he squinted at the illustration. "That does *not* look like me."

"It absolutely does." She couldn't help but giggle. "You've already made that exact face. At least twice."

"Oh yeah? Well…" He took the book from her and flipped to a random page. "This one's you, then."

He pointed, cocky—right up until he saw what he'd picked.

It was a deer. *Sort of.*

The creature stood upright, humanoid in shape but unmistakably deer-like: distinctive ears, soft brown fur, expressive eyes. Her body was graceful, curved beneath the fur. One hand held a pine branch like a scepter; the other rested on her hip. Her hooves gleamed.

Annabelle blinked hard, then snatched the book back. "Why—how is that me?"

He froze, every word he'd ever known deserting him at once. "I—uh—no, that's not—I didn't mean—"

"Oh, I get it." Her grin curved slow and smug. "You think I'm pretty."

The shock lingered only a second, replaced by a fragile kind of bravery. "I do."

"Ha, I knew—wait. What?"

"I think you're pretty, Annabelle." He said it like it was the simplest truth in the world.

She wasn't expecting the honesty. Or maybe she'd forgotten what it felt like to hear something like that without an edge.

"Oh—um..." She shifted and looked away, trying to regain her composure.

Valen followed her gaze, if only for a second—then let it drop.

The shirt had ridden high on her thighs, offering only partial modesty. The neckline dipped with each breath—hinting at the shape beneath.

If the book slipped, or she leaned even a little closer, he wouldn't stand a chance.

And if he stayed much longer, he knew he'd stop trying to keep his composure.

He stood abruptly.

"Would you like to..." He cleared his throat. "See where you'll be staying?" he said, too fast.

He'd been close enough to steal her breath, and now he was halfway across the room. The sudden distance left her off-balance.

"I—yes. That would be... yes."

She pushed to her feet too fast, fumbling with the book as she set it aside.

"Let me grab my things," she mumbled, already heading toward the sitting room.

Her clothes and cloak were still damp from the rain. Her boots caked in mud.

She bent to grab her bag, then turned toward him. "All set."

"Right this way," he said, crossing the hall to the stairs.

She followed close behind, focusing on the railing instead of looking at him.

"I could still leave, you know." The words surprised her the moment they escaped.

"I'm not saying I will," she added quickly. "I just... I could."

Bracing for his usual sidestep, the vague detachment he wore like armor, she held her breath.

But he didn't deflect.

"The real question, Annabelle, is whether you'll choose to stay once you don't have to."

Plans for tomorrow were the furthest thing from her mind right now.

They climbed a few more steps.

"I want you."

He didn't look at her when he said it. Just kept walking, like he couldn't bear to see if she felt the same.

Her foot hesitated on the next step.

I want you here. I want you to stay. I want... you.

All of it folded into three impossible words.

Valen led her down a short hallway and opened a door on the right, one of several along the wall.

The room beyond matched the rest of the house: deep plum and gold softened by candlelight. A bed that looked like it belonged in a storybook. Lace curtains stirred at tall windows, framing the rain and dark beyond.

She stepped inside, eyes drifting over everything, then back to him.

"So, um… what if I need anything?" She set her bag on the floor beside the bed.

He didn't budge from the doorway. "Just call."

"What if I get hungry?"

That coaxed a laugh from him. "Morning isn't that far off."

Her hand skimmed the velvet coverlet.

"And if I need…" She closed her eyes and swallowed. "You?"

His jaw tightened. One hand curled against the doorframe—he needed the contact. "Then you say so."

"Will you hear me?"

He hesitated, then nodded. "Always."

The silence between them buzzed with a question neither dared voice.

Valen looked at her. "Sweet dreams, Annabelle."

The door clicked shut behind him. A sudden hush pressed in around her.

She took a deep breath, trying to relax. But the shirt she wore smelled like him—and that only made things worse.

For a moment, she considered taking it off. But the idea of bare skin against his sheets made her heart stutter.

She slid under the blankets, heavy and warm, and let herself sink. The mattress creaked beneath her.

Her thoughts spiraled as she stared at the ceiling.

I want you.

She shifted restlessly—first to one side, then the other, each movement more useless than the last. Her pulse was too loud. Her skin too aware.

Even after the fire had burned to embers, after the blankets molded around her, she lay wide-eyed in the dark.

Sleep finally found her, but it came hollow and left her wanting.

In the hall, right outside her room, Valen leaned against the wall for a long time. *In case she needs something*, he told himself. But really, he wasn't sure what to do now.

Eventually, he got tired of standing and slumped to the floor.

He ran his hands through his hair, like he could untangle the mess she'd left in his head.

"Why did I give her that damn shirt," he muttered.

His mind raced—replaying every shift she made throughout the night, every breath, every inch of bare skin he wasn't supposed to look at.

He leaned back, desperate for anything else to think about.

Finally, he went downstairs. He usually spent his evenings in the library anyway.

He picked up the book from the sofa and flipped through it, hoping for distraction.

But every page reminded him of her. The rabbit who kept wishing. The badger with his stormcloud. The deer that made him freeze.

It didn't matter where he looked—she was there, in the margins, in the silence, in the space she'd left behind.

She teased, she challenged, she opened up. And he wanted more.

For the first time in who knows how long, he actually wanted something. For himself.

CHAPTER 4

The Garden

His breath warmed her neck, fingers sliding down her spine, hands settling at her hips like they belonged there.

Her skin lit up, nerve by nerve, with every touch, and he touched everywhere.

His face stayed blurred—a jaw's shadow, the tilt of lips before it found her collarbone.

She gasped into the dark, but no sound came.

Pressing her into the mattress, his mouth trailed from shoulder to stomach, then lower. Each kiss slowed, drawing a tremble from her.

Just before she broke, he whispered something against her skin. The words slipped past her, yet they made her moan.

She woke with a gasp, the sheets twisted around her legs, damp with sweat.

Her chest rose and fell in uneven waves; the chill of early morning air clashed with the heat burning beneath her skin.

"Mercy," she whispered, pressing a trembling hand to her forehead.

She threw off the blankets and crossed the room to a heavy wooden door set into the far wall.

Inside was an elegant bathing chamber: smooth marble floors, a basin beneath a tall mirror, and a clawfoot tub already filled, steam curling above the surface.

She hadn't heard anyone come in. Somehow, she wasn't surprised.

Leaning over the basin, she splashed cold water on her face. Her palms braced against the basin's edge, trying to steady herself.

She stared at her reflection—flushed cheeks, wide brown eyes, and a mess of brown hair, frizzed and flattened in all the wrong places—and couldn't stand how much she still felt him.

When she finally got in, warmth soaked into her limbs. She lowered to her collarbone and closed her eyes.

All she saw was him: his voice in her memory, his gaze, the breath of space between his mouth and hers. The words he didn't say.

I want you.

She sank deeper, exhaling shakily, willing the heat to quiet whatever was building inside her.

Annabelle lingered longer than she needed to, chin above the surface, gaze unfocused.

Eventually, the chill found her. She rose, reaching for a towel folded neatly by the tub.

Back in the bedroom, she froze. The fire had been stoked, and two sets of clothes lay across the bed. They hadn't been there previously.

One was soft gray wool, modest in cut, with a high neckline and clean lines.

The other was... not.

Still tasteful and elegant, but finer, smoother to the touch. A green rich as moss or pine, shifting in the light.

Annabelle stood with the towel clutched tight, staring at them both.

She knew what choosing either meant, or what she quietly hoped it might suggest.

Her hand moved to the second. The fabric slipped over her skin like water. The neckline dipped slightly.

It clung at her hips more than expected, and she had to shift it twice before it settled.

She paused at the tall mirror beside the wardrobe, her reflection catching her off guard.

The dress fit perfectly. Of course it did.

It wasn't scandalous. But she could feel it everywhere: her skin, her spine, the pulse at her throat. As if the dress had learned her shape before she had.

Her hair was damp, already beginning to curl at the ends. A few freckles scattered across her nose, barely visible with the color high in her cheeks.

Hands braced against the mirror's frame, she took a few steadying breaths.

She had never wanted anything this much—and never hated herself so little for it.

"You're being ridiculous," she whispered. The reflection stared back, unchanged.

After a final sigh, she reached for the bedroom door.

Her fingers hovered on the handle. She wasn't ready, but she wondered if he'd look at her differently. Or if he'd already known what she'd pick.

The hallway was silent as she made her way to the stairs.

Her bare feet padded against the polished wood, each echo louder than it should've been. She winced. The quiet judged her anyway.

In the sitting room, she found her clothes and cloak neatly folded. Her boots, previously caked in mud, had been cleaned.

Slipping them on, she felt a flutter rise in her chest.

The dining room was quiet too, the long table undisturbed, chairs tucked in.

She turned toward the only room she remembered: the library.

Pushing one of the doors open, she peered inside.

The chess table remained untouched, the game frozen mid-moment. Her knight angled toward a toppled king—a quiet echo of the night before.

She stepped back into the corridor and continued past a few closed doors.

The end of the hall curved in a wide horseshoe. This stretch was similar to the last: velvet drapes, ornate trim, mirrors that caught her reflection at angles that felt too sharp.

She was about to give up when she saw sunlight spilling from an open archway.

Drawn toward it, she forgot what she'd come looking for.

Beyond the arch, the space opened wide, glowing with warmth. Ivory walls trimmed in gold, windows stretched from floor to ceiling.

A door on the far wall was ajar.

She slowed, as if even blinking might break the spell. A breeze slipped in, sweet and floral. Reaching for the door, she eased it wider.

The garden unfolded before her like a dream.

Winding paths cut through towering hedges and willow trees with long, draping branches. Flowers spilled over stone borders in vivid, unruly bloom. Birdsong drifted on the stillness.

She forgot the dress, the hallway, even Valen. For a while, there was only color and scent.

Passing a pale rose bush, she inhaled its sweetness, pausing beside a cluster of lilac.

The curve continued; she followed, the hedges growing taller with each turn.

She turned in place, but nothing looked familiar.

The willow trees were gone. So were the flowerbeds. And the door she'd entered through was hidden behind the green.

Each new route mirrored the last, every fork leading to more of the same.

Unease crept along her spine as she continued past the next curve in the hedge.

She heard the trickle of water ahead and followed it to a narrow stream cutting across the walkway, sunlight glinting on the surface.

It had to lead somewhere. Anywhere.

She stayed near the stream until it bent sharply around a hedge, then stopped. Turning in a slow circle, she scanned the hedges, the trellises, the endless paths.

A bird flapped past too close, wings loud in the hush. She flinched, heart jerking—then silence again. Even the breeze had calmed.

She hesitated, then spoke. "…Valen?"

Only the birds responded.

"Valen?" Still nothing. A chill crept up the back of her neck.

"Valen!" The shout came louder than intended. She froze when a voice answered behind her.

"You called?"

She turned slowly. Tucked in the garden's farthest corner, shaded and overgrown with ivy, Valen rose from a weathered bench beneath a low stone arch.

He must've already been there when she arrived.

The sight of him: tall, composed, half-shadowed by ivy. Heat bloomed under her skin. Her eyes widened and she looked away.

There was a quiet certainty in his expression, as if he already knew.

He drew closer, partially hidden in the archway's shadow. "Did you sleep?"

She folded her arms across her chest, suddenly too aware of the dress. The way his attention hadn't left her since she turned.

"I... didn't sleep much," she said, a little too sharp.

"Mm."

"That's not an admission of guilt."

"I didn't say it was." He brushed past her and she followed.

"Do you always sneak up on people?" she muttered, falling into step.

"I wasn't sneaking."

"Lurking under ivy counts as sneaking, by the way."

"I was just sitting. If anything, you snuck up on me."

She shot him a look. He continued walking, unbothered.

Her fingers curled tighter into the fabric at her ribs. But every few steps, her gaze flicked sideways—brief, careful glances she prayed he didn't catch.

He looked the same as last night: broad shoulders and that posture, like gravity owed him something. In the sunlight, his eyes were greener. Not the gold she remembered from the firelight, but softer.

And now she'd dreamed of him. Her cheeks burned, wondering what he'd do if she moved closer.

"This way." He guided her along a curved trail where light filtered through the trailing limbs of weeping willows.

They walked in silence, the stream winding alongside them, until it narrowed at a bend and slipped beneath a single, flat stone laid like a stepping path.

It was only wide enough for one. Damp with dew, worn smooth by time.

Annabelle slowed. The water was shallow, just a few inches, but it glinted as if it could pull her under.

Valen crossed without pause, his weight shifting easily, coat catching in the breeze. He turned and extended a hand.

She hesitated. Her gaze dropped to the stream, then briefly to his fingers, the pause saying more than she meant it to.

"I've got it," she said, a little too quickly.

He lowered his hand and waited. After a moment, she stepped onto the stone.

Her foot slid on the damp surface—she flailed, then caught herself. She held her arms out for balance, then took another step and cleared it.

She walked past him with an edge of confidence that didn't quite fit.

"See?" she said over her shoulder, their gaze meeting briefly. "Not that hard."

A willow branch disagreed. It struck her across the face with a feathery thwack.

She gasped, flinched, and stumbled backwards. "What in the—what was that—"

He let out a chuckle, then coughed lightly, as if trying to swallow it.

She spun toward him, mouth agape. "You saw that, didn't you? Why didn't you say anything?"

He raised a brow. "I thought you had it."

Her expression twisted into something between a glare and a laugh. "Next time I'll let you smack into a tree."

His grin tugged at one corner, maddeningly smug. "I'll look forward to it."

They rounded a bend, then another, the path winding endlessly ahead.

The stream veered behind a cluster of reeds, and the hedges gave way to a wider gravel trail. Birds flitted through the branches above them, and somewhere in the distance, wind chimes stirred.

She glanced around. "How big is this place?"

"Large enough that most guests don't find their way back on the first try."

"Comforting."

His mouth twitched at the corner, but his eyes lingered on the path ahead.

"My mother loved the garden," he said after a pause. "We spent most of our time out here when I was young. She was always picking flowers for the table or reading to me. Sometimes we'd find a sunny patch and stay there for hours."

They followed the path around a quiet turn.

Annabelle's expression softened. She looked over at him, lips parting. "Is she—"

To the right, nestled behind a low iron gate, was a smaller section of enclosed hedges. A wooden sign arched above the entrance: *Family Graveyard*.

One gravestone stood immaculate. The ivy surrounding it trimmed back. A neat bouquet of white lilies rested at its base. The rest of the markers were aged and half-swallowed by green.

Annabelle faltered, a quiet ache blooming in her chest. But Valen kept walking, gaze fixed forward, as if the act of not looking was its own kind of remembering.

She caught up quietly and matched his stride.

The air felt cooler now, as if the garden itself had turned solemn.

They reached the glass doors. Without a word, he opened one. She stepped inside.

Warmth greeted her immediately—sunlight slanting through tall windows, the scent of something buttery and sweet already drifting across the room.

But for a moment, her mind lingered behind them. On the moss, the flowers, and the single grave still remembered.

CHAPTER 5

The Ascent

"You didn't sleep." Valen set a platter of pastries and fruit on the table.

"We've established that." Annabelle sat across from him, filling a small plate—unsure if the knot in her stomach was hunger or something else.

He poured her coffee. "You dreamt of me."

She nearly choked mid-sip.

"I didn't say it was a bad thing." He looked far too pleased. "What did you think of the room?"

She cleared her throat. "It was... lovely. More than I needed, really."

"And the clothes?"

"A little presumptuous."

"Presumptuous?" he echoed, the edge of a smile playing at his mouth.

"You left me two options."

He tilted his head. "And?"

"You made both fit me perfectly," she said, leaning back. "It was clearly a test."

He smiled into his cup. "You could've stayed in the shirt."

Her cheeks flushed. "That would've been worse."

"For whom?"

She gave him a look and sliced into a piece of fruit, a bit too precisely.

Valen didn't blink. "It served its purpose."

He took a slow sip from his mug, still watching her.

She paused mid-bite, chewing slowly.

"What would you have said," he asked, "if I'd left you only one outfit?"

"That you're arrogant."

"Accurate."

"And manipulative."

"Only slightly."

She tried not to smile, but the corner of her mouth betrayed her.

"And what would you have thought," he asked, "if I hadn't left you anything?"

"That you were very confident."

He let the silence stretch, sipping from his mug. A smile crept in—like he could see that version of the morning and hadn't entirely ruled it out.

Her pulse kicked somewhere low. The worst part was how much she liked that answer.

A breeze stirred one of the curtains. The room didn't cool.

He leaned back in his chair, watching her with that same infuriating stillness.

"So," he said, "what would you like to do today?"

A simple question. But it landed like more.

Annabelle set her fork down. She didn't mention the rain or the broken carriage. The storm had passed, and her clothes were dry.

It should've been easy: ask to leave, find her way to town, keep going.

Instead, she looked at him. "Show me something."

"Something?"

"Yes. I want to see more of you."

Her voice stayed calm, but there was a glint in her eye. She knew exactly how that sounded.

Valen didn't blink, but his grip on the mug tightened. "Is that what you want?"

She held his gaze. "Yes."

His mouth curved, part smile, part secret, as he stood.

He didn't say where they were going, as he led her out of the sunny dining room. Their footsteps were muffled by the long hallway runner.

They paused at a narrow door, half-hidden behind a velvet curtain. He opened it to reveal a tight spiral staircase, the stone steps worn smooth with age.

She hesitated, staring up the spiral's curve. He glanced back and offered his hand.

They ascended in silence, her skirts brushing his legs with each stride. The stone groaned beneath their feet, the sound echoing up the narrow walls.

Her grip tightened without meaning to. The higher they climbed, the thinner the air felt—not from exertion, but something else.

Anticipation, perhaps.

At the top, the stairs opened into a round tower room bathed in soft, golden light. Books lined the lower walls: some shelved neatly, others stacked haphazardly on windowsills and benches.

A cold fireplace curved along one wall, the faint scent of ash still lingering. Near the tallest window stood a telescope, and beside it, a chaise in pale blue toile, the fabric faded at the edges. A single armchair faced the hearth, a book resting on its arm.

But it was the balcony that pulled her.

He pushed open the doors, and morning air swept in. Annabelle stepped outside, and the view stole her breath.

Mountains unrolled in layers of blue and gray. A river shimmered below, catching light like broken glass. Beyond the forest, the rooftops of the town blinked through the trees.

She rested her hands on the railing and leaned forward. The metal was cool beneath her fingers.

"I had no idea…" she whispered.

Valen joined her.

"This is stunning," she said too quickly, as if silence might press too close if she let it. "You must be up here all the time."

His gaze stayed on the horizon. "No, not really."

"If I lived here," she murmured, "I'd be up here every day."

The wind caught her dress as she traced her fingers along the rail, drinking in the view again.

"This would be the perfect place to read," she said. She smiled, a small, private one she rarely offered anyone. "Or sketch. Or sit with tea and pretend nothing else exists. And—"

Valen wasn't looking at the mountains. His gaze was on her.

That same focused intensity—still there, but different now. Like he wasn't studying her anymore. Like he saw what he wanted.

"You don't come up here often."

"No."

"Why not?"

He looked almost puzzled, as if the question brushed against something long-unused. "I'm up here more than I used to be. But I stopped really seeing it a long time ago."

Annabelle frowned. "But it's beautiful. Doesn't that... help?"

"On occasion, I suppose. But solitude has a way of turning beauty into background."

"...Why did you bring me here?"

His eyes dropped to the strain in her arms. Then returned to her face.

"Because this is the one place in the house where I can see everything," he said. "And for once, I didn't want... to look alone."

She looked back at the horizon, but the view had blurred. She tried to trace the ridgelines, name the colors, let the sun mean something. But every contour redrew itself around him.

It was like trying to reread a familiar line and realizing the meaning had changed.

A bird cried somewhere in the forest. The breeze caught her hair, pulling it across her face. She swept it back out of the way.

"So... how long did it take you to collect all those books downstairs?"

"I lost track," he murmured. "But I remember why I kept the first one."

"What was the reason?"

"It reminded me the world could be bigger than the walls I knew," he said. "It stayed with me. When other things... didn't."

"Must've been an interesting book."

She glanced over and found him right behind her, his breath warm at her neck. A sharp kick pulsed in her chest.

Her grip on the railing tightened.

"It wasn't nearly as interesting as you," he whispered.

That word—*you*—hit her like a spark. Her heart thundered, instinct screaming to run, but her reckless curiosity kept her rooted.

Her lips parted, but no sound came. She wanted him to close the distance. That scared her more than she'd admit.

Annabelle faced him, tilting her chin to meet his eyes.

He held his breath a moment too long. A pause that gave him away.

"It feels like you want to... kiss me," she said.

His shoulders tensed. His mouth twitched, fighting a smile. A crack in the stillness.

For a flicker, he looked caught off guard.

But then it passed. And Valen was Valen again.

He held her gaze. "...Do you want me to?"

The words slid between them like velvet over a blade.

Her balance shifted. She couldn't tell if it was the floor or her resolve.

"I haven't because I wasn't sure if I should," he said, low.

Now she was the one on the edge.

"W—wait... you actually want to kiss me?" she blurted.

"You already know I do." His eyes held hers. "But I want to hear it. From you."

He leaned in until his breath grazed her lips. The space between them barely counted as space at all. "I want you."

She stayed frozen. Even the air went still, waiting with her.

Her mind raced, torn between sense and surrender.

The warmth of his breath curled along her mouth, and the rest of the world slid out of focus. Every sound faded: the river below, the wind through the trees, all giving way to the steady, impossible rhythm of her own heartbeat.

Then, hardly more than a breath—too soft to carry if he hadn't been so close—she said it. "Please."

That was all.

The decision settled in her chest, fragile as glass, every breath a risk of breaking it.

His hand found her jaw, fingers brushing her skin. He tilted her chin and closed the last inch between them.

Their shadows merged on the stone, the faint scent of sandalwood wrapping around her, warm even in the mountain air.

Lips touched hers, light as a whisper, careful in the way first things often are.

Then he kissed her deeper, slower, like he meant for her to remember it.

His mouth on hers was unfamiliar, but nothing had ever felt more right. She didn't know where to put her hands, her thoughts, her heart.

For a moment, nothing moved. Not the wind, not her breath, not the ache in her chest that said this was the first time she'd felt wanted in the exact way she needed.

The kiss broke. Too soon.

He drew back just enough. His lips ghosted hers, one last trace of warmth before the air returned.

Annabelle stood motionless, eyes closed, chest rising in shallow waves. Somewhere far below, the river kept moving. She didn't.

Behind them, a tall pane of glass caught their reflection in the morning light. For a moment, the glow shifted, as if the space itself had tensed. Then it stilled.

When she opened her eyes, Valen was already watching her. His expression was softer, but no less intense.

CHAPTER 6

The Echo

They stood still. The space between them felt changed, the air settling differently.

Annabelle's pulse was loud in her ears. She tried not to lean into him again.

Valen looked at her as if the world had narrowed to this.

A breeze moved faintly through the open tower, brushing against her skin. She wasn't sure if the shiver that followed came from that or from him.

Then he took her hand, laced their fingers, and led her to the stairwell.

They descended in silence, her heels tapping softly. Mid-step, his thumb brushed hers—a touch that felt like a kiss in its own right.

On the main floor, he bypassed the library and opened the next door. She hadn't expected a music room.

A grand piano anchored the space, black lacquer catching the light. Along the right wall, glass-fronted shelves held violin cases, a cello, a harp, and stranger instruments she didn't recognize.

The walls were deep maroon, patterned in narrow stripes that shifted as she moved. Beneath the window sat a small desk, sheet music scattered across its surface.

Valen stepped inside without a word. She let go of his hand and drifted further in.

She hadn't known what to expect, another library, perhaps, but this was different. Intimate in a more personal way.

Instruments lined the wall. Some gleamed. Others lay forgotten under dust. A violin rested in velvet, its bow set beside it with quiet care.

The room smelled of old wood, varnish, and something faintly floral.

Her fingers grazed the piano's edge. She left it untouched, but the silence felt expectant.

"Do you play?"

"When I want to."

She gave him a look. "That's not an answer."

"Yes. I play."

Her eyes trailed over the polished bodies and edges of instruments she couldn't name.

She paused at a long-necked, stringed thing with dark wood and brass frets. "What is this?"

"A theorbo."

She blinked at him. "You're making that up."

"I wouldn't dare."

"Do you play it?"

"No," he said. "Not that one."

"So, which one's your favorite?"

"The cello."

"Oh?"

"It's quite versatile. But I like how expressive it can be."

"I took a few violin lessons as a girl. I wasn't that interested, but my mother insisted. After the third tutor stormed off, she finally stopped forcing it."

She wasn't sure why she'd told him that. But the words were out now, hanging between them.

He made a soft sound—surprise or amusement, she couldn't tell. "Maybe it just wasn't a good match."

"Perhaps..." She nodded, but her mind was elsewhere. The echo of his kiss clung to her like a held breath.

"Are we... not going to talk about what happened back there?"

Valen watched her for a long moment. "Do you want to talk about it?"

Annabelle turned too fast and caught her foot on the piano leg. The strings hummed, breaking the silence. Her thoughts a mess of heat and confusion.

"I just..." She stopped. "If it didn't mean anything to you, that's fine. It's just—"

She folded her arms. "You kissed me, Valen."

He nodded once. "I did."

"You say that like it's nothing."

"It was a kiss."

"Right," she said quietly. "Of course."

She turned away, because looking at him too long might confirm what she was starting to suspect—that the moment had meant more to her than to him.

It hadn't been nothing. Not to her. And maybe that was the problem.

Each blink sharpened the sting in her eyes. His silence was louder than anything else.

"I just—" she faltered. "I can't tell what's real with you. One minute you're looking at me like I'm the only person who's ever existed. The next, you're answering as if you're carved from stone."

She took a breath. "I'm trying to understand what this is. But you give me just enough to wonder—not enough to know."

"And now we're here, in this absurdly tragic music room, and you kissed me like it meant something. And then said 'it was a kiss' as though we brushed sleeves in passing."

Her voice cracked. She winced.

"I don't know what you're doing to me," she whispered. "But it's not nothing."

The words lingered, fragile and unresolved. She rubbed her arm, like she could smooth out whatever had come loose beneath the skin.

His hand settled on her shoulder from behind. "Annabelle."

She turned, caught off guard by the openness in his face.

"I didn't kiss you because I could," he said. "I kissed you because I couldn't not. I've waited a long time to feel anything. And then you arrived."

He hesitated. "Now everything's louder, and I don't know what to do with it."

The words echoed, and something inside her gave way—like pressure easing behind her ribs.

"I'm sorry," she said softly.

"For what?"

"For needing answers. For... pushing so hard. I barely know what this is yet. But not knowing what I meant to you... it got to me."

She stepped forward and reached for his hand.

His fingers closed around hers without hesitation, like they'd always meant to.

A moment later, he pulled her close.

He held her like she mattered, her cheek against his shoulder, his warmth bleeding through the fabric.

As if the world couldn't be trusted with her, and this was the only safe place left.

And she gave in.

CHAPTER 7

The Intrusion

"Well," said a voice from the threshold, smooth as silk and twice as sharp. "Isn't this sweet."

Annabelle flinched.

A woman stood in the doorway like she was posing for applause, draped in red from her dress to her pointed heels, not a drop of subtlety in sight.

Heels too high for a house this old. Lips painted a red that dared you to question it. A smirk that stopped short of her eyes.

"Seraphine," Valen said her name as though it were a warning.

She walked in with the confidence of someone who'd never heard the word no.

Her gaze skimmed the room like a stage she'd already performed on. She barely paused on Annabelle—a flick of attention, the kind you give a stray reflection.

"Didn't realize you were entertaining," she said, trailing a finger across the piano lid. Her nail clicked once. "Though I suppose even you'd get lonely eventually."

"What are you doing here?" Valen said, each word clipped and cold.

Seraphine turned, all feigned surprise. "What, I can't visit my lover?"

The word fell heavy between them.

Valen stepped forward, blocking her path. "Outside. Now."

"Oh, Valen," she purred. "Still so dramatic."

He led her into the hallway.

Annabelle stayed in the quiet that followed.

She stared at the closed door, her heart sinking with every second.

Muffled voices drifted through the walls, faint but too clear to ignore.

"You don't get to show up like this—"

"Oh, please. You missed me."

A low laugh, barbed with amusement. "You didn't tell her about me? That's cruel, even for you."

Annabelle pressed a hand to her chest, as if to hold it in place.

She caught fragments: *lovers*, *a city of lights*, *a shared room*.

Waiting by the piano, she stared at the ivory keys until her fingers curled into a fist.

Of course he had a past. She just hadn't expected it to walk in wearing heels.

The echo of her footsteps followed, sharp and smug, clicking like punctuation. The rhythm faltered briefly, then resumed its perfect poise.

The door slammed, louder than it needed to be.

Valen returned, jaw tight. "Annabelle—"

"I'm fine," she said, too fast.

She angled away, rubbing her arm with her opposite hand, seeking steadiness.

"She has a talent for..." He paused. "...lingering where she isn't wanted."

Annabelle let out a breath of laughter. "That seems to be a theme around here."

He flinched. "I should've warned you about her. What she can be like."

"I'm not upset."

He moved closer. "Let me explain."

"I—" She swayed. "Sorry. I'm not feeling well."

"Annabelle—"

"I just want to sleep. Please. I'm fine."

He hesitated. His expression twisted—concern scraping against instinct. "Do you want me to stay?"

She gave him a weary glance. "No offense, but... I'm not sure what I want right now."

Instead of waiting for a response, she stepped past him. He didn't stop her.

At the door, she paused, one hand on the frame.

"I'll go in the morning," she said. "I think I've stayed longer than I should have."

He nodded, barely.

She moved down the hall as though the air resisted her, unwilling to call it jealousy. But that smile. That voice. The way Seraphine said *lover*—like she still owned the word.

A sour twist curled low in her gut.

She reached the bedroom and went in.

The fire was lit.

At the far side of the bed, Seraphine waited, holding the other dress. The one Annabelle hadn't chosen.

Seraphine turned slowly, lips curling. "Not my style, but I'm sure it's very becoming on you." She tilted her head. "Rough night?"

"What are you doing in here?" Annabelle asked. Her voice barely reached past Seraphine's dripping confidence.

Seraphine stood, letting the dress drop onto the bed.

"I thought I'd check in on the new favorite." She slinked forward, gaze sliding over Annabelle as though she was sizing up the damage. "Making sure you weren't crying into his pillow or anything tragic like that."

Annabelle opened her mouth, but nothing came out.

Seraphine's sneer widened. "Poor thing. You really thought this meant something."

"We're meant to be together," Seraphine said, matter-of-factly. "Always have been. You're an intermission. That's all."

"That's not true," Annabelle said, but the words were raw.

Seraphine raised an eyebrow. "You think you know him? Because he gave you a room and let you play dress-up for a few nights? Darling... you've only seen the pieces he wants you to."

Still smiling, Seraphine leaned in. "I've seen what he is when the lights are out. When no one's watching. When he's not playing house."

Annabelle shook her head, as if it might clear the smoke curling through her thoughts.

Seraphine's words were sweet and toxic. "You're beginning to wonder, aren't you? What he hasn't told you. What you haven't asked."

Annabelle pressed both hands to the dressing table. The wood was cool beneath her palms.

"Don't worry," Seraphine whispered, closer now. "You won't be here long enough for it to matter."

Annabelle turned, heart hammering. The room was empty.

The fire crackled, but the flames didn't answer. One popped, spitting a fleck of ash to the stone.

She crossed to the bed, ignoring the dress Seraphine had handled as if it were a dare. She let it lie.

Her fingers fumbled with the fastenings. She loosened her dress enough to stop feeling caged.

Curling onto her side, she wrapped her arms around herself, focus fixed on the firelight dancing across the wall.

You're an intermission.

Her eyes closed. She didn't remember falling asleep, only that time blurred.

All she heard was a single repeating note, punctuated by heels clicking on the floor.

Valen was farther down the hall. She attempted to reach him, but the hallway stretched.

Red silk wrapped around him, pulling him into shadow as the light dimmed to nothing.

She tried to call out, but only smoke left her mouth.

Glass shattered in every direction.

She woke up with a gasp.

The room had dimmed. Violet shadows stretched across the ceiling like bruises.

Her skin was cold; the fire had gone out.

She sat up slowly, thoughts dragging. Seraphine's words echoed.

Swinging her legs over the side of the bed, she stayed there for a moment.

Then got up: refastened her dress, pulled on her boots, grabbed her bag, and pulled her cloak tight.

Stepping into the hall, she found the house quiet.

She walked down the stairs toward the sitting room she'd first entered yesterday.

The way out was ahead.

She reached for the handle. It didn't budge.

Pressed her shoulder to the wood. Still nothing.

The locks weren't engaged.

"You can't leave unless you ask," Valen said from behind her.

She whipped around.

He stood near the hearth, arms loose at his sides, face unreadable.

It sounded like something a villain might say. But when she studied him, there was only sadness. And a loneliness deeper still.

Her pulse ticked faster. "Am I a prisoner?"

"No," he said gently. "You stepped inside. I don't let many do that."

She searched his face for a lie.

There wasn't one.

"You're welcome to stay, Annabelle. As long as you want."

"I think I've already overstayed my welcome."

She faced him, cloak still wrapped like armor. Her hand snagged in the sleeve. She shook it free.

"I suddenly feel like I was never meant to be here," she said.

That broke something in him. The stillness—that careful, sculpted calm—fractured.

He looked at her like she'd struck him.

When he finally spoke, the words dropped low. "If that's what you would like, I won't stop you."

He paused. Took a shallow breath. "But just know I don't want you to go."

That was it. Simple. And somehow it hurt more than a plea.

Annabelle remained there, hand lifted toward the door, pulse pounding as if it might run even if her body stayed.

Valen's eyes were lowered, a faint crease between his brows.

And in that moment, she saw the distance in him, threaded with a muted kind of sadness. The kind he never named.

It showed in the slope of his shoulders, in the quiet understanding that whatever she chose, he wouldn't fight it.

Her hand dropped. She stepped away from the door and took a few slow steps toward him.

She shrugged off her cloak, let it fall over the arm of a chair, and set her bag beside it.

"Are you alright?" she asked.

His gaze lifted to hers. It wasn't the right question. Or maybe it was too close.

For a moment, he said nothing.

"No."

She hadn't braced for honesty.

He shifted his attention, lips pressed together. "She knows exactly where to cut."

Annabelle stepped a little closer. "She hurt you."

"Yes. But not the way she wants you to think."

He didn't elaborate.

She waited.

He only stared into the fire, as though it might speak for him.

"You don't have to tell me everything," she said. "But you don't have to carry it by yourself either."

Her attention drifted to the carved leg of the chair—a detail that required nothing from her.

"She was in my room," she said quietly.

His gaze snapped to hers, the shock breaking his stillness.

"Or... I think she was," she said, rubbing her temple. "It felt like a dream. No—a nightmare."

"I walked in, and she had the dress I didn't choose." She let out a short, unsteady breath, not quite meeting his eyes.

"She was mocking it. Mocking me. Saying I didn't belong here. That you and she were... meant to be." Her voice thinned. "She said this was fleeting. That I don't even know who you really are."

He closed the space in two strides. "This is not fleeting."

"Were you really together?"

His jaw tightened. "We were... entangled. She doesn't like not being wanted."

"So yes," Annabelle said. Sharper than she meant.

"She called herself my lover. I never did."

She rubbed her wrist absently. A small motion, but it grounded her. "But you didn't stop her, did you?"

Valen looked drained in a way she hadn't seen before.

"I was lonelier than I realized." He didn't apologize. But he wasn't proud.

He reached for her, then stopped. His arm falling back to his side.

"She gets inside people's heads," he said. "She feeds on it."

Annabelle bit her lip. "She did a good job."

"You're not temporary," he said, firmer now. "She wanted you to believe that. To leave. So I'd be alone again."

He stepped closer, brushed his hand lightly along her arm.

"I don't want to be alone anymore. I'm tired of shutting the world out just because it's easier." His gaze held hers. "That's why I opened the door for you."

She stayed frozen—trust flickering in her chest.

Valen felt it. He didn't push. "Are you hungry?"

"No," she said. "...Maybe."

He nodded as if that made perfect sense. "I'll have something waiting in the library."

"That's not necessary."

"I want to." He turned and left the room.

She followed, sheathed in her own quiet defenses. Doubts threaded through every step.

CHAPTER 8

The Embers

The library was warm, firelight holding the dark at a distance. Shadows stretched across the shelves, settling in for the night.

A modest spread was laid out on the table: fruit, bread, soft cheese, maybe spiced ham.

Annabelle sat in silence while Valen poured her tea.

She tore off a piece of bread and took a bite. He didn't eat, watching her instead.

"Are you going to sit there like a statue or try the strawberries?" she said.

"I'm more of a blackberries-in-the-wild type."

She caught the twitch of his mouth and laughed.

He picked one up, turning it as though it might be plotting something.

Annabelle sipped her tea, studying him.

He glanced up. "What?"

"Picturing you foraging in some dramatic cloak."

He raised an eyebrow. "You think I'm dramatic?"

She tilted her head and bit into an apple slice. "You have a spiral staircase, a tower with a telescope, and a library big enough to drown in. The shoe fits."

Valen made a low sound, almost a laugh.

"Fine. I'm a little dramatic," he said, taking a bite.

She smiled, cautious at first, but it stayed.

They kept eating. The quiet softened between sips of tea and bites of fruit. A log cracked in the grate.

Neither wanted to admit the meal was over.

Annabelle folded the edge of her napkin, then unfolded it again.

Valen broke the silence. "I'm sorry. About Seraphine."

She blinked, then met his eyes. "How did you end up with her?"

He didn't answer. Enough time passed that she nearly took it back.

"I was young. Stupid." He stared at the table. "I thought being with her would... I don't know. I thought it would fix something in me."

"And did it?"

"No. The opposite, actually." He leaned forward, elbows on his knees. "Took me a long time to realize that."

Since Seraphine walked in, she'd doubted everything. But this felt honest.

"Did she mean anything to you?"

Valen's gaze shifted over. His fingers twitched on the armrest. "Yes. No. I'm not sure. I thought she did."

"But was it just loneliness?"

"Yes."

"If I could undo it, I would," he said. "I thought it was what I wanted. What I needed. It wasn't."

She leaned back, tired from everything she didn't say.

It was the ache of wondering whether she'd ever be someone's first choice or merely a consolation prize.

She stared into the embers, as if clarity might rise from the ash. But all she heard was Seraphine's voice: *You won't be here long enough for it to matter.*

"I'll never compare to someone like her," she said. "Gorgeous. Elegant. Every hair in place. She walks into a room and it belongs to her."

"Perfect," she finished, the word bitter on her tongue.

She didn't need to look to know he was watching. When she met his gaze, his expression had changed.

"If that's perfection," he said, "I'll take flawed."

"Everything was a performance with her—every word, every smile, every touch. Nothing was real. Not even the way she looked at me."

His voice dropped. "In the end... all she wanted was for me to want her."

Annabelle's throat tightened. *And you didn't want her?* she almost asked. But it didn't matter. He wasn't saying this to patch things over. Or to keep her here.

He seemed unguarded. And she believed him.

The fire faded to embers. Only the occasional pop disturbed the stillness.

She folded her hands in her lap.

Valen reached out and brushed her cheek. He searched her face. "Do you believe me?"

"I... I think so." A moment passed. "Yes." She meant it. Mostly.

A sliver of doubt lingered—she'd spent too long believing she wasn't enough. That a man like him couldn't mean her.

She moved to the shelves, ignoring the way everything felt different now.

"Alright," she said, voice light. "You have an entire kingdom of books. Which one's your favorite?"

He crossed to the far side, trailing along the spines with the kind of familiarity that came from love, not habit. Then he stopped.

Pulling a well-worn book from the shelf, he handed it to her. "This one."

She took it gently, as if it held more than paper and thread.

The leather was soft from years of use, still warm from his touch. The cover was plain: deep brown, bordered in gold.

"What is it?"

"A story I've read a hundred times," he said. "And always come back to."

Annabelle turned it over, thumb brushing the softened edge. The title had been re-gilded by hand, slightly uneven, the gilt too bright in places. The stitching along the spine was careful, but not expert.

"...Will you read to me?"

It caught him off guard, like she'd asked for something more personal than a secret. "Alright."

He took the book, opened to the middle, and began to read.

"She told herself not to hope—not for love, not for anything lasting—because hearts like hers didn't get endings, only chapters that faded before the story could finish."

He paused. The words sat too heavy. He cleared his throat and turned the page.

"There was something in the way he looked at her—like she hadn't just passed through his life, but had always been part of the plot. The kind of woman stories were written around and never quite recovered from."

This time, he didn't keep reading. He just let the words sit.

She blinked. "...Is it all like that?"

Valen lifted his head, off balance. "I forgot that part."

She wasn't sure if he meant it. But the way he read it... maybe that was his way of telling her.

He closed the book.

"I'm sure there's something less... dramatic." He turned toward the shelves.

She didn't let him off the hook. "But you said it was your favorite."

The tension in his posture gave him away as he paused over the spine of another book.

Annabelle saw him pull back and stepped in, slipping it from him.

"If you won't read it," she said, "I will."

Flipping it open, she read aloud, "*He touched her hand like it was a question he didn't dare ask out loud...*"

She giggled. Couldn't help it.

"Annabelle," he sighed.

Grinning, she held it just out of reach. "*She looked at him like an answer—*"

"Give it here."

She laughed. "Why? Embarrassed?"

"Mortified." He reached again.

She twisted away, reading between fits of laughter.

"*—and he thought, if this was ruin, then let it take him—let it strip him down to something unrecognizable, as long as it meant she was the one undoing him.*"

"Annabelle."

"Too poetic for you?" she teased.

He stepped closer, reaching for the book. She turned too fast and collided with him.

Their lips met before either of them meant it.

They froze for one breathless second. The book slipped from her grasp, forgotten.

Her hand slid to the back of his neck, urging the kiss deeper.

He kissed her back like he'd been holding his breath and finally got permission to breathe.

Full of every word they hadn't spoken. Every moment they'd kept their distance. It poured into this.

She held his shirt tight, needing anything to hold onto.

Valen sank into the armchair and guided her into his lap. She straddled him without thinking. Her pulse still uneven from the shift between laughter and whatever had taken its place.

His hands found her waist. Her body pressed close, tense with want she hadn't meant to show.

Their mouths met again, slower this time.

She moved against him, and his hand slipped lower, under the hem of her skirt, warm against her bare skin.

The falter in his breath, his grip tightening at her hip, the firm press of him—unmistakably wanting—stilled her.

His lips parted, maybe to apologize.

But she beat him to it.

"Not yet." She offered a smile, flustered but fond.

He nodded, swallowing hard, like instinct had taken the lead.

"Sorry," he said, voice unsteady. "I didn't mean to push—"

"I know." She touched his jaw, steadying them both. "I just don't want to ruin this."

She wasn't used to setting the pace. But this time, she did. And he didn't pull away.

CHAPTER 9

The Crescendo

Over the next few days, they settled into an easy rhythm.

Mornings began with citrus tea, flaky pastries, and Valen reading aloud from the book she'd picked the night before.

Afternoons drifted into quiet talks about childhoods, half-forgotten stories, music, and things they rarely said out loud. She told him about a nickname that still made her cringe. He shared a memory worn from practice.

Sometimes they didn't talk. The silence was just as close.

They spent long meals and unhurried walks in the garden together. Their hands brushed more often now, no longer by accident.

One night, she fell asleep with her head on his shoulder, his arm around her like it had always belonged there.

Trust built quietly: in the space he gave her, the way he waited, never asking her to be less.

Though she caught herself on occasion, half-expecting the wince or the sharp look that usually followed from others. It never came.

She laughed too loud. Interrupted. Said too much, or not enough. But he never looked at her as if she was too much.

He stayed.

One afternoon, after the sun had passed its peak, Annabelle finished her book in the garden and went inside. Near the library, she heard music. A careful melody drifting into the air.

She slid the book onto a shelf and followed the sound to the music room.

Valen sat at the piano. He looked up when she entered, their eyes meeting before he turned back to the keys.

A few bars in, something wavered—a wrong chord, a pause, then movement again.

By the end, the song was quieter, uncertain. His hands hovered over the piano a moment too long. "I thought you were outside."

"I was," she said, stepping further in. "I didn't mean to intrude. I heard the music and just... followed it. I should've knocked, but... it was beautiful."

He glanced at her, something in his face easing, briefly, before it vanished. "You weren't supposed to hear that."

"I'm still glad I did."

He looked at her for a moment longer, then shifted aside. "Sit with me."

She hesitated. "I've never played."

"That's alright."

She smiled and sat beside him.

He reached across her and picked out a few notes. A simple melody filled the quiet between them.

"Here," he said low.

He turned toward her, slid his arm around her, and guided her to the keys.

"Just try," he murmured.

She shivered at his breath, warm on her ear.

Nudging her index finger, he said, "This one."

She pressed the key. A single note rang out, clear and soft.

He adjusted again, tapping her pinky. "Now this."

Moving too quickly, her ring finger struck another key as the first sound faded. The clash lingered long enough to make her wince.

His hand stayed warm over hers, like the noise didn't bother him at all.

"Sorry," she said.

Valen stifled a chuckle. Poorly.

She grinned. "Don't laugh."

"I'm not."

"You're terrible at lying."

He guided her through a few more notes, tapping each finger in turn. She followed: one key, then another, then a third. All clean.

Guiding her higher, he motioned to a note farther up. She moved too quickly.

Her pinky hit a black key instead of the white beside it, and she pressed both in quick succession.

A sharp chord bounced off the walls. It clashed so badly she snorted, then burst out laughing. "I warned you. I'm terrible."

"You're trying."

"That's not always enough."

"It is to me."

Her laughter stopped. Her smile faltered. He was closer than she'd realized.

Their knees touched, the narrow bench leaving no room for distance. His arm stayed behind her, his hand over hers on the keys.

The air between them stilled.

Their eyes met.

"You have this effect on me," she said softly.

One brow lifted. "What effect?"

She felt the flush give her away.

He didn't quite smile, but it was close. "You'll have to be more specific."

"You know exactly what I mean."

"I might. But I like hearing you say it."

She laughed, low and disbelieving. "Of course you do."

Valen tilted his head, still maddeningly calm. "I only want to understand you better."

"You understand plenty." Her hands froze above the keys.

"Then say it. What do I do to you?" he murmured.

Heat pooled behind her ribs. Her mind itched to do something reckless before the moment slipped away.

Before she could overthink or he could say one more smug thing, she moved. Her mouth found his like a protest—the only way to make him stop talking.

He gasped, off-balance for a second, then kissed her back.

His kiss was slow, full of the same quiet control he always carried. It cracked when her hand slid up his chest, curling into the fabric near his collarbone.

She leaned in, seeking out the shape of him, the coarseness of his beard, the inhale when her touch grazed his throat.

Her knee brushed his thigh as she closed the distance, barely registering the hard edge of the piano behind her.

He gripped her waist, fingers flexing as she shivered.

She blinked, dazed, as he stood and lifted her to her feet. She followed, warmth coiling low, silence thick with heat. The hallway felt narrower now.

Valen opened the door. Inside was a lounge: mahogany walls, a long sofa, deep purple, low to the floor, clearly meant for collapsing into. She barely registered the rest.

She stepped in, tugging him toward the sofa.

Velvet hissed under them as the cushions sank. She pulled him down and kissed him, urgency replacing patience.

He hovered above her, half-braced. Her legs intertwined with his, one knee slipped beside his hip, her dress hitched high enough to feel the chill on her bare leg.

Staying close, he deepened the kiss with every pull, his touch sliding higher, leaving fire in its wake.

She gasped when he reached lace. He paused there.

Her hands twisted in his shirt as she pulled him closer. Her mouth trailed down his jaw to his neck. Teeth grazed skin and he breathed her name, barely a sound.

He drew back, their foreheads meeting. "Annabelle. Is this what you want?"

Her lips brushed his, just shy of a kiss. "I want you."

"Though I'm not exactly prepared for…" he gestured vaguely.

"Neither am I. But I don't care."

"Me neither."

He kissed her again, rougher this time. His hand slipped past the lace, finding heat. Tentative at first, his touch built slowly, coaxing her higher.

She moaned against him, sliding her palms down his chest, tracing the shape of him under his clothes, every inch sparking beneath her touch.

The world fell away. Nothing else existed.

Her dress rode up, bunched at her hips, forgotten. Somewhere, the fire cracked sharp in the silence—but neither flinched.

Buttons gave way beneath her fingers. She pushed his shirt open, skin meeting skin, muscles tensing under her palm.

Her nails scraped his side by accident. He grimaced, then laughed softly.

"Sorry," she whispered.

"Don't be."

He sucked in a breath when she drifted lower and found him, through fabric, then not.

"Are you sure?"

Her answer was quiet, but certain. "Yes."

Kneeling between her thighs, he shed the last barriers between them.

When he pressed into her, slow and unyielding, she inhaled sharply.

He paused, waiting for her body to catch up to her breath. His eyes searched hers, as if learning the shape of this alongside her.

Moving again, deeper, he was guided by how she clutched at him. Her eyes fluttered shut.

The rhythm built, slow at first, then faster, every motion fanning heat that left her aching.

Finally, he let go with a shudder. One hand cradled the back of her head, the other snug around her waist.

Annabelle blinked up at him, still dazed. He kissed her forehead, her temple, her jaw.

Beneath it, something trembled—a question he didn't know how to ask. She felt it in the uneven rise of his chest, in his stillness.

She brushed his cheek with trembling fingers and kissed him.

He exhaled softly, steadying himself.

She wrapped her arms around his shoulders, his weight settling over her. Her body sank into the cushions, the last of something unspoken unwinding from her.

They lay there, heartbeat to heartbeat, the quiet stretching between them.

Valen's breathing evened, soft against her collarbone, his arm draped low across her waist.

She blinked slowly, watching a sunbeam shift over the floor, golden dust in the air.

Her touch rested on his back, fingers spread across warm skin. Neither moved.

Annabelle stirred first. Sleep had come quietly. Her thigh stuck to his hip. She shifted with a quiet grimace, then smiled.

Valen groaned, tucking his face into the crook of her shoulder, refusing to move.

She ran her hand through his hair. "You're heavier than you look."

"Mm." He muttered, "You're dangerously soft."

She laughed, surprised by the sound of it. "That's not a compliment."

He lifted his head, eyes half-closed. "I disagree."

"Of course you do."

He brushed a strand of hair from her face.

"You drool, by the way," he said, deadpan.

Her jaw dropped. "I do not."

"You're a menace," she muttered.

He raised a smug eyebrow. "Mm. I've been called worse."

She laughed, muffled against him.

And for a little while—the world was small and safe.

Annabelle shifted, cheek against his shoulder. Her fingers traced lazy circles across his chest. "So... what are we now?"

He pressed a kiss into her hair. "Something real. If you want to be."

CHAPTER 10

The Steam

The sun was low when she woke. The space beside her was warm, but empty.

She ached, but not in a way she knew how to fix. It lingered—a low hum beneath her skin. Like her body hadn't quite caught up to her heart. A bath might help. Something warm enough to hold her.

Her dress lay where she left it. She pulled it on, bracing against the chill.

She padded barefoot through the hall and up the stairs, the quiet folding around her.

The bathing chamber was fogged with steam. Rosemary and citrus drifted up from the water.

She stepped out of her clothes and into the bath.

A few moments later, Valen slipped in behind her. The soft slosh was the only sound.

She leaned back into his chest, knees above the surface, toes curling. "I could get used to this."

His chuckle rumbled through her. "You already have."

She elbowed him.

He caught her wrist and kissed it, the water rippling around them. Her heart stuttered.

"Earlier..." he murmured, gently combing through her hair. "Did I—was that alright for you?"

The answer wasn't no. But finding the words was harder.

Behind her, he gathered her hair and poured warm water over it, letting it run through in slow, even passes. It was almost too much—gentle in a way she hadn't known she needed.

A bottle clinked softly as he poured something into his palm: lavender, and an earthier undertone. The scent wrapped around them.

Her eyes drifted closed as he lathered her scalp.

"I liked it..."

He traced gentle spirals through her hair. "But...?"

"It's just..." She exhaled. "I thought I'd feel different afterward. More... settled, I guess."

"Mm. I understand."

His fingers slowed, then gently skimmed the nape of her neck, barely a touch.

"You're enjoying this," she said.

"You have very... expressive shivers."

She laughed, sinking deeper, warmth blooming in her cheeks.

His hands followed, rinsing, then massaging with a slowness that said everything. His fingers combed the length to smooth it. Then they slid lower, coaxing heat with every deliberate movement.

"You're supposed to be helping me get clean," she teased, her voice already unsteady.

"I am," he said, completely unconvincing.

He lingered at her waist, thumbs skimming the edge of something not quite casual.

Heat prickled down her spine, the water suddenly hotter, her skin aching to be touched.

He had no business being that gentle.

His hand moved up her side, tracing the soft curve below her breast before gliding back down.

She tried to focus on the water against porcelain, but failed.

Her breathing faltered. Her body was far too aware of his touch.

"You're very quiet," he murmured, his voice low behind her ear.

"You're very smug."

One hand slipped beneath the water, skimming the inside of her thigh—a graze disguised as adjusting her leg.

She flinched. "Valen…"

"Yes?"

Her head tipped back, resting against his shoulder. "You know what you're doing to me."

He drew lazy lines from the nape of her neck to her collarbone, stirring more than just the surface. "I'm only helping you rinse."

"*That*," she breathed, squirming, "is not rinsing."

"You haven't complained."

She half-turned, water sloshing softly. His face was right there, smiling.

"Yet," she said.

His hand drifted higher, skimming the side of her breast with agonizing patience, like he was tracing constellations only he could see.

Goosebumps followed. His lips brushed the damp line of her neck, then her shoulder and back again.

Her pulse pounded. She shifted, legs tightening beneath the water, tension coiling low and deep.

"Valen," she breathed.

"Hmm?" he hummed close, like he hadn't heard the way her voice broke on his name.

"You're doing it again."

"Doing what?"

"You know."

He kissed her cheek. "I'm only washing you."

"Liar." The balance was tipping. Her restraint thinning by the second.

His fingers sank lower, tracing a path that lit every nerve.

Then he stopped. Completely.

Silence hit like a splash. She writhed—breath unsteady, hips tilting toward him, muscles tensing beneath the water.

"Is this what you want?" he whispered in her ear.

She stilled, a tremor in her throat. "...Yes."

That was all it took. His hand slid between her thighs and she shattered.

His fingers moved like he was discovering what she needed, one breath at a time, finding the rhythm that made her come undone.

Her head tipped back, mouth open, breath slipping out in place of words.

She gave in completely—hips twitching, knees drawing inward, back arching into him as the moment swallowed everything else.

He held her through it. He kissed her temple as her pulse began to settle. Her breathing slowed. She reached for his hand, fingers shaky as they closed around his.

"Told you I was just helping you rinse," he said.

She didn't need to look to know he was smiling.

Words failed her as she melted into his chest. Only the ripple of water and her uneven heartbeat remained.

"Was that... what you needed?" He kissed her cheek, the warmth of it lingering longer than the touch itself.

She nodded.

His shoulders loosened, relief easing into his expression. "Good. Glad I could help."

Carefully, he rose from the tub, giving her hand a final squeeze.

She barely registered it until his hand dipped back into the water.

"Come here," he said.

His voice steadied her. Her limbs resisted at first, but she let him guide her out.

Steam curled in the air between them.

He wrapped a thick towel around her shoulders, his hands warm and patient as they moved over her arms.

Her legs wobbled, not entirely convinced they could hold her.

"I'll give you a moment." He kissed her forehead, slipping out and closing the door behind him.

She stood for a while. Still warm from the bath, but warmer inside. Flushed from all of it.

The towel slipped from her shoulders and fell to her feet.

Two outfits waited on a nearby stool.

Both were elegant. More suggestive than what he'd offered before, but not overtly so.

One was a deep forest green, the neckline dipping low enough to be dangerous. The other was a sleek champagne silk, the kind of fabric that didn't ask questions.

She bit her lip, hesitated, then reached for the silk.

Slipping it on felt like surrender all over again. Only this time, she knew what she was giving in to.

She moved to the mirror, barefoot on cold tile, pressing the wrinkles flat with one hand.

Then she glanced up and saw herself. Her damp hair curled from the steam. The freckles across her nose stood out more than usual.

Her skin glowed and she looked... *beautiful*.

The woman in the mirror—Valen had touched her like she was made of stars.

He wanted her.

The one with flushed cheeks and tangled hair. With too many thoughts and a voice that didn't always stay soft.

And somehow, that had been enough for him.

She smiled at her reflection, then turned toward the door.

Valen stood just outside, leaning in the frame like he'd been waiting there the whole time.

The way he looked at her said everything.

CHAPTER 11

The Key

"I want to go to the market," Annabelle said. She hadn't meant to blurt it over breakfast.

Valen tilted his head. "Now?"

"Soon. Today," she said. "I don't know why exactly—I just... I need to. Paints, brushes. Maybe one of those ceramic palettes—the kind with wells."

His brow lifted.

"I have to make something. I've never felt this way before, and if I don't get it out, I'll explode."

He studied her—flushed cheeks, fidgeting with her napkin. She couldn't sit still.

"What do you want to make?" he asked.

"Anything, really. I just need to put this somewhere. All of it."

"You're going alone?"

"Yes?" Her pulse jumped, sharper than she preferred. She rushed to fill the silence.

"I won't be long. I'll stay near the market, just a few shops. I'm not planning to talk to anyone or go anywhere strange. I—" She caught herself. Bit the inside of her cheek. "I'm not asking permission."

"I could come with you."

"You'd slow me down." She tried for a smile, but it came out crooked.

"Would I?"

"Absolutely. I won't be gone long."

"You don't need to justify it, Annabelle."

That caught her off guard—more than if he'd argued.

"I'm not used to being allowed to just... go."

"The driver will be by today. Old habit. I'm sure he'd take you—if you want."

She shook her head. "No, thank you. I'd rather walk. You never know when inspiration might strike."

"Fair. One moment." He rose and left the room.

Her pulse hadn't settled. The mug was warm in her grip, but her hands stayed tight.

It was fine. She was fine.

She hadn't realized how hard she'd braced for a fight that never came.

A few minutes passed.

He returned holding a brass key: ornate, gold-toned, its ridges worn smooth with time. The bow curled in baroque flourishes. He set it beside her plate.

"For the side door," he said. "The one you came through before."

"Are you sure you can find your way back?" he asked softly.

"I... think so."

She picked up the key. It was heavier than it looked.

"You don't need permission to return," he said, almost offhand.

But she heard what he didn't say: she had freedom. And he was terrified of what she'd do with it.

She finished her breakfast slowly and stood. The key stayed with her as she went upstairs to gather her things.

Her cloak hung on the hook. She slipped it on and tucked the key into the pocket stitched into the lining.

Boots next. Then the mirror, her hair mostly behaving. She grabbed her bag on the way out.

When she came downstairs, Valen was already at the side door. He held out a folded sheet of paper. "In case you need it."

She unfolded it. A map, drawn in tight, elegant script—his hand, unmistakably his.

The lane to the road, the footpath through the woods, a dotted trail winding into the square. Even tiny illustrations: shops, garden walls, the stream.

A soft laugh caught in her throat. "Worried I'll disappear?"

"Yes." His jaw tightened, as though the words cost him.

Folding the map back up, she tucked it alongside the key.

She leaned in, brushing her fingers against his cheek. "I'll be back before you have a chance to miss me."

"I doubt that," he murmured, meeting her eyes.

He kissed her. The kind of kiss that lingered even after she left. The key was warm in her pocket, its weight comforting as the door clicked shut.

She crossed the gate, boots brushing the narrow path. The town's cobblestones wouldn't begin for another quarter mile. The sun was high and golden, warming her shoulders despite the morning chill.

Town stretched ahead in crooked rows, flower boxes spilling green from open windows.

She hadn't really seen it before. Last time, it had been all darkness, broken wheels, and fear.

Now it buzzed around her: vendors calling out, wheels rumbling over stone, a child's shout fading into the crowd. A dog barked, chasing a wagon. Someone haggled over a basket of too-ripe pears.

It wasn't a city, but it was alive.

More than the quiet village she'd come from. That place whispered. This one hummed.

She let the sounds and scents wash over her: bread, bells, laughter behind glass.

Between a bakery and a bookstore stood a narrow shopfront. *Sable & Thread: Fine Papers, Inks, and Supplies for the Artist and Tradesman.*

Her steps quickened. She pushed the door open as a bell chimed overhead.

The shop smelled of dust, linseed oil, and something faintly metallic. Ink, maybe. Shelves lined the walls, crowded with tools, powdered pigment, neat stacks of handmade paper.

Annabelle moved slowly, glancing over soft charcoal pencils, flat tins of paint, spools of twine, and long, delicate brushes too beautiful to actually use.

She didn't know what she wanted to paint, or where to begin. But it didn't matter. Everything felt possible.

Maybe she could catch the feeling that had been bubbling under her skin since dawn. The one that refused to stay quiet.

"Looking for anything in particular?"

She turned. An older man stood behind the counter—ink-stained fingers, wire-framed glasses perched on his nose.

"Just browsing," she said. "I haven't painted in a long time."

"Well," he said, nodding at the shelves. "You've come to the right place."

She gave him a practiced look that passed as warm.

Her gaze lingered another moment before she made her selections: a sketchbook, a tin of watercolors, and a set of brushes that fanned, delicate as bird feathers.

He counted them out slowly, commenting on paper weight and how a proper brush holds its shape in water.

"Haven't seen you before. Just arrived?"

She hesitated. She hadn't meant to say it, but the words escaped anyway. "I'm a widow. Passing through."

The lie settled too easily on her tongue. The familiar feeling of guilt followed.

His expression softened. "I'm sorry."

"I needed space. Time to think."

He tied the last bit of twine around her bundle. She placed a few coins on the counter.

"Well," he said, tucking them into a drawer, "you've picked a good place for it. Quiet enough when the market's not in full swing."

She took the supplies and slid them in her bag. "Thank you."

"Hope to see you again."

"Maybe you will."

In the square, she paused—bag tucked under her arm, the breeze catching at the loose ends of her cloak. A burst of laughter spilled from a nearby restaurant window. A bell rang out the hour.

She wasn't ready to return. Not yet.

Her gaze drifted before landing on the bakery.

The same one she'd passed her first night, when the world was rain-slicked and uncertain. Then, the windows had glowed in the distance. Now, she walked in as though she belonged.

It smelled of cinnamon, honey, and a bright note of citrus. A woman at the front of the shop smiled. "Morning! Can I help you find anything?"

"Just looking for something sweet to bring back," Annabelle said.

"Any favorites?"

"No... but I think I'll know them when I see them."

She chose a tart glistening with dark berries, a powdered spiral with lemon zest, and a layered square that looked utterly decadent.

The woman wrapped them in waxed paper and twine.

"For someone special?"

"Maybe." Annabelle smiled, sliding her payment across the counter. She tucked the bundle carefully into her bag.

"He's a lucky man."

She laughed, then slipped back out into the light.

The bookstore sat a few doors down, its sign faded but legible beneath a carved wooden awning: *Blackwell's Antiquities & Secondhand Titles.*

The air was cooler inside, dense with ink and old paper. Dust had settled into the corners.

Books filled every wall. The shelves rose high, some slightly crooked under the weight. A cat slept in a patch of sun near the back, unmoved by her arrival.

She liked the idea of surprising Valen—ideally finding something he didn't already have.

A shelf labeled *Fables & Folklore* caught her eye, and she slowed.

One book stood out: leather-bound, the spine cracked, gold lettering dulled. *The Prince with No Name.*

She skimmed some of the pages. A lonely ruler. A locked garden. A girl who refused to knock. It wasn't perfect. But it was close enough.

At the front, she exchanged a few coins with the sleepy-eyed clerk. Slipping the book into her bag beside the pastries and paint, she headed through the door.

The walk back felt shorter.

Behind her, the market square faded, the bustle softening into birdsong and the rustle of trees as she neared the edge of town.

Her stride slowed as the house came into view.

A black carriage rolled down the lane, cresting the bend from the estate. Its windows were shut, the horses moving at an unhurried pace.

As it passed, the driver tipped his cap, and Annabelle gave a small wave in return. She watched as it continued along the road, its wheels leaving soft impressions in the gravel.

At the house, the key turned easily, the door creaking open.

And there he was. Valen sat in the sitting room—still in the same spot, as though he'd been holding his breath the whole time.

Once she was inside, his shoulders finally dropped.

"You know I was gone—what, an hour?" she said, smiling.

"Two," he murmured.

"Heavens, you're dramatic." She laughed softly.

She'd meant it lightly. But his expression stayed guarded.

Her smile faltered. "I... didn't mean that the way it sounded."

"I know."

He said it simply. But it landed between them, solid as a stone in the path.

Crossing the room, she slipped her hand into his. "I'm back."

He closed his fingers around hers, an answer in itself.

Moving to the table, she pulled out the bakery parcel and the leather-bound book.

"I brought you something."

He glanced at her, then at what she held. "You didn't have to get me anything."

"I wanted to." She approached, offering it to him. "I hope you don't already have it."

The Prince with No Name. His thumb brushed the worn spine. His breath caught somewhere between his chest and his throat.

The way he looked at the book made her quiet. He opened it slowly and held it as if it might vanish.

She watched him for a moment longer, as if he wasn't entirely in the room yet.

"I also stopped by the bakery," she said, placing the parcel of pastries on the table. "I'll share if you're nice."

He glanced up, distracted. "Hmm? Oh—what do you mean, if I'm nice?"

"I mean exactly what I said." She grinned.

He set the book aside, as if on a pedestal. "Did you get your paints? I can't wait to see what you do with them."

She unwrapped a pastry, carefully. "Oh, I—I'm not sure what I'll create yet. Or if I'll want to share it."

He cocked his head.

"I mean," she added quickly, "I haven't painted in years. And when I did, it was mostly... safe. Landscapes. Flowers."

She turned the pastry slowly. "Never what I wanted. So this feels..."

"New?" he offered.

"Mine. But in a way that's still... scary."

"Then you don't have to share until you're ready."

She blinked, the tightness in her chest finally loosening.

"I'm sharing this, though." She passed him a still-wrapped pastry.

He took it with a faint smile. "Even if I'm not nice?"

"You're on thin ice."

That made him laugh.

She retrieved her bag on the way to the hall, pastry in hand. "I think I'll paint for a while."

Valen picked up the book she'd brought him, thumb resting at the place he'd marked with a ribbon. "I'll be in the library. If you need me."

She headed to her room. Her new sketchbook waited—blank and full of possibility.

CHAPTER 12

The Chase

Annabelle pulled on the deep green dress she hadn't dared wear yesterday. Hair pinned, sleeves smoothed, she left her room.

Valen stood outside. His eyes caught on her shoulders, dipped lower, then finally found hers. "Good morning."

She smiled, knowing exactly what effect she had.

They moved through the house together, down the stairs and past the library. At the far end of the sunny dining room, he opened the garden doors. A gentle breeze drifted in, rich with the scent of roses. Birds called overhead, hidden in the branches.

Outside, everything was in full bloom. Leaves glistened, dew clinging to places the light hadn't reached. The paths were already dry, sun-soaked and waiting.

Wandering deeper, past familiar beds and fountains, they headed toward towering hedges and sunlit archways she'd glimpsed from afar.

They walked slowly, fingers laced, shoulders brushing now and then as the trail narrowed between walls of emerald green.

"You really have a hedge maze."

"I do."

"Of course you do."

Valen shot her a glance, a brow raised. "You sound surprised."

"I'm not. I just want to see what's at the center."

"You'll have to want it enough to find out."

Heading into the tunnel of pale roses, she let her touch linger on the petals, hips swaying with the kind of intent that needed no explanation.

"I want it," she said, not looking back.

As she bent to pluck a violet, her dress slipped—gravity pulling where intention had already drawn his eye.

He inhaled quickly and cleared his throat.

She straightened with a grin, tucked the flower in her hair, and kept walking.

"You're insufferable," he muttered.

"Mm. And you love it."

He didn't argue.

The walkway narrowed, sunlight slipping through the hedges.

She slowed, voice soft, the teasing gone. "So. I'm just here now, then?"

He looked over, but she didn't meet his gaze. "Living in your house. Wearing borrowed clothes. Wandering through a private garden like it makes sense."

"You make it look natural," he said.

"That's the terrifying part," she muttered. "It's starting to feel like it is."

They turned a corner. A petal drifted down into her hair. He reached to brush it away, but paused and let it stay.

"Do you usually take in stray women with mysterious pasts?"

"Only the ones who come through my door in the middle of the night."

"So...?"

"You're the first."

She let the quiet stretch between them. "If I'm the first… what am I, exactly?"

He didn't answer.

"Because I keep waking up wondering what I am here. A guest? A secret? A… future scandal?"

He stopped. "You're not a guest."

"Then what, exactly?"

"…Someone I want to stay."

She paused a second longer, heart kicking up, then kept walking. "A secret scandal. Good to know."

He frowned. "That's not what I meant."

"Doesn't mean it's not true. I wouldn't want to ruin your reputation by association."

He laughed. "Please. Ruin the reputation of a hermit? I can handle the fallout."

"Perfect," she said, smirking. "Then we can be ruined together."

She reached up—tracing the line of his jaw, then down his throat, light as breath.

Her fingers brushed the open collar of his shirt: heat, breath, and something barely held in check.

He swallowed hard.

Then she took the next path as if none of it mattered.

They walked in silence, sunlight dappling through the roses.

The trail dead-ended, foliage closing in. She turned, mischief in her smile. Then she saw his face.

Tension radiated from him as he inched in, until breath and intent were all that remained.

She backed up, spine pressing into the hedge, hands caught halfway up, unsure if she meant to push him away or pull him in.

"That was cruel," he murmured.

"You'll live."

"I might not."

He braced himself beside her against the garden wall, arm sliding around her waist as he leaned in.

She smirked—then slipped beneath his reach, gone before he could stop her.

"What—"

By the time he turned, she was halfway up the garden walk. Boots scuffed the dust. She laughed, the sound bouncing off the hedges.

"Annabelle—"

"You can't corner me and expect me to behave," she called over her shoulder.

He sighed, then ran after her.

Her laughter rang out the moment she heard his footsteps behind her. She darted through the maze, flowers and sunlight blurring past.

Then she skidded to a halt in the clearing at its heart.

A stone-edged pool sat at the center, a simple fountain arcing water into steady ripples.

Benches lined the hedges in a ring, tucked into the shade.

Four archways stood at each point of the compass: tall, trimmed, threaded with vibrant azaleas and trailing wisteria.

Valen caught up moments later.

Her grin was radiant and reckless.

He couldn't decide whether to kiss her there or throw her onto the nearest bench.

"Don't even think about it," she warned, palm raised in mock defiance.

"Oh, I'm definitely thinking about it."

She stepped back—heel catching the fountain's edge. She wobbled, halted mid-step.

"Annabelle—"

His hand shot out, grabbing hers as she tipped.

Their fingers locked, but she was already falling.

Water closed over her in a cold rush, the dress blooming around her like petals.

The chill tore through crepe and skin, dragging her from flirtation into breathless clarity.

She glanced up as he reached for her, droplets sliding down her lashes. But instead of lifting herself, she grinned—and tugged. Hard.

There was a yelp, a curse, and then a splash.

Suddenly, Valen was in the fountain beside her: glaring, hair stuck to his face.

Water sloshed around them. A bird shrieked overhead, wings slicing the silence.

"I—what just—did you really—" he sputtered, flicking droplets away.

"You jumped in after me."

"You pulled me in!"

Her grin widened. "That's not the version I remember."

He stared at her, chin dripping, shirt plastered to him.

Despite the absurdity of it all, she laughed. Light, bright, and utterly unrepentant.

He scowled, unimpressed. "Was that your plan?"

"Not at first."

Valen sat up, shoved wet hair from his face. With a sharp exhale, he shifted to his knees and stood, water cascading off him. His clothes clung, heavy and unforgiving.

He extended both hands, offering surrender with the dignity of a mop with opinions.

She arched a brow. "Really?"

"Yes," he said. "Despite my better judgment."

She paused, narrowing her eyes. "You sure you want to risk it?"

"I've accepted my fate."

She gripped his hands. "Good."

Water streamed down her limbs as she stood, crepe clinging like a second skin. That green had never looked so indecent—and she knew it.

She tucked her hair behind her ear, droplets scattering, and lifted her chin in amused defiance, daring him to pretend he wasn't watching.

Valen's eyes raked over her.

Sliding in close, her gaze traced where wet fabric clung to his chest.

"What a mess," she said, feigning concern. Her voice dropped. "We've got to get you out of those wet clothes."

Reaching for the top button, she popped it open. Then the next. And the next.

She traced along his collarbone. "You're taking this very seriously."

He ached to touch her with more than his hands. She was standing there in a dress that might as well have been painted on.

Each button slipped free under her unhurried touch.

A button snagged. She muttered a curse under her breath, then smiled.

His gaze dropped. Just once. Then back up, sharp. That was a mistake. He tried to focus on anything else: the fountain, the breeze, the flowers.

By the time she reached the last button, he was barely holding it together.

She studied him. "So serious."

"I'm trying to be polite."

Her lips brushed his jaw. "Don't."

The final button gave way too fast. He flinched as his shirt fell open. She hadn't even touched it.

"Do you trust me, Valen?"

"…Yes."

"Then close your eyes and count to ten. Slowly."

He didn't move.

She leaned in. "Please?"

He let out a long sigh and closed his eyes.

"Out loud. And no peeking."

"…One."

She giggled. Nothing amused her more than his hesitation.

"Two."

Her footsteps faded behind him.

"Three."

A laugh, softer now, farther down the way.

"Four…"

When he reached ten, he opened his eyes and froze.

Her dress draped over a low hedge. Sunlight caught a drop still clinging to the fabric. He touched the green crepe—warm from her skin, damp at the seams.

His pulse spiked.

The walkway curved, thick with leaves and perfume.

He rounded the bend. Her underdress waited, sprawled over the curve of a mossy planter, pale cotton catching the light.

A few more steps, and her boots sat under a rose bush.

The trail ended with the last things a lady might take off when she wasn't trying to be one.

A final turn. A dead end.

And her.

She lounged on a stone bench, greenery rising behind her like a stage set for sin, the spotlight already hers. Sunlight spilled through the hedge above, covering her in nothing but light, and the smirk on her lips.

Reclining as though none of it was on purpose, she was all ease and angles, composed for the view without seeming to try.

Lifting a hand, she curled a single finger to beckon him closer.

He didn't hesitate. He was on her in seconds: hands at her waist, mouth against hers, body pressing her into the sun-warmed stone as every last thread of restraint finally broke.

Her gaze found his, flushed and breathless, back arching beneath his grip. Tangled in sunlight, roses, and the hush of a garden made for secrets.

"I wondered what it would take to make you come..." She leaned in, breath hot in his ear. "...undone."

He gripped her thighs, drawing her closer as need surged between them.

"You're overdressed," she whispered, tugging his shirt.

He complied, pulling the heavy fabric off, then stripped the rest: boots kicked off, the last of it tugged free until there was nothing left between them but skin.

This time, he didn't ease in. He pressed her into the bench and took her, hard and wanting and without hesitation.

Gasping, she tipped her head back, fingers digging into his shoulders. She barely felt the stone beneath her, too lost in how he moved.

His mouth found hers. Slow at first, then urgent.

Overwhelmed by the pressure, she arched into him, the ache he knew how to answer.

He drove deeper, a man caught between ruin and relief, each thrust a claim—as if stopping meant losing the only thing that still mattered.

She broke beneath him with a cry. Every thought gone. He followed with a shudder, her name rough in his throat.

They lay tangled in the aftermath: stone cool against their skin, sky bright above the hedges, his cheek resting on her chest.

Everything had been too easy. And easy things never lasted.

She couldn't say it out loud. He pulled her tighter, stillness giving her away.

His fingers drew slow, aimless patterns on her hip. "You knew exactly what you were doing to me," he murmured, voice low and spent.

She grinned into his skin. "Just like you knew what you were doing to me the other day. It was only fair."

He let out a short laugh. Then groaned. "For the record—this bench is a terrible place for—"

"Oh, thank you," she cut in, stretching with a wince. "I thought it might be romantic. My back disagrees."

He chuckled, but she was already watching him too closely.

She wondered if he saw the same thing in her she was starting to see in him: hope for something more.

Standing, he reached for his still-wet trousers. The fabric clung as he tugged them on. His feet squelched into his boots.

The hedge glistened. She stepped toward it, plucked his shirt from the ground, and handed it to him.

He draped it over her shoulders. "You're going to make this shirt indecent."

She slid her arms in, leaving it unbuttoned.

Picking up the violet where it had fallen, he tucked it gently back into her hair.

They talked quietly as they backtracked, gathering her scattered layers: boots, dress, and everything in between.

The twists were behind them now. The hedges gentler. The path, clear. It was as if the maze had been hers all along.

At the house, they left their boots by the door, hoping the afternoon heat would dry them by evening.

The sun was still high, early enough to pretend the day had only begun.

They washed, rinsing away the chill of the fountain, the warmth lingering under their skin.

Using a towel, he dried her hair, and made a complete mess of it. Laughing, she let him try again.

He offered her a shirt, deep gray and soft with wear. It slipped off her shoulder and hit mid-thigh. He didn't complain.

She slid under the covers.

He took the nearby chair, a book in hand, glancing up now and then.

Her breathing slowed as sleep took her.

He stayed there, watching her, not quite trusting the quiet to last.

ACT II

━━━━━━ ◆ ━━━━━━

ENTWINED

CHAPTER 13

The Silence

Amber light flickered from the sconces. The hallway still held the last of the day, but here it had dimmed.

Dinner waited: roasted vegetables steaming, warm bread stacked high, rosemary and smoke curling through the room.

Valen sat across from her, glass in hand, one leg loosely crossed, shirt half-buttoned. Comfortable in a way men rarely were around fire or feelings.

Annabelle stabbed a potato harder than necessary.

"You know," she muttered, swirling her wine, "you don't have to look like that while I'm trying to chew."

He glanced up, brow raised. "Like what?"

"You know exactly what you're doing with your face."

He paused, eyes dropping to her lips, then back. "Perhaps."

"Fine," she said, poking at her plate. "Keep your secrets."

"I'm not hiding anything. You just have to guess first."

She studied him over her glass. "Hmm... Let's start with your favorite tea. You strike me as an Earl Grey man. Black, no sugar. Very brooding."

"Darjeeling, with milk," he corrected, smile tugging. "But I'll take 'brooding' as a compliment. Let me guess—you're an Oolong drinker."

"Oh no," she laughed, brushing it off. "Etiquette classes ruined Oolong for me a long time ago. Jasmine."

"Unexpected." He refilled her glass, fingers lingering at the base.

"What's my favorite time of day?"

He tipped his head, studying her. "Early morning."

"Close," she said, leaning her elbow on the table. "Sunset. Sunrise too, if I'm awake for it. The light's just... sharper then. Colors you don't see any other time."

She stole a roasted carrot off his plate.

"Guess mine."

"You're a midnight kind of man," she said without hesitation.

"Twilight."

"Interesting. How come?"

"Because it's quiet, but not lonely yet."

A candle popped beside them, the flame flaring before it steadied. She poured the last of the wine between their glasses, sliding his across the table.

"Alright. Favorite season?" she asked.

"You guess first," he said.

"Autumn."

His brow lifted. "Yes, actually."

"I knew it. The leaves are dramatic."

He rolled his eyes. "That's not—I like the crisp air. Let me guess, you like summer? Longer days to seduce men in hedge mazes?"

"A close second, though you make a good point. Spring is my favorite. Can't beat the first flowers. You can smell them before you see them."

They kept going, guesses spilling easily, no real rules except to answer. The kind of back-and-forth that made the air feel warmer than the fire.

When the plates were empty, they cleared the table together, their hands brushing now and then—small touches that lingered a moment too long to be accidents.

It was easy with him. Honest in a way she hadn't let herself hope for in ages.

They finished as the lingering daylight slipped behind the trees. He guided her toward her room, his hand light on her back.

As they reached the top of the stairs, three sharp knocks echoed from the front of the house.

Valen stopped. His jaw tightened. A flicker of resignation crossed his face. As if he knew who it was.

He exhaled slowly, frustration barely concealed.

"I'll come say goodnight." He turned, already heading down the hall.

She nodded. A chill prickled down her spine.

In the washroom, she scrubbed harder than she meant to, not sure what she was trying to wash away.

She dropped onto the bed, brushing her damp hair with distracted fingers.

Eventually, she gave up and began pacing. The unease had grown into something gnawing and unshakable.

After too long, curiosity got the better of her and she crept barefoot into the hall.

Listening for a few seconds, she heard distant voices, and started down the stairs. Near the bottom, she froze as a familiar feminine voice drifted from the library.

She moved toward the door, slightly ajar, a sliver of firelight bleeding into the corridor.

Another voice followed, low and muffled but unmistakably Valen.

Her pulse quickened as she got closer.

A breeze stirred the curtain. The house felt colder.

Then the voices stopped. The silence was suffocating.

She inched forward. It was cracked just enough to see through.

Seraphine straddled him in the chair, red dress bunched around her thighs. Her hands tangled in his hair, their mouths locked. His hands gripped her hips, then slid to her chest.

Annabelle couldn't breathe. She backed off, a knot twisting in her stomach.

Seraphine moaned. He didn't pull away.

The sight was too much. She looked elsewhere before she could see the tension in his arms, the stillness of his mouth.

What she saw was enough. Her hand fell from the handle.

She turned and ran.

As if any hesitation might let the hurt lunge and drag her under.

She didn't stay to see him shove Seraphine back—hard—and rise, voice sharp with fury.

The latch clicked behind her, the sound barely registering over the thunder in her chest.

Still wearing the borrowed shirt, her body numb, she climbed into bed.

She curled onto her side, eyes open for a while before finally closing them.

Her hands knotted in the sheets. She didn't realize how tightly until her knuckles ached.

Footsteps paused outside her room. Then the hinges creaked.

She lay motionless, but felt him there, his presence shifting the air like gravity.

"Goodnight, Annabelle," Valen whispered, soft but not steady.

She almost said his name. Almost reached for him. But her lips stayed closed, hands curling tighter beneath the blanket.

The door shut again.

She waited until the silence settled, then turned her face into the pillow and fell apart.

Time passed. Or maybe it didn't.

"I know you're not sleeping."

Gasping, Annabelle sat up sharply.

Seraphine stood at the foot of the bed, a silhouette carved from shadow and silk, her red dress catching what little moonlight crept through the curtains.

Annabelle pulled the covers higher, as if they could protect her.

"Please," Seraphine said, tilting her head, voice dry. "If I wanted to hurt you, I'd do it properly."

Seraphine's smile didn't reach her eyes. "I just thought..." She stepped forward. "Maybe you finally figured out what I've known all along."

Annabelle's voice scraped the air. "And what's that?"

"He's very good at meaning it," Seraphine said, tone smooth as silk. "Until he doesn't. He plays pretend. Tells himself he's different now. But he always ends up back in the same pattern."

Annabelle's jaw clenched, but she didn't argue. Some part of her—the part aching—believed it.

Seraphine shrugged. "You can go," she said. "The door will open."

Annabelle blinked. "What?"

"I know how to make it open," Seraphine said. "Always have."

Annabelle didn't ask how or want to know. Her chest ached. But what else had she expected?

It had always been temporary. She'd forgotten that when it started to feel like home.

This wasn't her world. Wasn't her place.

She'd stumbled into something beautiful. Of course it was never going to last—not for someone like her.

Seraphine turned to go, fingers trailing along the dresser. "I'll be waiting downstairs," she added, glancing back once. "When you're ready."

Then she was gone.

Annabelle got up, found her bag in the corner: her house key and the last of her money.

She moved through the motions, as if her bones remembered how to leave.

At the far wall, she pulled out the dress she'd worn the night she arrived: dark blue, simple, hem frayed.

The green dress swayed in the wardrobe, taunting her.

She stepped out of his gray shirt and let it fall. Getting dressed took longer, fumbling with the side hooks, tugging it closed without fastening them all. It hung crooked, but she didn't care.

Reaching for her cloak, she shrugged it over her shoulders and snugged it close.

The room felt unfamiliar, the edges sharpened the moment she stopped pretending she belonged.

Her gaze drifted to the supplies: her brushes, the sketchbook, the little tin of watercolors she'd started hoarding.

Moving toward them, her fingers brushed the nearest handle, then stopped.

She straightened the desk with care, each motion more final than the last.

Then she turned away. Her boots waited by the threshold, but she didn't put them on, carried them in one hand instead. Perhaps she wanted to feel the ground.

She slipped into the hallway and moved quietly down the stairs.

The hall had deepened into shadow. Or maybe it had always looked this way, and she'd seen it through softer eyes.

Seraphine waited in the sitting room, silent, watching as Annabelle entered and pulled on her boots.

When Annabelle reached the threshold, hand on the handle, Seraphine said softly, "He'll say it meant nothing. Maybe even to himself."

Annabelle paused.

"He might even believe that," Seraphine added. "But you saw what you saw."

Annabelle didn't turn as she opened the door, took one final deep breath, and stepped into the night.

CHAPTER 14

The Aftermath

Valen never really slept. But last night, even stillness escaped him.

After Seraphine left—her presence like a storm that touched nothing but left everything wrong—he returned to the library. To the quiet. To the chessboard. Anything.

The board sat mid-play. He ran the same opener again and again. He knew it by heart, but his thoughts wouldn't stop.

Her repeat intrusion. The kiss he didn't want. The exit he hoped was the last.

By the time morning light stretched across the floor, he was already picturing breakfast: checking on Annabelle, making tea, letting the quiet be shared.

He knocked on her door and waited. No answer.

"Annabelle?" he called, opening it.

The blankets were tucked too tightly, as if she'd never slept there. But something rested on the covers.

A small stack of watercolor paper, pages carefully placed, the edges curled from dried dampness.

Every step made it harder to breathe.

Three, maybe four paintings. Each different, but unmistakably hers.

One showed a sky streaked with orange, rose, and violet. Wildflowers scattered along the bottom in vibrant, imperfect dabs.

Another was all color: swirls and splashes, like motion itself had been captured. As though she'd let herself feel without caring if it made sense.

A third was quieter: blues, mostly, forming a garden that could have been his.

The last... he wasn't sure what it was. But it *glowed*.

It ached with light. As if it were painted by someone who finally believed she could create something beautiful—and did.

She hadn't been practicing; she'd been confessing.

These were parts of her: honest, joyful, and free.

And she left them there. Deliberately.

He sank onto the bed, the paper soft beneath his fingers.

That's when he saw it: the key, half-buried in the sheets.

He left it alone. Touching it would make it real.

The ringing in his ears didn't stop.

She was gone. And she'd left joy behind—because she couldn't carry it anymore.

The weight settled. Not grief yet, but the shape of where it would grow.

"Aw," said a voice behind him: smug, syrupy, unmistakable. "Gone already?"

Seraphine stood in the doorway, smirking. Red dress still impeccable, like she hadn't left claw marks in her wake.

Silence clung to the room in the wrong way. As if Annabelle had never been there at all. Even the paintings looked out of place without her hands to anchor them.

He didn't trust himself to breathe.

Seraphine gave a delicate shrug, her voice thick with manufactured pity. "She looked exhausted. Poor thing. I felt bad and let her out."

Let her out.

His jaw locked. In his chest, the rot of old want crumbled to ash.

It wasn't her door to open.

But Seraphine had always known where to press. Where the lock was weakest.

So when she opened it anyway, without asking, it wasn't just cruel. It was familiar.

That same cold sense of being left behind. Again.

Annabelle was gone.

And Seraphine was still standing there, as if the emptiness might make him worship her again.

"She didn't even say goodbye," Seraphine went on, eyes wide with mock sweetness. "I suppose she finally realized what we already knew: you always ruin things in the end."

Silence stretched.

"There was never anything between us, Seraphine," he said, voice flat.

"I was never yours." He avoided her gaze. "I'd rather let the sea take me under if it meant I never had to see your face again."

Seraphine blinked, then flinched. Expression cracking before she could catch it.

"You didn't want me," he said. "You just didn't want her to have me. You were the last mistake I let define me."

Then he walked past her—without a glance—as if she wasn't there at all.

Seraphine stared at him, pale and open-mouthed. Then scoffed.

"You'll regret that," she muttered, more to herself than to him. "There are still six hundred thirty-seven men who'd kill for a chance with me."

She turned with calculation, one shoulder slicing the air like a blade, and swept out. A few moments later, the front door slammed shut with all the finality of a casket.

A vase near the stairs shuddered from the force, its water sloshing over and pooling across the floorboards.

Valen stood alone in the hallway.

Annabelle's boots were gone. Her bag. Not even the room remembered where she'd been.

And he didn't understand why.

He could've survived a fight. A slammed door. A bitter goodbye.

Not the silence that said nothing—and took everything.

He'd opened himself up. *Really* opened. Let her see him. Let her in.

Now he was hollow. Carved clean through, like joy had left its own grave.

He turned and walked to the library. The quiet closed in, dense as fog.

The sofa waited, the one where she'd once curled beside him, teased him over tea, leaned against him without hesitation. Now lifeless cushions. A fire that offered nothing back.

He stood again, crossed to the window. Outside, the morning mist clung thick to the glass, trees little more than shadows beyond it. No tracks. No lantern glow.

His hand found the mantle, then the doorknob, as if movement might trick his body into believing it still mattered. As if choosing a hallway and starting to walk would somehow lead him to her.

But there was nowhere to go. No clue. Not even a note.

He released the handle. The metal stayed cold.

As he leaned forward, his hand slipped and hit the table's corner, sharp enough to sting. He didn't react.

His thoughts twisted, hard and unforgiving.

He tried to rebuild the walls that had always kept him safe. The ones she'd slipped past like they weren't even there.

Every lock, he'd unlatched for her. Let her look, linger, laugh. But now, he couldn't close it again.

The hinges didn't fit anymore. They felt wrong.

Leather creaked beneath his weight. His boots scraped the rug, dragging a corner loose.

He pressed his elbows to his knees, fingers steepled at his brow, and sat there in the silence.

Empty. Alone.

Because that's what he'd always been. Maybe all he was ever meant to be.

———————— ◆ ————————

Elsewhere, in a room carved from glass and ego, Seraphine sat.

One shoe swung at the ankle. Too precise to be casual, too practiced to be relaxed.

Her crystal throne shimmered beneath her, sharp-edged and built to flatter.

The room held only what mattered: her seat, three mirrors, a glowing counter. Everything else was distraction.

Her gaze stayed fixed on the illuminated counter. Not a clock, though it resembled one: three narrow windows with ivory plates that flipped to reveal numbers.

637.

With a controlled breath through her nose, she steadied herself.

She'd spent the last hour like this: head high, shoulders set, waiting for the number to climb.

It didn't.

"Only one lost," she murmured. "No pattern. Nothing to read into."

Somewhere beyond the walls, a hinge groaned. Seraphine didn't flinch, but the sound crawled across the crystal floor like doubt.

She adjusted the line of her dress, smoothing a wrinkle that wasn't there.

Red silk took the light—too vivid for a room that reflected nothing but her.

She checked her nails. Let her hand trail the arm of the throne. One tap, then another. She caught herself.

"It'll be back to six hundred thirty-eight by morning."

But it hadn't changed. Not in hours.

Her mouth tightened. She looked away.

In the distance, the counter still burned.

637.

Her fingers flexed against the armrest, like movement might confirm something she wasn't ready to name.

She stood. Her heels clicked, echoing through the hollow chamber.

The mirrors waited. Her flawless reflection smiled from the center pane.

But the crack that appeared when the number flickered had deepened.

No longer a faint hairline. Now it carved down the glass, jagged and mean, from her temple to her collarbone. As if the mirror split under something it couldn't bear.

She stared, willing it to fade. Shifted her stance. Tilted her chin. Smoothed her hair.

The crack stayed.

It traced her face like a scar from someone else's memory. A version of her she'd never consented to.

She narrowed her eyes. Stepped closer. Lifted a hand to her cheek. Relief flickered when her fingers found only smooth, perfect skin.

But the mirror said otherwise.

Her gaze flicked back across the room. Just once.

The counter still burned.

637.

Her throat went tight.

Valen meant it. He didn't want her.

A thin splinter veined out from the crack. The mirror trembled—fragile and unmistakable.

She opened her mouth to deny it, to say something. Anything. Nothing came.

Only her reflection stared back at her, fractured and final.

Irrevocably alone.

CHAPTER 15

The Hollow

The carriage slowed as it rolled onto the familiar drive, the rumble beneath the wheels jolting Annabelle awake.

She blinked, groggy and disoriented. The driver opened the door and offered a hand.

"Will you be alright from here, miss?" he asked as she stepped down.

She nodded, barely.

"Any friend of Mr. Valen's is a friend of mine."

He tipped his cap and turned away, the carriage rattling off into the distance. The sun was sinking, the street quiet.

The gravel crunched beneath her boots, cold air slipping down her collar as she made her way to the walkway.

She tugged her cloak tighter. The fabric still held a faint trace of rosemary and smoke.

The windows watched her, dark and empty.

For a moment it felt as if it were a bad dream, but her chest ached, her eyes burned, and the wind carried the sharp memory of him.

She crossed the porch and reached for her key. It weighed more than it should have.

The key turned with a soft click and the wooden door swung open into the waiting silence.

Stepping inside, she shut the door and locked it without thinking. She set her bag down, pulled off her boots and cloak.

In the center of the main room, she lingered, gaze drifting over worn edges and empty spaces. It was still hers, but not home.

She collapsed onto the sofa, the sobs tearing out as if her heart had only just caught up to her body.

The tears stopped eventually, though she couldn't say when. Only that sleep dragged her under.

Pale gray sunlight filtered through the curtains as Annabelle stirred, stretched across the floor in uneven stripes.

She blinked, started to sit up, and froze.

Mason, her neighbor's grandson, stood a few feet away, watching her.

His posture was casual, but his gaze wasn't—eyes too small, giving his face a pinched look that knotted her stomach.

He didn't speak or move.

The blanket had slipped off in the night, leaving her sprawled across the sofa. Her dress had ridden up, twisted awkwardly at the waist, the neckline lower than she would have chosen.

She jerked it back into place, skin crawling under his gaze as she forced herself to clear her throat. "Mason. What...?"

He smiled, easy and uninvited.

"Didn't expect to find you here," he said, voice light, but his eyes never left her body.

She drew the throw tighter, willing him to look away. He didn't.

"I was swinging by. Checking on the place like you asked."

Right. She'd told him to check the house. It felt like something she'd done in another life.

"I got in late," she said, brushing a hand through her hair. "Wasn't really thinking ahead."

He shrugged, turning toward the kitchen. "Want coffee?"

She hesitated, then nodded, anything to break his gaze. "Sure."

The kettle clanked. Water sloshed. Cabinet doors opened and shut. She sat, listening to sounds she used to know by heart. Now just... wrong.

His voice drifted from the other side of the counter. "So... did you do what you needed to?"

"...What?"

"You left kind of suddenly. No explanation."

She didn't answer, staring at the wall until the kettle began to whine.

Several minutes passed before he returned, mug in each hand. The smell hit first—burned and bitter. He handed her the mug, fingers lingering too long.

She shifted, pulling one knee under the coverlet. The liquid was thin and scorched. She drank anyway, without meeting his eyes.

He sipped. "You back for good now?"

"Yeah. I think so."

He held her gaze over the rim of his cup, then set it down with a tap. "I've been meaning to ask you something. Didn't get the chance before you took off—"

"Can we talk later?" she cut in gently, raising the mug toward her face like a shield. "I didn't sleep much. Still a little out of it."

He paused long enough for her to notice, then smiled again, smaller than before. "Yeah. Sure."

She draped the blanket over her shoulders and stood.

"Thanks for the coffee."

She crossed to the door and nudged it open in silent suggestion.

Mason hesitated, mug in hand. His gaze flicked to hers, still sure he belonged here somehow.

Then he stepped in like it was allowed, and wrapped her in a hug before she could pull away.

Her arms stayed stiff, her shoulders tense. He pressed in hard—chest crushing hers, like he wanted to memorize her shape.

"Glad you're back, Anna."

He leaned closer, breathing in near her hairline.

"Still smells like you."

Her stomach twisted. The scent of him clung to her like a stain. She hadn't heard that name in over a week. It didn't fit anymore. Maybe it never had.

She tried for a small, brittle smile and said nothing. After a moment, he stepped onto the porch.

Closing the door, she turned the lock, the click loud in the silence.

The house was too still without him, and somehow not still enough. She didn't feel safer, only smaller.

Crossing the room, she climbed the narrow stairs to the bedroom. The bathing chamber opened off it, simple and spare.

She knelt by the small stove tucked against the wall, striking a match to light it. It caught with a sputter. The kettle was already near full. She set it over the flame to heat.

While the water warmed, her reflection waited in the mirror above the basin.

She wore the same dress she had left in, the same hem, the same worn buttons, but it hung differently now.

Heavier, as if it carried the weight of everything she'd tried and failed to outrun.

A stranger's face stared back: pale, hollow-eyed, the angles sharper than she remembered.

She touched her cheek, half-expecting her hand to pass through.

Behind her, the kettle rattled, steam curling into the room like breath.

She peeled off the dress slowly, then poured the steaming water into the tub, tempering it with a splash from the nearby jug of cool water.

The bath was angry, as though it was trying to boil the grief from her.

Lavender drifted up with the heat, catching her off guard.

His scent hit next, rising from her skin like punishment.

She almost forgot where she was, almost believed he was still there. The scent coiled around her as though it might anchor her, but faded fast, like everything else she tried to hold.

Her jaw clenched, a pulse ticking in her neck.

She let her head fall back against the tub rim and closed her eyes.

Silence pressed in, choking her—behind her ribs, turning breath into effort.

There was a hole in her chest where he'd been.

The water was cold when she woke, her fingers pruned, her skin chilled.

She got out slowly, wrapped herself in a towel.

The warmth from earlier was gone. The house felt dimmer, off in a way she couldn't name.

She dressed in simple clothes, enough to look alive if no one looked too closely.

As she went downstairs, she spotted the art corner. She moved the screen and slid inside.

A watercolor sat on the table, a piece she barely remembered painting. A sun-warmed path through trees, pale wildflowers on either side.

Or it should have been.

Now the color was stripped out, as if the paper had forgotten how to hold warmth.

She stared for a moment, then tucked it beneath the others.

The next few were the same: watercolors. A lake at dusk, a garden walkway, a windowsill with overripe fruit. Each dulled, now drained to gray.

Toward the bottom were charcoal sketches. Trees again: trunks and twisted branches, some with dark hollows carved through them.

Her hand hovered over one, brushing the edge. It smeared, leaving a mark across the paper.

She lingered on it, the hollow echoing in her chest.

Placing the pages down, she backed away. She couldn't imagine showing them to anyone, but didn't have the heart to throw them out.

Maybe a walk would help.

Outside, the air cut sharper than expected, slipping under her cloak and biting at her skin as if even the breeze wanted her gone.

The town looked the same but smaller, frayed at the edges, as if it had shrunk while she was away.

People passed with polite nods, quick glances, the flicker of recognition without memory.

She smiled when she was supposed to, said hello, kept her head down and steps steady. She didn't offer more, didn't ask for it either.

The streets felt narrower, the shop windows duller, the buildings hunched against the gray sky.

She walked on to stay ahead of the ache chasing her. It didn't help.

Stopping at the grocer, she picked up a few essentials absently. She managed small talk with the shopkeeper and nothing more.

By the time she turned the last corner home, the sun was low and bruised, the streets long and empty. Her head buzzed with the beginnings of a headache. Her feet ached with every stride.

She wanted warmth, a quiet nook to disappear into. But someone stood on her front step.

Mason waited, arms locked against his chest.

Straightening when he saw her, he brushed at his sleeve like he needed something to do with his hands.

He was dressed too carefully, shirt tucked tight, hair slicked back the wrong way—aiming for casual and missing by a mile.

Her stomach sank.

"Oh," she said, stopping short. "I wasn't expecting company."

He smiled as if he expected her to be impressed.

"Didn't want the evening to get away," he said. "Dinner? I dropped by the restaurant—told them to expect us. Figured I'd save you the trouble."

She hesitated, shifting her weight. "I... Mason, I'm still tired from the trip. Yesterday was long. Today too."

His smile faltered. A pause hung.

"Oh. That's... great," he said quickly. "Guess I'll go back... again. Maybe tomorrow night?"

A practiced curve touched her lips. "Tomorrow. Sure."

He nodded, overly satisfied, as if he heard a yes that never left her mouth.

"I'll come by tomorrow evening?" he asked, already assuming the answer.

She gave a slight nod, reaching for the handle.

He lingered long enough to sour the silence. Then he smiled once more and turned away.

Waiting until he reached the bottom step, she watched him disappear around the corner without another word.

Only then did she exhale and slip inside.

Securing the door out of habit, she let the bolt slide home with a dull click. But the lock didn't matter. Nothing did.

She dropped the bag and forgot it.

The remainder of the day, she moved through the motions mindlessly: tea she didn't drink, a book she didn't read, a house too empty to feel hers.

Sleep came eventually, shallow and restless, curling sharp behind her ribs.

CHAPTER 16

The Fog

She drifted through the next day like smoke—washed a dish, folded a towel, took a seat at the table, forgetting why she'd sat in the first place.

The world felt muted, as if someone had lowered the volume on everything that used to matter.

At some point, she found herself in the art corner. Sunlight caught the dust. The air smelled of dried pigment and old paper.

She touched the sketchpad, picked up a brush, but set it down again.

Charcoal sticks scattered. She stepped on one as she turned, smudging the floor.

She shut the folding screen behind her. The quiet didn't belong to her anymore.

Somewhere outside, a window slammed. She didn't flinch.

It was as if she were watching herself in a dream she'd already forgotten: brushing cabinets, closing drawers she never meant to open.

She stood in the doorway, unsure why, then lay on the bed fully dressed. The ceiling hadn't changed. But she had.

Once, she'd been someone else, somewhere else. Now that person felt too far to reach.

The pillow smelled faintly of sandalwood. Or maybe she wanted it to.

She shut her eyes. There was nothing more she cared to look at.

Morning bled into afternoon. She woke sore, heavy, no closer to clarity.

Outside, life kept moving. She wanted to care, but couldn't.

By late day, she'd changed, only because the fabric itched. She hadn't eaten. Or spoken. The only sounds were the house creaking and the steady tick of the clock.

She barely registered the first knock. The second was harder to ignore.

Eventually, she pulled the curtain just enough to see out. Cold air leaked through the frame.

Mason stood on the porch, smiling like he'd practiced.

His hair was combed, shirt tucked, boots polished—like he'd dressed up to be someone else and missed the mark.

She answered the door, then remembered what night it was, and how easily she'd agreed to something she didn't want.

"Evening. You ready?" His voice was much too chipper.

She blinked at his clothes. "Didn't realize this was a formal event."

He laughed, loud enough to make her wince. "You look fine."

"Thanks."

She paused before stepping outside. The cold bit at her arms.

"Give me a second." She stepped inside to pull on her boots and shrugged on her cloak. It still smelled like Valen.

She locked the door and slipped the key into her pocket.

He offered his arm. She ignored it, walking beside him instead.

The local restaurant was small and cozy, almost uncomfortably so. Candles everywhere, oil lamps tried to warm the corners.

He held the door with too much flair. She walked past him without a word.

The host led them to a corner table by the window, private and tucked away. The kind of spot that started whispers. Someone always noticed.

She nudged her chair until the distance felt tolerable.

The menus hadn't even arrived before Mason began talking. "So what did you do while you were gone? You never really said."

She reached for her water. "I needed a break. A different view."

He nodded as if that explained everything. "Bet it was peaceful. This town gets so boring."

He launched into gossip: who might be pregnant, which shop was barely staying open, the price of corn.

She gave the expected nod, offered the occasional polite comment, but none of it stuck. The words drifted past, thin and meaningless.

"You know, some folks would call this courting." Mason grinned over the rim of his glass.

"...What?"

He laughed, trying for charm. "I asked you to dinner. You said yes. Just wondering where we stand."

She drank instead of answering. "I'm not sure, Mason. I'm still sorting myself out."

"Right. Of course." He tipped his chair back. "Though I wouldn't be surprised if half the town thinks we're courting after tonight."

A sick weight settled behind her ribs, but she smiled anyway, the kind her mother taught her to use instead of speaking her mind.

The waiter arrived. "We'll both have the lemon herb chicken," Mason said, handing over both menus.

"I was actually going to—"

"Figured you'd order the usual." He winked.

She hadn't even decided. But somehow he had.

The drinks he'd ordered were brought out. She sipped hers. The bitterness lingered on her tongue.

Dinner dragged. Mason filled every silence as if her voice didn't matter.

Pretending grew too heavy. She pushed her chair away. "Excuse me for a moment."

He stood halfway, as if he might follow.

The washroom was too bright. The surfaces too stark. She doused her face with water. Her reflection blinked back, pale and not quite hers.

Even the soap smelled wrong—too sweet, out of place. It slipped from her hands, splashing in the basin.

She dried off and straightened her dress. Lifted her chin, though her shoulders stayed hunched.

On her way out, a shadow shifted outside. She squinted, uneasy, then glanced toward her seat.

Mason leaned over her plate, sawing off another piece of chicken. "Thought you were finished," he mumbled, mouth half-full.

She recoiled at the scrape of silverware. "It's fine. I was."

The last of her appetite dissolved.

Valen came to mind again, uninvited. The weight of his voice: *Goodnight, Annabelle.* The way he didn't just look at her but saw her.

Mason, on the other hand, looked at her like something he already owned. A prize he'd waited long enough to claim.

She realized, with a sinking certainty, that being near him made her skin crawl.

Through the window, a black carriage sat across the street, lanterns low, nearly swallowed by dark. She stared. It seemed familiar, but she couldn't trust her eyes.

She focused on her glass instead and let the silence thicken.

The waiter brought the bill. She didn't ask for him to pay, but he grinned as if the night had gone exactly as planned.

She threw on her cloak and stepped outside.

The air was brisk, but she barely noticed. All she wanted was to get home and forget the evening ever happened.

"Hey, I almost forgot—I wanted to show you something." He veered off the main road, guiding her with a hand at her back.

"What? Can't it wait?" She didn't want to spend another second with him. She nearly said no, but followed anyway.

"Nah, it'll only take a minute."

The street narrowed into an alley. The gas lamps thinned, leaving more shadow than light. Something twisted in her gut.

"So... what is it?" she asked, hoping to hurry him along.

He muttered, too low to catch, then turned. A cheesy grin plastered across his face.

"Anna, sweetie. Can I call you that?" He didn't wait for an answer.

"I've been holding this in too long." He shifted his weight. "I love you, Anna. Always have."

"Since the day I met you." He stepped closer.

"I waited the best I could, what with you being a widow and all. But it's time we stopped pretending." He opened his arms, expecting a hug—or maybe a fanfare.

Her brain stalled. "...What? Is this—"

He advanced a half-step. "You basically admitted we're courting at dinner. I'm just giving you what you've always wanted."

"Mason, I—" She tried to retreat, but there was nowhere left to go.

He smiled as if she'd confirmed it all. "I know, it's scary. But you've been alone too long. You need a man in your life."

She wondered how long he'd been rehearsing this. How long he'd been rewriting her life into his.

He hovered nearer. She edged down the wall, trying to stay calm. Stone scraped the backs of her legs.

"I've been fine. And I'm not sure I'm ready—"

"You won't know unless you try. Our love is strong—I feel it. I see how you look at me."

"No, Mason. I don't love you. You don't even know me." Her shoulder clipped brick. She was trapped between buildings.

He kept coming, a flicker of anger breaking through before it vanished.

"I know plenty about you. Like your morning baths. How you always leave the curtain open for me."

She stared. "You... watched me?"

"Or how you kept that shawl I gave you?"

She'd hidden that in a hat box in her closet. The thought of him in her bedroom turned her stomach.

"You went through my things." The air felt thinner, too sharp to breathe.

He'd been inside her life in ways she hadn't even known to fear.

Reaching up, he brushed the side of her face. "You make me feel special, Anna. That's what I love about you."

"Mason, I don't think..." She turned, reaching to knock his arm away.

He caught her by the wrist, pushing it aside. "Thinking complicates things. Let me handle that. You focus on being happy, staying home, and keeping things warm."

She glanced over his shoulder, toward the glimmer of light behind him.

"Now, what do you say we take 'us' to the next level, hmm?" He leaned in, eyes closed, lips already reaching for hers.

She shoved him hard. He staggered, cursing. She ran.

But he caught up fast, yanking her by the elbow.

"What is wrong with you?" Whatever charm he had left slipped. Only anger remained.

"Let go of me, Mason!" She struggled, but he only tightened his grip, shoving her into the wall.

"Why'd you make me do that?" His voice was too loud, as though he needed the echo to agree with him. "It's always the same with you."

She reached up to try to fight: scratch him, slap him, anything. But he grabbed her and pinned her arm above her head.

"This will be much more pleasant for both of us if you accept it." He moved in, aiming for her mouth as if he deserved it.

His breath smelled like molasses and meat—sweet rot and arrogance.

She closed her eyes, bracing for impact.

"Unhand her."

Mason froze, as if disbelief alone would erase him.

A tall figure stood at the alley's end, dressed in black. Light caught the sharp angles of his face.

"One second, sweetie. Man business." He let go of her arm and tousled her hair, mock affection that made her clench her teeth.

Mason scoffed, turning halfway. "This doesn't concern you, alright?"

That was all she needed.

She dropped and drove her head into his jaw, hard.

He staggered back, cursing. One hand pressed to his face, the other fumbling against the wall.

Annabelle stumbled, catching herself on rough stone. Her heart thundered.

Pain flared in her skull, but she didn't care. She'd do it again.

Her knees buckled. The alley tilted. She dropped, hitting the ground harder than she expected.

Before Mason recovered, Valen stepped in close.

His voice was low. "Stay away from her. Leave this town. You won't get another warning."

Mason looked between them: bleeding, breathless, pride leaking faster than his spit.

Then he ran. Footsteps echoed down the alley as he disappeared into the dark.

Valen didn't wait. As soon as Mason vanished, he dropped to her side.

His hands shook, giving him away. "Annabelle."

"...Valen? What are you...?" she barely managed. The world was slowly coming back into view.

She'd run from him, too. But somehow he'd come for her.

He looked her over, quick and frantic, then exhaled as if he'd been drowning.

"Thank goodness. Are you alright?" His voice cracked. "Did he hurt you?"

"I'm... fine. I think. Where did he...? How did you...?" She trailed off, rattled.

"He's gone, but you hit your head pretty hard. We need to get you out of here. Can you stand?"

She rose halfway before the strength drained out of her. He caught her.

"Hold onto me." He slid his arm around her waist.

"How... how did you find me?"

He hesitated, the explanation cluttered on his tongue. "I'll explain later."

She clung to him, unsteady, as he led her through the shadows. Each step jostled the ache in her skull.

The carriage waited where he'd left it.

After a moment, the driver jumped down, brows knit, and opened the door. "Everything alright, ma'am?"

"Yes, I'm fine. Thank you," she said.

Valen climbed in first, then turned to help. She gripped the side for balance as he lifted her in—one hand steady at her waist, the driver ready in case she faltered.

She collapsed into the seat, trembling from more than the cold.

Without thinking, she leaned against him, her head finding his shoulder.

He didn't move at first. Then his arm came around her.

Outside, the driver waited. Valen knocked twice. "Take the long way."

She let her eyes close. The knot in her chest started to loosen. Her breath left slow and deep, and exhaustion pulled her under.

CHAPTER 17

The Mend

The carriage rocked gently, the town slipping past in silence. The driver followed the long route.

Only the creaking frame, hooves on cobblestone, and the weight of what had just happened filled the hush between them.

Annabelle stirred, breath shallow. Her fingers curled near his lapel, as if her body still clung to safety even in sleep.

He held her, hand warm against her back.

The wheels slowed onto a familiar lane.

"We're back at your house," Valen murmured. "You're safe."

She sat up too fast. Her head throbbed. "Ow... right. Mason."

"That was him?"

"Yeah."

The driver helped her down.

A door opened and shut nearby. She whipped around. "Oh no..."

"What is it?"

"Might be Mason. He lives next door," she whispered.

"Silas, stay with her."

He tipped the brim of his driver's cap in reply.

Silas steadied her as she sank onto the carriage step, then handed her a small paper-wrapped bundle.

She unwrapped a piece of bread. Stared for a moment, then took a bite—more reflex than hunger. It hit her stomach as if it had forgotten how to take food at all.

Valen crossed to the other end of the duplex. An older woman with a lantern appeared around the corner.

"Apologies, ma'am, thought you were someone else."

"Looking for Mason, I expect," she said, drawing her shawl closer, like she hadn't meant to be out long.

"Yes, ma'am. Have you seen him?"

"Came and left in a hurry. Made quite a ruckus." She peered past Valen toward the carriage. "Did something happen?"

"He was... being untoward. With Annabelle."

"Annabelle...? Oh—Anna. That poor girl's been through enough."

"If my Thaddeus were still here—rest his soul—he'd have given that boy a proper spanking. Doesn't matter how old he is. Never too old for a paddlin', he always said."

She drifted for a moment, then caught herself. "Anyway—are you a friend of hers?"

"Yes—how rude of me. Valen." He gave a small bow. "I was worried about her. Glad I got there when I did."

"Is she alright?"

"She hit her head. She's a bit shaken, that's all."

"Would you mind keeping an eye on her, then? I doubt Mason will be back—if he knows what's good for him—but hard to say with that boy. Head's thicker than a walnut."

"Of course, ma'am. I wasn't planning to leave her alone."

"Good, good. Let her know I'm here if she needs anything."

"Will do. Thank you, ma'am." He bowed again.

She waved to Annabelle and headed back inside.

When Valen returned to the carriage, Silas gave Annabelle a quiet pat on the shoulder, then went to tend the horses.

She half-rose, then settled again. "Was that Mrs. Linton? What did she say? Is he here?"

"He was, but he left. She doesn't think he'll come back."

Annabelle exhaled, her shoulders easing—but the knot in her stomach stayed.

"Will you... stay? Just in case?"

He extended an arm. "I came to make sure you were safe. I still mean to. Even if it means sitting on your porch all night."

"You don't... have to stay out here. You can come inside."

She pulled the key from her cloak and stepped inside. The house was dark, but streetlight filtered through the curtains.

"My room's just up here," she said, gesturing to the stairs. "You can take the sofa. Or whatever you need."

She hesitated at the first step.

"Valen? Could you... help me? I'm not sure I can..."

She turned, and he was already there, arms braced on either side.

"I've got you."

He steadied her as they climbed, one careful step at a time.

At the top, she leaned into him, guiding herself to the mattress.

"Let me," he said, turning down the covers.

She crawled into bed and let out a slow breath. "...Thank you. I—I don't..."

"It's okay. We can talk tomorrow. Just rest." He pulled the blankets gently over her.

Crossing the room, he dragged a chair closer. "I'll be right here."

She was already half-asleep when he sat down.

Later, she shifted, softly moaning, limbs tense.

"I'm here," he whispered, brushing dampness from her brow. "You're alright."

She didn't wake again.

Valen kept his eyes on her.

By mid-morning, Annabelle stirred—body aching, head pounding in time with her heartbeat, mouth dry. She blinked against the light spilling through the curtains.

Her throat tightened. She tried to sit up, but dizziness forced her down.

"Easy," he murmured, rising to steady her. His hand hovered near her shoulder. "Take it slow."

She sank into the pillow. "Can we... talk now?"

"Only if you're up to it. I can wait."

She turned to face him. "Why are you here?"

"I had a bad feeling. I couldn't ignore it. I just—I had to know you were safe."

"The carriage," she murmured. "I thought I saw it through the window."

"I didn't know if you'd want to see me." His voice was slow, as if the words didn't want to leave his mouth.

"After everything, I'm surprised you still care."

Valen stilled, the hurt flickering behind his eyes. "Why?"

"Because I left," she said.

"I thought you were asleep when I said goodnight. But in the morning you were just... gone. I had no idea what happened. Or what I did wrong." His words frayed at the edges.

The silence deepened.

She whispered, "I saw you. In the library. With Seraphine."

He froze, his face shifting—from confusion to clarity to horror.

"She was on your lap, Valen. Kissing you. Your hands—" Her voice cracked. "It looked like..."

She looked away. "I left. Because it looked like you'd made your choice."

He exhaled slowly, as if the air had been knocked from his lungs.

"She showed up uninvited. She always does when she wants something. She said she just needed a minute," he said, tone low and controlled. "I told her to make it quick. She went toward the library. I followed, thinking I could shut it down, get her out, and return to say goodnight."

His fists tightened in his lap. "That must've been the moment you came in. Right on cue for her... performance."

"She was—" Her throat burned as she tried to form the words. "On your chest. Your hands..."

"No. I was pushing her off. I shoved her hard enough to knock over the chair." His tone wavered. "She planned it. Wanted you to see. To leave."

"I didn't just tell her to get out—I tore her apart. Told her there was no us. That there never had been. That I'd rather drown than spend another second with her. She's all but dead to me," he said.

"I didn't choose her, Annabelle. Not then. Not ever."

Annabelle sat there, stunned, Seraphine's voice still echoing in her mind.

The memory was burned in. She wasn't sure she could unsee it.

But looking at him, she saw something else.

He wasn't hiding. He wasn't trying to charm his way out of it.

Her eyes dropped to his fists, clenched tight. As if letting go would make everything come apart.

If he was lying, it was the worst performance she'd ever seen.

But if he wasn't... maybe she'd already broken something far more important than she realized.

"Will you... lie down with me?" She met his gaze.

He blinked, as if he couldn't quite believe what she was asking. "Oh... of course."

Moving to the other side of the bed, he slipped beneath the covers.

She turned slowly, nestled her cheek against his chest, and let her arm settle around his waist.

He froze. Then pulled her close, careful not to mistake comfort for keeping.

Their breathing slowed together, quiet deepening between them as they slept. Sunlight slanted through the curtains, thick with afternoon haze.

Annabelle stirred first, her face tucked under his jaw, limbs loosely tangled under the blanket, still folded into his warmth.

The rise and fall of his chest beneath her cheek was the most peaceful rhythm she'd felt in days.

His scent surrounded her: leather, spice, something unmistakably him. She breathed it in, let it fill the last broken spaces inside her.

He hadn't let go. But he'd taken no more than she gave.

Somehow, that made her feel even safer.

She lifted her head just enough to look at him.

The words slipped out before she could stop them. "I missed you."

Valen stirred, his arms tightening instinctively at the sound of her voice.

Without thinking—still half-lost to drowsiness—he kissed her. Like he'd forgotten what had been broken.

Then he pulled back, blinking hard as realization caught up.

"I—I'm sorry," he breathed, sleep-rough and guilt-laced. "That wasn't—I wasn't—"

But she was already leaning in. Her hands cupped his face. And this time, she kissed him.

He exhaled against her mouth, a fragile sound. Like permission and apology wrapped into one.

She shifted closer, her body melting into his. He let out a breath of relief.

He drew her in again, the kiss saying everything he didn't have words for. He traced along her waist, settling at the small of her back.

She curled into him, fingers threading into his hair. "I need you."

He pulled away, searching her face as if he wasn't sure he'd heard right. "Wait—what? Do you mean—?"

"Please," she whispered, tugging gently at his shirt.

For a breath, nothing moved. Only the hush of their breathing. Her hand rested over his heart, feeling it race under her palm.

"Are you... sure? We can wait—"

"I *can't*, Valen. I need you now."

He studied her for a moment, needing to be positive this wasn't something he'd dreamed.

Then he moved over her, relearning the lines of her body.

She gasped softly as his hand slid beneath her dress, gathering fabric and breath alike until nothing was left between them.

Then his mouth found her skin, trailing slow worship down her throat, across her collarbone, over the swell of her breast.

He took his time, easing into her, their bodies fitting as if they'd always meant to find each other again. The heat of skin on skin, the ache of everything unsaid, pressed between them.

His forehead met hers, their breath mingling.

She held his face in her hands as if it grounded her. Like he was the only thing tethering her to the world.

He moved within her with aching care, each thrust a promise not to lose her again.

Her legs wrapped around him, drawing him deeper, closer.

His name escaped her lips, a prayer shaped like a whisper.

And when she came, it was surrender, a letting go she hadn't known she needed.

His release not long after, burying his face at her shoulder with a groan that sounded as if it had been waiting since the day she left.

Afterward, they stayed wrapped together—limbs tangled, breath steadying.

Her fingers traced idle lines across his back.

He eased onto his side, one arm still around her, then nuzzled into the crook of her neck, brushing the softest kiss to her collarbone.

"I missed you too," he murmured.

She gave a small laugh. "I noticed."

That earned the faintest grin against her skin.

Eventually, her stomach spoke up. "I think I forgot what hunger felt like."

"You're not the only one."

She looked up at him. "Should we...?"

"Yeah. We should eat."

They untangled themselves from the bed, slow and reluctant.

Annabelle threw on a dress, while Valen grabbed his shirt and tugged his trousers into place.

Downstairs, the kitchen was dim. They found something simple to eat, enough to settle the quiet ache in their stomachs.

She sat at the small table, legs curled beneath her, as he poured the tea.

"Annabelle?"

She looked up from her cup. "Hmm?"

"...What are we doing?"

"Eating...?"

"No." He frowned. "What are we doing—you and I?"

"I—" she sighed, smoothing out her napkin. "I don't know..."

She stared into her cup like it might give her the words.

"I miss you. I miss us. I just..." She swallowed. "Did I ruin everything?"

"I'd be lying if I said it didn't hurt," he said, after a moment.

"...I'm so sorry, Valen. I—"

"I know." His voice softened. "It was Seraphine. I get it. It'll just... take me some time. That's all."

"So..." she asked quietly. "Do you still want me?"

"I never once stopped wanting you, Annabelle."

CHAPTER 18

The Warmth

They'd meant to get up hours ago, but the bed was cozy, the quiet too kind, and neither wanted to break it.

Annabelle stretched, a small sound escaping as his arm tightened around her waist in protest.

"Hungry," she murmured.

"Mmm."

"Something warm and filling," she added, already imagining pancakes.

Valen hummed into her hair, lips curving against her shoulder. "Then I suppose I'm breakfast."

She snorted. "Tempting. But not unless you come with syrup."

"A narrow escape," he said under his breath. "For now."

They got up slowly, brushing against each other with every movement—touches needing no excuse or explanation.

She padded into the kitchen, straightening her dress. Her head swam for a moment.

The way she moved around the room felt... at ease. He sat at the table, arms crossed, watching her gather the ingredients.

She reached for a bowl, tossing a glance his way. "You're just going to sit there?"

Valen leaned back in the chair. "I've never done this before."

She blinked. "You've never made pancakes?"

The flour hit the bowl first, followed by the rest of the dry ingredients, loose and unmeasured.

He tilted his head. "I haven't made anything in… I can't remember how long. I usually just have things appear."

Huffing a laugh, she returned to the counter. "It's easy. Watch."

She cracked an egg into the bowl with a clean, one-handed motion.

"Come here," she said, topping off the mixture with a splash of milk.

He hesitated, then stood. "Is this some kind of test?"

She smiled faintly. "Only if you're terrible at it."

He joined her, peering over her shoulder. "This becomes pancakes?"

"Well, they will."

"For dinner?"

She shrugged. "No one's here to say otherwise."

He gave her a long look. "You are absolutely drunk on power."

"Not yet. That's what the syrup's for."

She offered him the whisk.

He took it like she'd handed him a sword. He held it as if it meant something, then stirred once, flour exploding into the air.

It landed on his chest and in his hair.

She blinked at him. He blinked at the whisk. Then she burst out laughing, arms around her stomach, laughter echoing off the walls.

Valen stood motionless in a small cloud of powder. "I meant to do that."

She gasped through giggles. "You are *spectacularly* bad at this."

"And yet," he said, dusting off his chest with regal dignity, "you're still making me dinner."

She wiped a tear from her eye. "We're making it together. You're part of this now, flour prince."

He cracked a smile despite himself.

For a while they were simply two people in a worn kitchen—shoulders brushing, batter on their fingers, laughter filling the cracks left behind.

The pancakes were uneven, thick in the middle, but golden and warm, smelling like comfort.

They sat at the table across from each other, plates full, butter melting in soft pools, syrup glistening.

Annabelle took her first bite. "Not bad for a first try."

Valen cut into his with exaggerated caution, as if the pancake might retaliate. Then he ate, like a man starved.

"You're actually eating," she said. "Without me having to scold or bribe you."

He gave a slow, satisfied nod. "After all that work? I've earned this."

She grinned. "You whisked for ten seconds and got flour on the ceiling."

"Yes. Heroically." He took another bite, licking syrup from his fork with mock solemnity. "You saw me. I was majestic."

For a while they ate together, pancakes and stolen smiles, a quiet that asked for nothing more than presence.

They finished their meal slowly, neither in any rush to end the moment.

Eventually, Annabelle pushed her empty plate back with a satisfied sigh. "Alright. Dishes."

Valen looked mildly alarmed. "They don't disappear?"

She stood, gathering the plates. "Not in this house, apparently."

"What a cruel and inconvenient domain."

"You'll live."

"I'm not convinced."

She gave him a towel and turned toward the sink. "You dry. I'll wash."

He took it as though it would disintegrate. "What do I dry with this?"

She blinked. "The dishes. You dry the dishes."

"Oh. Right."

She rolled her eyes, ran the water, gave the plate a quick scrub, and handed it to him.

He stared at it like it might offer clues.

She offered him a fork next, but he still wasn't finished.

"Valen."

"Yes?"

"You're taking forever."

"I'm just being thorough."

She arched a brow. "You don't need to be thorough with everything."

"Didn't hear you complaining last time."

She froze. Then handed him another plate a little too fast.

Turning back to the sink, she smiled to herself. A sudden worry snagged.

This felt... easy. Too easy.

If she leaned too far into it, the warmth might slip through her hands.

The thought coiled tight, but she shook it off.

She wasn't going to mistrust joy simply because no one had let her keep it before.

Running her fingers over the rim of a submerged glass, she grounded herself. Then she pressed her palms together just right, sending a perfect arc of water into his side.

"Hey!" he barked, looking at the soaked spot on his shirt.

She snorted without apology.

"Then you want a fight, do you?" He scooped some from the sink and flicked it her way.

It splashed across her arm and shoulder, and she gasped.

Then it was chaos.

Flicks turned into palm splashes. The towel was weaponized.

By the end, her sleeves were rolled, his shirt clinging to him, and the kitchen looked ransacked.

Leaning against the counter, she was dripping and breathless, grin playing at her lips.

He stood across from her, towel useless in his hand, a damp curl pasted to his forehead.

They caught each other's eyes and dissolved into laughter.

She wiped her wet hands on her dress.

Valen watched her.

Her cheeks flushed with delight, hair dripping from their kitchen skirmish, gaze shining. Completely unguarded.

Something shifted behind his expression. The teasing drained away and he crossed to her.

He kissed her suddenly, as if her joy had caught him off guard in the deepest part of himself.

She melted into it, fingers curling into his soaked shirt, tugging him closer. When they parted, her voice was gentle. "The rest of the dishes can wait."

He didn't hesitate, following her upstairs, their hands laced, footsteps faint on the wooden steps.

The moment they crossed her bedroom threshold, he pressed her to the wall, his mouth on hers with none of his earlier restraint.

His fingers worked hastily at the buttons on her dress, pulling it over her head before she even finished unbuttoning his shirt. Her back stuck faintly to the wood paneling.

They kissed like the space between them had been the real agony all along.

He lifted her, her legs wrapping around his waist as he carried her to the bed, kiss unbroken.

They landed in a sprawl of limbs and breath, her laughter spilling into his mouth.

Clothes fell away piece by piece, their bodies chasing heat. Sheets twisted under them, soft and cool where their bodies hadn't met.

What followed wasn't gentle or quiet.

It was heated hands, bitten-back moans, her name whispered like a promise against her skin.

The room was silent. Only the hush of cooling touch, steady breath, and warmth still clinging.

Then she murmured, barely audible, "I forgot what this felt like."

He kissed her shoulder. "Then let's make sure you remember."

CHAPTER 19

The Threshold

The smell of cinnamon and butter drifted lazily through the house, making Valen stir with a soft groan.

He stretched, one arm flopping into empty space. The sheets still held her warmth, like she'd only just stepped out.

Downstairs came the faint clatter of dishes and the sizzle of a pan. Thank heavens he didn't have to cook again.

Barefoot and sleep-ruffled, he padded into the kitchen. Annabelle stood at the stove, flipping a slice of French toast with casual precision.

He paused, one hand braced on the counter. "Is this a thank-you breakfast or an apology for attacking me with water?"

She shot him a look over her shoulder. "Can't it be both?"

He crossed the room and kissed her cheek. "Smells amazing."

"Try not to cry when it turns out better than your pancakes."

"I make no promises."

They ate at the table, sunlight spilling across their plates, the world steadier with every bite.

Midway through his second helping, he leaned back. "So. What happens now?"

She sipped her coffee. "I want to come back. If you'll have me."

"I'd love nothing more."

"Or," she teased, "we could stay here. You seem to enjoy the simple life."

Valen muttered about needing fine linen sheets and privacy.

She laughed. "I'll take that as a no."

Pushing her plate aside, she rose. "I'll start packing after we clean up. Just a few things. I should be ready soon."

"I'll be ready whenever you are."

The morning passed gently. Once the dishes were done and the kitchen cleaned, Annabelle stood in her bedroom doorway.

It felt different this time—less like escaping and more like choosing to move forward.

She opened the wardrobe, pulled out the travel bag she'd used before, then set it aside.

At the tall chest of drawers, she slid open the top one and pulled out a velvet pouch. She poured the contents into her hand: a necklace from her mother, a ring she never wore but couldn't part with, and earrings from her sister's wedding. She tucked them back inside with care.

Next came the photo album, its cracked spine and sticking sheets familiar under her fingers. She flipped through: friends, family, faces she hadn't seen in so long they felt like another life.

She smiled at a picture, slipping it between the pages, then closed the book and placed it on the bed.

At the bottom of a small box, buried under a mess of old keepsakes, she found the photograph Mason had given her, from a time when she was too tired to argue.

He stood stiff for the camera, chin lifted, one hand on the back of a chair as if it were a throne. The certainty in his gaze said he had already won.

She stared at it, feeling nothing—only weight.

Crossing to the fireplace she nudged the embers to life. When the flames caught, she dropped the photo in. It curled and blackened. She didn't watch it burn.

With the last trace of Mason reduced to nothing but ash and memory, she went back to packing.

She folded the clothes she loved, the pieces that still felt like her. A few favorite books joined them, though she left one out. A worn pair of boots. A cardigan faintly scented of pine and old paper.

When she fastened the satchel, it was heavier.

Her gaze swept the room a final time. She had outgrown this life. And now she was ready to go.

The bag hung from her hand, the book tucked under her arm. At the bottom of the stairs, a faint shift of light caught her eye.

The screen in the main room corner was ajar, leaving a gap. She slowed, brow furrowing.

Near the door, she set her things on the side table and stepped forward.

Valen stood in the art corner, surrounded by sketches: some finished, some warped with water damage, others abandoned mid-stroke. A few were clipped to boards; more lay in uneven stacks across the desk.

He stood beside the table, slowly flipping through a stack of papers. The top few were stark and skeletal—charcoal trunks, branches, hollowed forms.

A few pages in, the tone shifted: color, light, movement. Brushstrokes that didn't ask permission. Shapes that didn't care to be understood.

He lifted one toward the light. "These look like you."

She gasped. "What are you doing?" she snapped, sharper than she meant. Heat rose to her cheeks.

"I thought—" She stopped herself.

"You don't have to hide from me," he said. "I saw the ones you left."

She hadn't expected him to mention those. She'd half-forgotten they existed.

He looked at her with quiet understanding. Somehow, that made it worse.

Heat surged behind her eyes; she clenched her jaw to hold it back.

Valen flipped to the next one, still holding the stack.

She stepped forward, then froze. Her fingers hovered near the papers, as if touching them might confirm how much they said. Then she snatched them from him.

He blinked, looking down at his empty hands. "I'm sorry. I didn't mean to pry. I thought... I shouldn't have touched them."

Crossing to the wastebin, she dropped them in without a glance. Her heart thudded, but her composure stayed steady.

She faced him, her voice quieter but sure. "I'm ready when you are."

Nodding, he stepped back to give her space to pass.

She picked up her bag and the book from the table. By the time she straightened, Valen was at the entryway, holding the door open.

The sun was climbing above the rooftops as Annabelle stepped outside, her satchel brushing against her skirt.

Valen stood beside the carriage, catching her eye as she approached, his hand resting on the frame.

She handed him the book, then faced Silas at the reins, passing over her bag. He nodded and secured it on top of the carriage.

Her hands empty, Annabelle turned toward the house next door.

Mrs. Linton stood in her garden, pruning with clippers too dull to be useful.

Annabelle crossed the narrow strip of grass. "I'm leaving for good this time."

Mrs. Linton looked up, blinking behind thick glasses. "I figured," she said, not unkindly. "You've been packing with the windows open. Half the neighborhood knows."

Offering a small smile, Annabelle reached into her cloak pocket, and held out the key. "Thank you—for renting me the space. For giving me a chance when I needed one."

Mrs. Linton took the key and closed her fingers around it. "You were never any trouble."

Annabelle swallowed. "Do whatever you'd like with what's left. The books, the kitchen things, the garden... I won't be back."

Mrs. Linton nodded. "Then I'll make sure it's looked after. And dear?"

"Don't let that one get away. He's got sense in his head. And those hands look like they know how to build a shelf. Rarer qualities than you'd think."

"I—I won't. Thank you." Annabelle didn't wait for more. She gave another small, grateful smile, then turned, her cheeks warming.

Valen waited by the carriage door, hand extended. "Ready?"

He gave Mrs. Linton a nod.

Annabelle glanced back: the porch, the quiet windows, the door she'd closed behind herself too many times.

"As I'll ever be." She nodded.

He helped her climb in. Valen stepped in after, taking the opposite seat—until she reached across and tugged at his sleeve. Their fingers brushed as he passed her the book.

The silence between them was warm, full of things that didn't need saying. Her head found his shoulder before the hills gave way to the forest.

He turned, pressing his cheek to her hair, and inhaled. She smelled of lavender, ink, and a scent only he could name.

As his arm settled loosely around her, he let out a breath.

With her, sleep came easily.

A sharp axle creak cut through the hush. Valen shifted, pulling her closer at the sound.

The rhythmic sound of hooves on stone blurred into her breathing.

Until it stopped.

The stillness outside wasn't silence exactly, but the kind that waited. Even the birds were quiet.

"Annabelle."

She blinked awake as the last gold light slanted through the window.

Valen looked at her. "We're here."

She sat up slowly, stretching the sleep from her limbs.

He stepped out first and offered his hand. She took it, and he lifted her down.

As her feet found solid ground, Silas passed her things down to Valen.

The carriage clicked shut as the horses pulled away.

Valen opened the door to the house and set her bag inside.

"Allow me," he said quietly.

She blinked. "You're serious?"

He smiled, then swept her into his arms.

"You're not hauling me across the threshold for appearances, I hope," she said, laughing against his shoulder.

"Of course not," he murmured into her hair. "I'm doing it because you're mine."

Her smile didn't slip, but a faint chill moved through her. She brushed it off.

He carried her over the threshold.

As the carriage disappeared down the drive, the door behind them closed with a soft, final click.

Annabelle exhaled, her shoulders dropping. "It's so nice to be back."

Valen turned to her, eyes still unsure, like he hadn't dared believe she'd returned.

"That first night, after you left…" he said, voice rough. "I thought that was it."

He hesitated, then said, more raw, "I didn't think I'd see you again."

Annabelle's exhale faltered, her chest tightening.

He studied her. "Come with me."

Before continuing, he stooped to retrieve her bag.

She followed, their footsteps muffled against the carpet as they moved down the corridor, past the dining room, up the stairs, past the guest room she'd once stayed in.

At the end of the hall, he opened a door and stepped aside for her to enter.

She shifted the book in her grip as she entered and slowed. The bedroom was larger than she'd expected.

Valen crossed to one side, struck a match, and lit the small oil lamp on the mantel. A gentle glow spread through the space, brushing the shadows warm.

Dark wood anchored the walls, softened by velvet drapes in deep black and muted silver. Windows lined the far wall, sheer curtains still, catching the low light. A bed sat at the center—plush, too big for one person.

She turned slowly. "Wait…" Her voice caught. "Is this your room?"

He nodded, eyes never leaving her. "Ours," he said, then, barely above a whisper, "…please stay."

So much quiet now. No flour in their hair, no laughter off kitchen walls. The air thick with fragile hope.

She took the bag from him and set it down.

Crossing to the bedside table, she froze.

A small framed painting sat there, one of hers, glowing softly, as if it still believed in something.

Next to it was the key.

She glanced over and found Valen by the door, silent. She placed the book beside it, an answer in its own right.

"I didn't know if you'd come back," he whispered. "I kept hoping."

His voice dropped. "Are you sure this is where you want to be?"

Annabelle swallowed, gaze dropping. She looked away, and his brow furrowed, as if bracing for a no.

She hesitated, then stepped toward him.

Her tone was low, rambling in a way that betrayed how much it mattered. "I thought going home would help. It didn't. It just felt... hollow."

"Everything felt smaller... quieter. Like I kept comparing it to being here. With you."

His face didn't change, yet something in his eyes softened.

Her laugh was gentle, almost embarrassed. "I still don't get it. You could have anyone. And I've always been told I take up too much space."

Valen moved closer, his hand resting at her waist, steady and grounding.

He met her gaze. "Then it's settled. I've got more space than I know what to do with."

His touch slid up her side, fingers light. He leaned in until his forehead rested against hers, their breath mingling in the warm hush between them.

She kissed him, and all the noise quieted.

CHAPTER 20

The Edge

Annabelle stood in the quiet of his—now their—room, heart full, mouth still tingling from the kiss they hadn't needed to explain. The air remained charged.

Then, from somewhere low and human, her stomach growled. She blinked at the sound.

"You must be famished," Valen said.

She let out a soft huff, almost a laugh. "Apparently."

He smiled, offered his hand, and together they went downstairs, the hush of the house wrapping around them.

The dining room looked the same as her first night: familiar now, but different somehow. The hearth crackled softly in the quiet.

She sat across from him, not directly, but close enough their knees might've touched at a narrower table.

Her gaze caught on her wineglass, her reflection bent at the rim, like she was still adjusting to her own shape.

"The town felt smaller this time," she said, half to herself.

Valen glanced at her, waiting.

She nudged a piece of fig around her plate. "Not physically. Just... duller. Like the edges had faded while I was gone."

Her voice dropped, almost fragile. "I tried to care. I walked the streets. Passed the old shops. The same faces."

"But it didn't matter. None of it did." She shook her head, a breath of frustration escaping. "I didn't belong there anymore."

Their eyes held longer than necessary, his gaze steady in a way that made her pulse trip.

She looked away, her fork idly nudging at her food. "I didn't expect everything else to feel so... flat," she murmured. "Like the colors had been drained out."

Shifting in her seat, her foot bumped hard into his leg under the table.

She gasped. "Oh—sorry, I didn't mean—"

He didn't move.

She felt the brush of his hand at her ankle, then the other, holding her in place.

When she looked up, he was already watching—steady, faintly amused, his silence an unbearable weight.

She dropped her eyes, burying her face in her wine glass as if it might save her.

His fingers curled around her, the touch speaking volumes.

A prickle of nerves climbed her throat. She focused on her plate, stabbing a piece of roasted carrot with unnecessary force.

"So anyway," she said, words tripping over themselves, "I guess I won't miss the market either. It's always crowded, and someone ends up knocking over the apples, and—"

She faltered. His fingers slid higher, up the curve of her calf.

"—and, um... those little stands," she went on, "the ones with the jewelry made out of spoons? I mean, who actually wears that?"

She tried for casual. Failed completely. Her voice pitched up, a shade too bright.

Valen's hand climbed another inch.

Her fork slipped, clattering too loud against her plate. She snatched it up, cheeks burning.

Grabbing her water—wine would absolutely betray her—she gulped as if it might cool her down. It didn't.

His fingers curved behind her knee, gentle, with no intention of letting go.

She set her glass down, both hands braced against the table.

"Do we... have dessert?" she asked, too cheerful, eyes fixed on her plate.

Valen's lips twitched, not quite a smile, as his thumb traced a line along her skin.

She was still pretending composure when he broke the silence.

"What would you like for dessert?"

She hadn't noticed him move: now he was beside her, closer than she'd braced for.

One hand rested on her thigh, his touch burning through her dress.

She set her fork down as if even a shift might give her away.

He looked calm, devastating enough to make her forget her own name.

"I..." she faltered. "I don't know."

His thumb moved, a soft, barely-there stroke up her leg.

"I could offer you something sweet," he murmured, voice low and coaxing. "Something rich and warm you'd lose yourself in."

A flutter shivered through her chest.

He leaned in, his mouth brushing below her ear.

"Or perhaps," he breathed, "you already know exactly what you want."

A flicker of hesitation stole through her. She turned her head, lips near his. She still hadn't answered, and he was waiting.

She inhaled, steadying herself.

"Trifle," she blurted.

Valen arched a brow. "Trifle?"

She nodded, too enthusiastically. "Yeah. Creamy and rich, like you said. So... trifle."

He hummed, the sound rumbling through her. "I see."

Then, he turned her chair until their knees slotted together, one of hers between his, one of his between hers.

His gaze met hers. "We both know that's not what you really want."

She stared at him, flushed and breathless, without a retort.

Her heartbeat hammered, loud enough for him to feel.

Valen's fingers skimmed down her arm—the faintest, most maddening touch—without breaking eye contact.

She tipped her chin up despite the flush, letting a flicker of challenge show in her eyes.

"Oh?" she asked, her voice too breathy to sound smug. "And what is it you think I want?"

Valen's smile deepened. He leaned in until their breaths tangled.

"I know it's not trifle," he murmured, "because your cheeks are flushed..."

His hand brushed up her arm, a slow tease along her skin. "Your breath's been ragged since I touched you under the table..."

His thumb glided over her collarbone with aching patience. "And you haven't looked me in the eyes for more than three seconds since I sat beside you."

"And now?" he added softly. "You're trembling."

She hadn't noticed until he mentioned it, and now it was all she could feel.

Annabelle swallowed hard, painfully aware of his closeness, his gaze never wavering even as hers darted away.

Desperate for some scrap of dignity, she straightened enough to sass back, though her voice wobbled. "Well, what about you, then?"

Valen tilted his head, the corners of his mouth curving as if savoring her struggle.

She pressed on, reckless. "I know what you want. Why don't you admit it?"

He didn't blink. "I want you," he said simply. "All of you."

Her chest tightened, rising with the force of her breath.

He leaned closer, his gaze devouring, his voice a rough caress against her.

"I want the way you tremble when I touch you. The way you fight staying composed. The sound of my name when you stop trying."

His hand slid beneath her dress, slow and sure, fingertips grazing bare skin, stealing whatever words she might've had.

"And I want inside your thoughts," he murmured, "the way you never left mine."

She shifted, her knee brushing the hard, undeniable press of him through his clothes.

He wasn't hiding it. He wanted her to notice.

When she spoke, her voice was breathless but brave. "Take what's already yours."

Their eyes locked, wild and unsteady.

Valen stood in one fluid motion, his chair scraping against the floorboards.

He cleared the table in a single sweep. Dishes clattered to the floor—some slid, some shattered—but neither of them flinched.

He turned back and lifted her onto the cleared surface.

She gasped as he coaxed her down, guiding her to lie against the warm wood.

Her head bumped the table with a quiet thunk, sharp enough to sting.

Firelight spilled across the walls, echoing the heat between them. Her heart thundered, pulse quickening, breath coming faster.

He slipped his hands beneath the fabric, drawing it up with care, easing the last barrier aside, baring her inch by inch until she gasped at the cool kiss of air on her skin.

His lips traced along her inner thigh, then his mouth was on her.

She arched against him, a startled sound slipping past her lips as she gripped the table edge.

For a flicker of a second, she stiffened, a last fragile resistance against the flood rising inside her. It crumbled quickly, swept away by him, by this.

Her head fell back, a moan escaping as she melted for him, undone under his mouth.

She reached for him blindly, fingers curling into his hair like it was the only steady thing left.

Annabelle shuddered beneath him, trembling through each wrecking wave.

Valen lifted his head, his expression composed.

He kissed her deeply, tasting her sigh as his hands made quick work of the clothes still between them.

When he entered her, a broken breath escaped him, low and rough.

She gasped, gripping him, and he stilled, letting her feel every inch.

Even as her body ached with need, she felt his restraint, the careful way he touched her, patience threaded through each movement.

Then he moved, savoring the shift in her rhythm and each sound she gave him.

The table creaked beneath them, the fire cracking softly nearby.

When she whispered his name, he kissed her, slow enough to steady her breath.

Then, she felt it—the falter in his breathing, the tremble in his hands.

Valen moved faster, urgency bleeding into every thrust. Almost desperate beneath the control he fought to keep.

He gripped her hips, pulling her closer.

She rose to meet him, gasping, dizzy with the rough, relentless pace he set.

He was letting himself need her: every piece, every breath, every part she'd been afraid to offer and he now held without hesitation.

His hand slid up her side into her hair. He kissed her, devouring what little distance remained.

"I need you," he whispered, voice rougher and more ragged than she'd ever heard. "Say you're mine."

"Valen," she whispered. "I'm yours."

The rhythm broke apart as he pressed into her with desperation.

He buried himself in her as he came, his hands clutching her hips like she was the only thing keeping him from coming undone.

Collapsing beside her, his breath slowed, rough exhales giving way to quiet.

They sprawled shamelessly across the table like royalty after a feast. Or survivors after a storm.

Annabelle turned her head toward him, hair sticking to her cheek. "So. No trifle then?"

Valen laughed. "Maybe later."

She smiled wider, and for a long stretch they didn't move—only the faint shifting of the fire and the quiet pulse of their hearts, finding the same rhythm again.

The world felt small in the best way, as if nothing outside the circle of firelight could touch them. For now.

She curled beneath his arm, both too spent to do more than breathe and hold on to the quiet between them. They stayed there, tangled and drowsy in the low light.

Eventually, they cleaned up what they could, laughing as they draped napkins over broken dishes, and salvaged two spoons and a half-full wineglass from the mess.

Finally, they picked up their scattered pieces of clothing and made their way upstairs, back to the room that was already theirs.

They collapsed into the bed, still warm from each other, and finally let sleep take them.

The future could wait. This quiet was a choice she hadn't made in a long while.

CHAPTER 21

The Future

The next few days blurred in a slow stretch that made everything seem suspended: warmth in the sheets, sunlight through the window, the smell of bread or firewood or rain depending on the hour.

Sometimes he read. Sometimes she painted. Sometimes they didn't do anything at all.

They took long walks through the orchard, left chess games half-finished, turned meals into stories.

Some mornings they didn't speak until noon; some nights hummed with barely-touched wine and glances across the hearth.

She started keeping a brush and a jar of pigment on the nightstand again, in case the urge to paint found her.

One morning, she was quiet—gaze fixed on the window, hands idle in her lap long after breakfast. The brushes stayed untouched as she watched the breeze catch the budding trees beyond the glass.

Later, as they walked the garden path, her fingers slipped from his, halfway to the arbor. He let her go. When she didn't loop back, didn't offer some teasing glance or coy remark, he looked for her.

She was staring at a patch of low, flowering shrubs past the gate. Their blooms were white with a faint flush at the center, like a secret blushing to be kept. Her face had gone distant.

"Annabelle."

She didn't look at him.

"I used to get excited when the trees bloomed," she said softly. "Like the blossoms meant something. Like it was the start of something good."

Valen stayed quiet.

"I remember the exact day they started to flower last year." Her voice dipped. "I pointed it out. Just said, 'oh look, they're blooming already.'"

"And Dominic told me to shut up." She exhaled, almost a laugh. "He said if I couldn't behave in public, he'd make sure I learned how."

Valen's posture shifted.

The memory clung, sharp as citrus.

She finally turned toward him, dry-eyed but worn, like a bruise not yet surfaced. "That was the day I left."

"I tried so hard to be who he wanted," she said. "But it never mattered. There was always more to fix, something else to hide. He'd call me raw material. Said I'd make a fine wife once I was shaped properly."

Her mouth moved—an echo of a smile that never made it. "I lost myself trying to become who he wanted to marry."

Valen moved closer.

"I haven't told anyone that," she said.

"So your family didn't know?" he asked, gently.

She shook her head. "They were thrilled just to have a suitor for me. I think they thought something was wrong with me. That I was too much. Too picky. Too difficult to place."

"You weren't."

"I was," she said. "But not in the ways they thought."

He watched her with quiet patience, the kind she was still learning to trust.

"Have you thought about seeing them?" he asked.

Annabelle hesitated. She had, more than she liked, more than she'd admit out loud.

She wondered if they'd packed up her room. If her sisters had filled the gaps she left. If the little ones still remembered her at all.

"I don't want to be that girl again," she whispered. "The one who painted what she was told, wore the dresses they picked, and smiled like it didn't hurt."

Valen's gaze softened. "You don't have to be."

She glanced up at him.

"You could go back," he said. "You don't have to stay. Just see what's there."

Annabelle looked out over the garden, at the blooming branches, the place she'd started to feel like herself again. "I don't know if I'm ready."

"That's alright. But when you are—I'll go with you."

She reached for his hand, the thought of him beside her steadying her breath.

Evening came soft and gray, the hearth casting hushed shadows. Rain earlier had left the windows beaded and the air smelling of stone and damp moss.

They were already in bed, her head beneath his chin, one arm folded under her shoulders, the other tracing quiet lines down her spine.

Annabelle had stayed silent, her fingers working the weave of the blanket in slow, repetitive motions, like unwinding a thought.

"How far is it to Dunbridge?"

Valen didn't open his eyes, but he stilled. "About half a day. Maybe less, if the roads are clear."

He gave her a moment, then another. "Do you want to go?"

"I think I'm ready," she said, quiet but firm.

He looked at her, his hand brushing a few loose strands of hair from her temple. Her gaze met his, clear in the dim light, steady yet fragile—like glass that hadn't cracked but might.

"How soon?" he asked softly.

"As soon as possible. Before I get cold feet."

"Then I'll make arrangements first thing in the morning."

She tucked herself closer, pressing her forehead to his collarbone. She was still wound tight, shoulders tense, breath shallow.

His fingers moved through her hair, as if calming the thoughts beneath.

After a while, her breathing deepened, her grip on the blanket loosening. One leg hooked instinctively around his.

He kept his hand there until she went slack with sleep. Even then, he didn't stop.

Morning came early, paler than she'd expected, still hazed with leftover mist. Somewhere in the garden, a chickadee sang too cheerfully for the hour, and Annabelle groaned quietly into the pillow before dragging herself out from under the covers.

Getting dressed, she kept silent.

In the kitchen, they ate standing up. Toast. Fruit. A bite of cheese. She wrapped a few extras in a soft linen napkin without thinking, then blinked down at her own hands as if she'd surprised herself.

"Snacks," she said, too flatly.

Valen only nodded and handed her the tin of dried cherries. "For the road."

Later, Annabelle paused in the middle of the bedroom, the bed buried beneath a mess of fabric: wraps, undergarments, three pairs of boots, six nightgowns, and enough dresses for a monthlong trip, though they'd be gone at most four nights.

One glove dangled from her hand, her knuckles white around it as she stared at the heap.

Her breath came thin and uneven.

It started slow, trying to choose something respectable. Something her mother might approve of. Something modest but nice.

Bold felt like rebellion. Plain felt like surrender. Dominic's voice lingered in every hem.

Except Dominic wasn't here. He hadn't been for a year.

But the voices didn't care.

Old reflexes hummed under her skin. Her hands trembled as she reached for another skirt.

Every option was wrong. Too loud. Too lifeless. Too much like her.

She didn't realize her knees had met the mattress until she was sinking into the pile of clothes.

Her breath thinned. She froze—as if her mind had too many signals and chose none.

The door eased open behind her, but she didn't look up.

Valen paused inside the threshold. Took in the bed, the floor, the tension in her shoulders.

Then, he asked, "Are we staying a month?"

Her head lifted.

He almost smiled, a faint curve at his mouth.

She blinked against the sting in her eyes and swallowed hard.

"I don't know what to bring," she whispered.

Valen drew closer and settled at the foot of the bed.

"You don't need to convince them of anything," he said. "You're not going back to be someone else."

She let out a shaky breath. "I don't know who I am with them anymore."

He took her hand. "Then bring what makes you feel like you."

He paused.

"And take your time," he added. "We're not in a hurry."

Exhaling slowly, her shoulders eased.

Still, she packed too much. On purpose, this time.

She left a single dress on the bed—the one Dominic always liked.

He carried the bags out to the waiting carriage, handing them to Silas, who stowed them neatly on the roof. She hesitated on the steps for just a moment before she followed.

By the time they set off, the sun had lifted behind them and morning light sifted through branches still damp with last night's rain.

The wheels bumped over the path as they pulled away.

Silence carried her, the air between them heavy with nerves.

She sat upright, hands in her lap, eyes tracing the hedgerows as if trying to commit them to memory.

Valen gave her space, watching the trees blur past.

She almost spoke, then changed her mind.

The road narrowed as they entered a stretch of woods. Light flickered through the canopy, dappling the seat beside her.

"I don't know what to say to them." Her voice was barely audible.

"It's been a year. I left in the night. No explanation. No goodbyes. I didn't even take everything." Annabelle stared out the window. "I don't know if they're going to be angry. Or relieved. Or... disappointed I came back at all."

Valen's hand rested on her knee. "They don't get to decide your worth just because they knew you first."

ACT III

WELCOMED

CHAPTER 22

The Return

The carriage slowed, wheels crunching over gravel as the estate came into view: weathered stone, ivy-climbed corners, shutters askew.

Nothing about the grounds had changed. But she was different now.

Annabelle leaned forward before they stopped, scanning the garden, fingers twitching at the latch.

Then the door opened, and she was out—boots on the ground before Silas could move. The air smelled of heather and firewood. A dog barked somewhere beyond the hedges.

The front door swung open. Her mother stood frozen in the doorway, hand to her chest. "...Annie?"

Annabelle ran before her voice could catch up.

She crashed into her mother's arms with a choked laugh, burying her face in her shawl. The scent of lilac and starch wrapped around her like an old quilt. Her mother held her tight, hands trembling against her back.

Voices called out behind them. Footsteps echoed on stone.

Her sisters were next. Eliza barreled into a hug—and missed, her cheek colliding sideways into Annabelle's temple.

"Ow," Annabelle laughed.

"Sorry," Eliza gasped. "I forgot how short you are."

Beatrice, the youngest, wept openly, one hand resting over the soft curve of her belly.

Two small children clung to her skirts, blinking in confusion before joining the chaos. "Auntie!" the smaller of the two squealed.

Someone stepped on her foot. Hard. No one apologized. It was too much joy for neatness.

Her brother came last, wearing a smile she hadn't seen in years. He pulled her into a rough hug, palm cupping the back of her head like he wasn't sure she was real.

Laughter mixed with tears. Questions tumbled out over one another. Was she well? Was she safe? Why had she left? Where had she been?

She couldn't answer them all at once.

Nobody noticed the figure still standing at the edge of the gravel path.

Valen hadn't moved. His hand rested on the carriage frame, the other tucked into his coat pocket. A polite observer. Almost distant.

Her mother glanced past the others, a crease forming between her brows. "Who... Who is that?"

She could lie. Pretend he was a traveler, a friend. But she decided against it. "That's Valen."

There was a shift in the air as awareness settled. A new rhythm to the silence.

Valen came forward, boots crunching softly over gravel.

"Valen Eldcroft," he said, offering a shallow, precise bow. "It's an honor to meet you."

"Welcome," her mother said, coming to greet him.

Her father appeared in the archway, his expression caught between shock and relief. He said nothing at first—just gave Annabelle a once-over, as if checking she was whole, before turning to the stranger.

"Edward Greenwick," her father said, offering a firm handshake. "You're the one who brought our daughter back."

Valen met his eyes. "She brought herself."

Her father nodded. "Well, then. You'd best come inside. Supper's just about ready."

Annabelle followed everyone back toward the house, bustling and chattering—willing to rewrite everything if it meant she was back.

Inside, the warmth hit. Stone floors gave way to worn rugs, and the air smelled of beeswax and something faintly scorched, like bread nearly forgotten.

The entryway hadn't changed: the same creaking floorboard by the umbrella stand, the same scuffed bench beneath the coat rack.

Behind her, hooves clattered on gravel, then quieted as the carriage pulled away.

Valen followed at a modest distance, bags in hand. He looked too large for the space: tall and quiet in his dark coat, careful not to track mud.

A wall mirror caught his reflection as he passed, slightly out of place against the silver-flecked glass.

As the front door closed behind them, her mother smoothed her apron like she didn't know what else to do with her hands. "How long will you be staying?"

"A few days. If that's alright," Annabelle said.

Her mother looked at her for a moment, then managed a worn smile. "Of course it is. We'll ready the guest room for Mr. Eldcroft."

"Thank you," Valen said.

"And Annabelle... we left your room the way it was."

Annabelle didn't trust herself to speak. She nodded silently.

From deeper in the house came the clatter of dishes, children's laughter, her sister's voices. Domestic life kept moving, even after the tectonic shift at the door.

Glancing between them, her mother said, "If you'd prefer something else, we can—"

Valen stood beside her, silent, bags in hand like a sentinel.

"No, that's perfect." Annabelle took her bag from Valen.

They headed down the corridor in a loose cluster, voices echoing off stone and plaster. Her mother called for someone to turn down the beds.

A housemaid led the way, skirts whispering across the floor. "This way, sir."

Valen nodded and followed. When they reached the guest room, he went in and set his bag just past the door.

Her mother hovered a few paces away, speaking to the maid.

Annabelle lingered in the hallway, carrying her things.

"I can take that for you," Valen offered, voice low.

"No need. It's just down the hall."

"Supper will be ready soon," her mother said. "Best wash up while there's still hot water."

Valen murmured his thanks, the door clicking shut behind him.

The housemaid disappeared down the hall, and Annabelle was alone.

She turned to the familiar weight of her bedroom door.

The room was dim, dust-dappled in the slant of evening light. A vase of dried lily of the valley sat on the sill, exactly as she'd left it.

She set her bag on the bed.

"Annabelle?"

She spun around. "Yes?"

Her mother lingered in the doorway, too still. "You're thinner. Are you eating enough?"

"Yes, Mom."

"You're safe? Where you've been—it's respectable?"

"I haven't disgraced myself, if that's what you're asking."

"And are you... are you happy?"

"Sometimes," she said, studying her hands. "But I don't trust it yet."

Crossing the room, her mother pulled her into a tight hug.

Annabelle stiffened, then gave in, resting against her mother's shoulder.

"I thought we'd never see you again," her mother whispered. "I thought you were gone for good."

Annabelle let herself be held a moment longer before the hug loosened.

Her mother eased away and brushed her thumb along Annabelle's cheek. "Supper soon. Come down when you're ready."

Then she left, closing the door with a low click.

Annabelle exhaled slowly. The air felt heavier now, like it had been waiting to settle.

The wardrobe opened easily. Her fingers found a stiff collar in pale colors she hadn't chosen. One still had the dressmaker's tag.

It felt like visiting someone else's life.

She went to the bookshelf by the window. The worn spines from her lessons looked foreign now: literature, natural history, a few volumes on etiquette. Most had paper slips marking chapters she'd struggled to care about.

On the desk, her old paintbrushes sat in a chipped ceramic jar. A half-finished sketch peeked from beneath a notebook—some courtyard she'd once loved enough to try and keep. The colors had faded.

Near the pillow, a small stuffed fox. The fur was matted in places, one button eye barely hanging on. She hadn't realized she'd left him.

But here he was. Waiting.

Annabelle picked him up, brushing a thumb over the seam behind his ear. A smile ghosted her lips.

She set the fox back down and stood in the heart of the room.

It was still hers, but she wasn't the girl who lived here anymore. She didn't want to be. Even the curtains felt unfamiliar against the dusk.

She let the truth settle. Then she returned to the hall.

Annabelle descended the stairs slowly, trailing her fingers along the banister. The scent of roasted meat and rosemary drifted up from the dining room. Her stomach clenched. She hadn't realized she was hungry.

"...My family's estate is outside of Westmere." Valen's tone was polite. "My grandfather was in shipping. My father carried on the trade until his health declined."

Her father's voice followed. "Westmere, hmm? I've passed through a time or two. So the money comes from boats, then."

"Among other things," Valen said, with a faint smile she could nearly picture. "He traveled often. Worked more. I spent most of my childhood with a series of tutors and housekeepers."

"Hm. And yourself?"

"My work is quieter," Valen said. "I restore and transcribe rare books. Mostly for collectors or archives. I don't need to work, but I prefer to stay occupied."

Annabelle reached the bottom step just as her brother leaned in with a knowing grin. "So, you're wealthy *and* brooding."

"Isaac," their mother said sharply, swatting at him with a napkin. "Don't tease."

Valen gave a mild shrug, his voice dry with amusement. "It's not brooding. It's quiet."

Annabelle felt a tug at the corner of her mouth, at how precisely, un-apologetically true that was.

Her father made a thoughtful sound. "And your mother—is she still living?"

"She... passed when I was very young," Valen said. The words came with the same practiced ease as everything else. Like something long since packed away.

Annabelle's hand tightened on the banister. She knew that tone—how much effort it took to make pain sound like closure.

Valen's thumb traced the base of his glass.

"Oh. I'm sorry to hear that," her father said, voice softening.

"Thank you."

The fire popped faintly in the hearth.

"So you grew up in Westmere?" her father asked, shifting gears with the polite efficiency of a man who knew when not to pry.

"Yes. The estate's a few miles east of town. I'm an only child."

"Mm." Her father took a sip of wine. "Must've been quiet."

"It suited me. Solitude is its own kind of company."

Her father nodded slowly, weighing whether that was admirable or cause for concern.

Annabelle peered into the dining room. Valen sat at the far end of the table: posture straight, relatively at ease, wine untouched.

"He's striking," a voice whispered beside her.

Eliza edged close, arms crossed, one brow lifted in open appraisal. Her smirk said she'd been watching longer than she let on.

Annabelle narrowed her eyes. "Stop."

Eliza leaned in. "Tall, brooding, mysterious... honestly, he might as well have been tailor-made."

"You're incorrigible."

"Mm. I get it now, though." Eliza's gaze flicked toward the dining room. "The disappearing act. Running off to elope with a smoldering stranger..."

"We didn't elope."

"Yet."

"Eliza—"

"When's the wedding, then?" she whispered, grinning wickedly. "Is that why you're back? To make it official?"

Heat bloomed behind Annabelle's ears. "No."

Eliza gave her a look of exaggerated pity. "Oh. So he's living with you, then."

"He's not—" Her voice snagged on the lie she didn't want to tell.

But Eliza was already sauntering off, tossing a wink over her shoulder. "Mom's gonna love that."

Eliza sauntered into the dining room, her voice folding back into the clatter of silverware and conversation.

Annabelle straightened her dress, took a breath, and stepped in after her.

Candlelight made the room feel cozy, long shadows flickering across wood-paneled walls. The table was set: roast meat, buttered vegetables, warm bread, and several mismatched serving platters crowded the space between family mid-reunion.

Warmth, flickering light, the smell of rosemary: it felt like something she'd dreamed of, only to wake and find it still here. Waiting.

Conversation dipped as she entered.

Valen looked up first, a trace of weariness crossing his face before he turned his gaze politely back to the carving knife in front of him.

Her father cleared his throat. "There you are."

Annabelle took the open seat between Beatrice and their mother—not beside Valen, of course. That would've been too pointed.

Bread and butter made their way around the table. The butter so soft it nearly melted at the touch of the knife.

Valen's hand hovered briefly over the bread, then drew back, as if unsure it was his to take.

Her brother reclined in his chair, eyeing her like someone trying to solve a riddle. "Where've you been all this time?"

"Living in Creswell," she said finally. "A little duplex near the end of the main road."

It wasn't even a full lie. She had lived there. She just didn't anymore.

Something in her voice faltered—barely—but her mother noticed. She gave a gentle touch to Annabelle's elbow, then returned to filling her plate as if nothing had happened.

"Small place?" her father asked.

"Cozy. But enough." It had been. Once.

The rest of the meal passed in a slow, easy rhythm: wine poured, laughter shared, questions asked in fits and starts.

Isaac brought up the time Annabelle had tried to make a birthday cake from scratch and nearly set the kitchen curtains on fire.

Eliza chimed in with a dramatic reenactment, knocking over the milk in the process. She dabbed at the spill with a napkin, never breaking stride.

Beatrice rolled her eyes fondly and handed a piece of bread to one of the children who had slipped beneath the table like a fox hunting scraps.

Now and then, someone glanced toward Valen. Nobody asked why he was here. Or what he was to her.

It lingered in the room, unsaid but present.

Her mother looked at them once or twice, her mouth pressed thin. Her father stuck to practicalities.

A quiet tension threaded beneath the clink of silverware.

They made it feel like she'd never left at all. And that was the part that stung the most.

CHAPTER 23

The Dragon

The parlor was chaos.

Crayons littered the floor. Paper crowns sat crooked, plastered with bright stickers. One of her nephews wore a throw blanket as a cape. Another clung to Annabelle's arm, demanding a three-headed pegasus "but scary."

She laughed, tucking a wisp of hair back as she leaned over the coffee table. Sleeves rolled, cheeks flushed. The most relaxed she'd looked in days.

Valen stood in the doorway. A faint smile tugged at his mouth—the kind he rarely let others see.

"You're gonna get stuck there if you don't make a move," said a voice beside him.

He turned, startled.

Nathan, Annabelle's sister Beatrice's husband, friendly in a way Valen wasn't sure how to replicate, appeared at his side, sipping from a mug.

"You've been standing there forever," Nathan said.

"Just watching." Valen's gaze drifted back to the scene. "I wouldn't even know what to do."

Nathan shrugged. "You don't have to know. Let them lead."

Annabelle glanced up. Valen remained frozen in the doorway, gaze fixed on the room as if afraid to step into it.

The children always looked so sure of where to put their hands, their voices, their wonder. She couldn't remember ever feeling that way at their age, certainly not with adults watching.

Nathan raised his voice. "Hey! Valen wants to play too! Says he wants to be the dragon!"

Heads whipped toward him.

"THE DRAGON?" Vincent's eyes lit up as if it was the best idea he'd ever heard.

"You have to chase us!" Aurelia demanded, crossing her arms defiantly.

"Can you breathe fire?" Graham bounced on the sofa, gesturing at imaginary castles.

"YAY!" Celeste cheered, excited by the commotion.

The children scrambled up in a rush of wooden swords, paper shields, and a dish towel that might've once been a flag, shouting plans and pointing at Valen as if they'd just discovered a treasure map.

Valen froze, wide-eyed and completely cornered by joy.

Annabelle looked up from the floor, surprised, then saw his face. Like someone had handed him a door to a place he didn't believe existed.

He stared, overwhelmed. She giggled, the sound warm enough to tug at something deep in his chest.

They closed in on him from every direction, all talking at once, brandishing weapons and rules he hadn't agreed to. For a moment, he felt like a man trying to read a map in a storm—buffeted by noise and motion until his only choice was to start moving.

Still stunned, Valen glanced at Nathan, who grinned, raised his mug in salute, and winked. "Have fun, dragon."

Valen turned to the children, still wide-eyed, arms stiff at his sides. "Rrrr-rrrraaaaaaahhhhhhrr!"

He hunched forward and growled awkwardly, but earnestly.

Shrieking with glee, they rushed him. One fell over in a fit of giggles. Another lunged, wielding a sword.

And just like that, he was surrounded. Chasing. Laughing. Letting go.

Annabelle watched from the floor, caught between awe and amusement.

Valen—stoic, terrifyingly composed—was crawling on all fours, howling like a monster. Swarmed by children who thought he was the best thing that had ever happened.

It was ridiculous, and so impossibly endearing she wanted to memorize every second.

She couldn't stop smiling.

He ended up standing like he'd been summoned to court without warning, four little voices shouting over each other with conflicting demands.

"Roar again!"

"No, chase me!"

"Wait—he's supposed to guard the castle!"

"Can he fly? Do we have wings?"

He blinked, the rules shifting faster than he could follow.

A blow landed on his knee.

"Tag, you're it!"

Valen peered down at the sword, then at the child.

Another tapped his other leg.

He raised his arms in baffled surrender, eyes darting between the small assailants.

Behind them, Annabelle tried to hide her grin.

He crouched, unsure what to do next.

"Rrrr… ahhhhr?"

The growl came out more like a confused cat.

Silence.

"That didn't sound very dragon-y," one of the children said.

"He needs practice," another added.

Valen opened his mouth to respond, but Annabelle beat him to it.

Clutching her chest, she said, "Oh no! A fearsome dragon has invaded the castle! Who will save me from such a terrifying beast?"

She collapsed into a pile of pillows with a theatrical swoon.

Aurelia, bold as ever, announced, "Uncle Valen has to save Auntie Annabelle!"

The children squealed.

Valen's eyes caught hers. She smirked, and his tension eased.

Then he let out a proper roar. "RRRRRAAAAAHHHHHHHH-HHHHRRRRRGHH!"

One of them yelped and stumbled back, wide-eyed.

Then chaos erupted.

He lunged, arms raised, growling in full force. The children screamed in delight, scattering like birds. One darted under the sofa. Another tried to "protect" Annabelle with a makeshift shield, giggling uncontrollably.

Valen roared again, chasing with exaggerated stomps.

Annabelle, still draped on her pillow-throne, caught his eye as he passed. She gave him a tiny, knowing smile. He smiled back, a little bigger this time.

Roars gave way to yawns, stomping replaced by the slow sprawl of limbs and lullabies.

The sun had dipped low behind the trees, casting the parlor in soft gold. Toys lay scattered, crowns abandoned, capes rumpled in corners.

Valen settled into the armchair. One child in his lap, another perched on the armrest. The third stretched on the rug with a pillow under his chin, and the final one leaned against his leg, half-asleep.

A book rested loosely in his hands, *The Golden Prince*, judging by the cover.

He read aloud, haltingly at first.

"...and so the prince crossed the cursed sea, not because he was promised a throne, but because the girl he loved lived in the tower at the end of the world."

His voice had settled into a steady rhythm, too formal, as if he didn't want to sound as though he meant it.

Across the room, Annabelle leaned against the doorframe, pretending to watch the story when she was really watching him.

The curve of his mouth softened with the next line.

"He didn't slay the dragon for glory. He did it because no one else ever tried to love her."

Something in her chest stilled. Her fingers went still against the wood, the nail of her thumb pressing into the grain.

Valen glanced up, met her gaze, then quickly looked back down at the book like it had wronged him.

She bit her lip to keep from smiling too wide.

One of her nieces shifted in his lap, blinking slowly. "Is there more?"

Eliza's voice came from the kitchen. "It's bedtime!"

A chorus of groans filled the room.

Valen almost sighed in relief.

"But—one more page!" one of them begged, tugging on his sleeve.

"Uncle Valen hasn't read the ending yet!" another said, already curling against his side.

Her sister appeared in the doorway, arms crossed, teasing smile on her face. "Alright. One more."

The children cheered.

Valen's shoulders slumped in mock defeat.

Annabelle couldn't help it; she giggled.

He gave her a flat look. She only grinned and winked.

Clearing his throat, he kept reading.

"She didn't need rescuing. Not really. But he came anyway, because the tower wasn't the thing keeping her caged. It was everything she'd been made to believe about herself."

One child nestled her face into his shoulder, another curled beside him. The last two were both softly snoring on the rug.

Valen paused on the final line.

"And when she opened the door this time, it wasn't to escape—"

He looked up and met Annabelle's eyes.

"—it was to go home."

The room was silent except for tiny breaths, shifting blankets, and one small hand still resting on his sleeve.

Valen eased the book shut so the sound wouldn't stir them.

"You're good at that," Annabelle said softly.

He raised an eyebrow. "Reading?"

"That. And getting trapped under a pile of children."

He glanced down at the heap of drowsy warmth. "I don't think I can move."

"Don't," she whispered, tucking a quilt over the one in his lap. "I don't think they want you to."

He settled back. Let one hand rest on the blanket, the other still holding the book.

Annabelle stood beside him, smiling down at the strangest, softest man she'd ever known. Surrounded by storybook pages and the smallest bits of trust he hadn't even realized he'd earned.

Footsteps padded in from the hall, and the children's parents began peeling them away one by one. Eliza scooped the final child from his lap, shooting Annabelle a look equal parts smug and knowing.

By the time they'd picked up the final toy, the room was mostly in order, only crumbs and echoes left behind.

Valen was standing at the bookshelf, straightening a stack of mismatched books the children had pulled out.

Annabelle leaned a shoulder against the wall, watching him with a small smile.

"You're still thinking about it," she said softly.

"About what?"

"Them calling you Uncle Valen."

His hand paused on the book spine. "It's just a word."

"Maybe. But you didn't hate it."

His eyes veered away.

"They were... a lot," he said after a moment, like he needed to ease into the truth sideways. "Louder and stickier than I thought they would be."

"You forgot glittery."

"Yes. That too." He looked down at his sleeve like it had personally betrayed him. "I think I'll be finding glitter in my clothes until I die."

She stepped in closer. "But you didn't hate it," she said again, quieter this time.

He didn't respond right away.

"I didn't know I could do that," he murmured, almost to himself. "I felt ridiculous. But they didn't care. They just... pulled me in."

She nodded. "Children are good at that."

"I've never been around them. Not like that." He hesitated. "And it felt... strange. Like walking into a room that's supposed to be locked."

She could see the tension in his shoulders now. The softness he wasn't sure he was allowed to hold onto.

"Did it hurt?" she asked.

His mouth quirked. "No. But I wasn't ready for it to feel like... something I could want."

She reached up, smoothing the collar of his shirt where a small elbow had wrinkled it. "You were good with them, Valen."

"I felt like I was pretending."

"But they didn't see a pretend version. They saw you."

His gaze met hers.

"I used to want it," he said quietly. "A family. A house that wasn't just filled with silence. I gave up on that a long time ago."

She let her hand rest over his chest. "Maybe it's not too late."

His eyes lingered on her for a moment. "They... called me uncle."

She laughed, warm and close, resting her forehead against his. "You'll live, Uncle Valen."

"Barely." But he was smiling now, edges softened.

He let himself feel the weight of what it could mean to want something again—and maybe not be punished for it.

The door to that life hadn't been locked at all.

He'd just never tried to open it.

The house held its breath with him: soft voices down the hall, a door creaking shut, the distant clink of dishes marking the end of the day's chaos. Outside, a breeze stirred the garden.

Valen sat alone in the guest room, the scent of linen and old wood in the air.

Still in his shirt, sleeves rolled, he remained motionless. Hands clasped loosely between his knees, posture hunched just enough to suggest he wasn't truly there.

He stared at nothing.

His shoulders curled in, like the walls had shrunk around him and he was trying to take up less space.

A faint knock came before the door opened without a sound.

Annabelle slipped inside, barefoot, hair still damp from washing. She wore something soft, her cheeks pink from the warmth of the hall or maybe the quiet audacity of the moment.

She hesitated just past the threshold, voice barely above a whisper. "I couldn't sleep."

Crossing the room, she settled beside him, resting her head on his shoulder. One arm looped around his, warm and steady, anchoring him.

They sat in stillness for a while.

"It's hard to believe all of this is real," he murmured. "Or the things that could be."

She didn't move.

"I was doing alright," he said, softer now. "I'd come to terms with... having you. Somehow. That still felt like more than I deserved."

"But today—" His voice cracked. "Today I let myself wonder what it would be like to really have that kind of life. It's been years since I let myself want something like that."

She shifted enough to look at him. His gaze stayed on the floor.

"A home full of laughter. Love that doesn't leave." He blinked, eyes stinging. "But it scares the hell out of me. Because the last time I dreamed that big... it burned."

Her hand slid into his.

He finally looked at her. "And my body still remembers how that felt. Even if my heart is starting to forget."

She squeezed gently. "It's alright to be scared."

"What if I reach for it and it vanishes?"

"Then we reach again."

"I think I want that," he whispered. "Even if it breaks me."

She leaned in, resting her forehead to his. "It won't."

They didn't speak after that. There wasn't anything left to say.

He stood slowly, pulling back the covers, waiting until she slid in first. Then he followed, as if even now, he still didn't quite believe he was allowed to be here.

Silence filled the room, shadows pooled in the corners. The kind of quiet that only comes after children go to bed and memories are stirred up.

Annabelle turned toward him without hesitation, pressing her body against his side.

She draped an arm across his ribs, cheek beneath his shoulder.

Only her breath moved, soft and steady. For a long time, Valen didn't sleep.

He stared up at the ceiling, eyes wide in the dark. He felt the weight of her hand, the warmth of her skin, the way she fit so easily into the space beside him like she'd been made for it.

It terrified him. And it soothed something ancient.

The steady rhythm of her breath became the lullaby his body had never known it needed.

CHAPTER 24

The Blush

The sun hadn't crested yet, but light filtered through gauzy curtains, painting gold on the floorboards.

Annabelle stirred first.

Her body was warm, limbs heavy, but it wasn't the bed that made her linger, it was the man beside her.

Valen lay on his back, one arm curved toward her, chest rising and falling slow. His face was unguarded in sleep. Softer than she'd ever seen it.

She watched him.

Usually all sharp lines and control, he looked almost boyish in this light. A tiny furrow between his brows, like even dreams didn't know what to do with him.

She brushed the hair from his forehead, careful not to wake him.

Then she leaned down and kissed him—the kind that asked nothing and meant everything.

He shifted as she pulled the blanket over his shoulder and slipped from the bed.

Downstairs, familiar voices reached her, muffled at the edges, unmistakably familial.

She padded into the kitchen.

Her mother was at the stove, Beatrice at the table nursing tea. Eliza stood by the counter, effortlessly put together, as always.

They all looked up as Annabelle entered.

"Morning," Eliza said, overly casual.

"Sleep well?" her mother asked, handing her a cup.

"Mmhmm," Annabelle murmured, wrapping her hands around it. "Thanks."

Beatrice leaned in. "So. Uncle Valen."

Annabelle groaned. "Please don't call him that."

"The children do," Beatrice said innocently. "Eliza said they wouldn't stop talking about him before bed."

"They're probably *still* talking about him," Eliza added. "Aurelia said she's going to marry him when she grows up."

"Sounds like big competition," Beatrice said. "You might want to lock that down."

Sighing, Annabelle picked up an orange from the bowl. "You're both ridiculous."

She dug her thumb into the peel. The scent was bright and almost cheerful, out of place in the heavy silence.

"He looked like he was enjoying himself though," Eliza said.

Annabelle snorted. "He nearly had a heart attack when they swarmed him."

"And yet," Eliza said with a knowing smile, "he didn't run."

Her mother glanced up. "So maybe there will be more grandchildren after all."

Annabelle stopped peeling, juice tacky on her fingertips.

It wasn't a question, but it settled like one. Her mind reached for an honest response and found the only safe one.

"It's too soon to say," she said.

But the truth sat quiet in her chest—wanting something she wasn't sure she deserved.

"You don't need to have it all figured out," her mother said. "But I caught a glimpse of you yesterday. The way you looked at him."

Annabelle blinked. "What did I look like?"

"Like you already knew."

It hit too close.

She sipped her tea, pretending to think of something else, even as her mind replayed Valen growling at the children. Laughing as they tackled him. Reading the fairy tale aloud, glancing at her as if he was afraid of what she'd see.

Conversation drifted like it always had: updates about old acquaintances, mutual friends, half-forgotten gossip.

It felt easy. Too easy. Like a song she used to know by heart—but couldn't quite hit all the notes anymore.

She was setting the silverware when Eliza cut in, voice low and too casual to be innocent. "...but just picture him holding a baby."

Annabelle's spine stiffened. "Eliza."

"What?" Eliza grinned. "You can't tell me you didn't think it. Last night—he had one sleeping on his chest and didn't even move."

"That's enough."

"Come on. It was adorable. That brooding dragon-man curled around four tiny humans like it was nothing."

Annabelle turned to the counter, hands moving without purpose. Her ears burned.

"I'd melt if someone looked at my kid the way he looked at—"

"Eliza, I swear," Annabelle said, half-laughing, "I will throw this cup at you."

"But honestly," Beatrice said. "You can picture it, right?"

Annabelle brushed the cup's rim as if she could stir the heat away.

It wasn't children that scared her—it was how easy it was to see him there. As if they'd begun something neither of them could name.

Her mother, quietly amused, said, "Well now she's pink as a rose."

"Not you, too," Annabelle mumbled.

A throat cleared, loud enough to hush the clink of silver.

Everyone froze.

Annabelle turned slowly, her heart in her stomach.

Valen stood barefoot in the doorway, sleep-rumpled and stunned. His expression teetered between bemused and betrayed by the universe.

"Morning," he said, dry.

They looked like children caught whispering past bedtime.

Annabelle blinked. Still flushed. "Good morning."

Her mother recovered first, smoothing her features. "We were just talking about—uh—pancakes."

Eliza didn't miss a beat. "For babies."

Beatrice buried her face in her hands.

Valen arched a brow, his gaze settling on Annabelle—absolutely guilty, and radiant in her embarrassment.

He stepped into the room, slow and graceful, like he hadn't just walked into his own nightmare and her daydream.

"Did I miss anything important?"

"Nope," Annabelle said. "Nothing."

He glanced at her. Then the table. Then back again. "You're blushing."

"You're impossible," she muttered, her cheeks blooming hotter.

He grinned, lazy and smug, reaching for coffee as if the room hadn't just imploded.

Passing behind her, he brushed her shoulder.

His touch lingered—just long enough to answer what no one dared ask.

CHAPTER 25

The Crossing

The kitchen was loud in that particular family way—overlapping voices, clinking plates, and the occasional clang of silverware hitting the floor followed by a chorus of "leave it, it's fine."

Annabelle's cheeks still burned.

Valen did his best to pretend the conversation about holding babies hadn't detonated around him.

He was halfway through his coffee when the front door opened.

Her two brothers-in-law entered first, chuckling over what sounded like a bad fishing story.

A few moments later came her brother, and behind him, her father, stoic and quiet as ever.

The room's temperature shifted.

"Morning," her father said with a nod, reaching for the coffeepot.

"Look who's up," Eliza's husband, Peter, added, eyeing Valen. "Slept through the fishing trip, didn't you?"

"That wasn't on the schedule," Valen said.

"Must've gotten lost in the mail," Nathan said.

"You missed five hours of nothing biting," Isaac said. "A real loss to the ages."

"But don't worry," Peter said. "You're not getting out of the hunting trip tonight."

Valen glanced up. "Hunting?"

Her brothers grinned in unison.

"We head out at dusk," Isaac said. "Camp overnight. Start early."

"Part of the tradition," Nathan said.

"And yes," Peter said. "That includes you."

"*Especially* you," Isaac said, pleased.

Valen gave Annabelle a long look. Her shoulders shook with suppressed laughter.

"This feels personal," he said.

"It is," Isaac said. "We want to make sure you can hold your own."

Valen didn't flinch, but Annabelle caught the faint pause, like a chess player rethinking his defense.

"Out in the woods," Isaac added. "With knives."

Valen arched a brow. "Ah. A trial by wilderness."

"That's one way to put it," Nathan said with a wink.

"Or," Annabelle said sweetly, "a character-building opportunity."

He looked at her. Then at them. Back again. "Are you going to save me?"

"You survived a room full of children," she said. "You'll survive four dads with knives."

"Three dads," he muttered. "And one very judgmental father."

Her father sipped his coffee, not denying it.

Valen picked up his fork like it might be the last weapon he'd see for twenty-four hours. "I'm going to need more pancakes."

As the laughter faded and the remaining plates were cleared, Annabelle stretched lightly and stood.

"I was thinking of showing Valen around town," she said, brushing a crumb from her skirt. "He hasn't seen much beyond the road in."

"Supplies?" her father asked, as if running through a checklist.

She nodded. "For tonight. And maybe a few things for the house."

"Better take someone with you," her brother said, grabbing more bacon. "Town's not far, but you'll want someone who knows the market."

Annabelle rolled her eyes. "I've been to town before."

"Yes, and last time you came back with a glazed goat and boots you never wore."

She looked at Valen. "He's exaggerating."

"I'm not," Isaac said.

"A glazed goat?" Valen turned.

"Don't," she warned.

"I'll go." Isaac stood, clapping a hand on Valen's shoulder. "You'll love the butcher. Great sausages. Smells irresistible."

"I can hardly wait," Valen said dryly.

Not long after, they rattled into town in a carriage that smelled more of damp upholstery than sausages. Geese called softly from the waterfront.

Market bells clanged faintly ahead: carts jostled past, shopfronts bustled, and someone was loudly berating a pig near the soap stall.

Isaac sat opposite them, chatting easily the entire time. Valen nodded politely but said little. Annabelle mostly stared out the window, pretending not to notice when their knees bumped.

Their first stop was the blacksmith: low stone walls, the smell of metal and soot thick in the air. Heat rippled from the forge before they stepped inside.

Isaac led the way, calling a greeting to the man at the anvil. "We've got a fresh recruit for the hunt."

The forge hissed as Valen headed closer, gaze drifting to the wall of knives—rows of them, each a little different. He examined them with the same calm intensity he gave to books.

Picking one up, he tested the balance and weight, then drew the edge lightly across the hair on his forearm.

Her brother raised a brow. "You've handled a blade before, haven't you?"

Valen let the silence stand, picking up another knife. Then another.

She watched him pass over the fancier knives, drawn to one with clean lines and understated strength.

When he chose, it wasn't the flashiest, but solid, with a curved handguard to protect his grip if things went poorly.

He turned to the blacksmith. "I'll take this one."

"Hope you won't need it," Isaac said.

Valen hesitated for a breath too long for the comment to stay light.

He met Isaac's eyes, not unkindly. "Hope you're right."

The blacksmith set about wrapping the chosen knife in oiled cloth, twine, and careful folds of brown paper.

Annabelle drew closer while her brother wandered off to examine an ornate horseshoe that absolutely didn't need examining.

Her hand brushed Valen's—innocent on the surface, but it lingered.

"You don't have to prove anything," she said quietly.

He glanced down at their hands, then at her.

"Too late," he murmured. "I already picked the one I wanted."

She let out a breath that might've been a laugh. Then, more seriously, "I'm not joking. You've never been hunting."

His gaze stayed steady on her.

"I've read plenty of survival manuals," he said, deadpan.

She tilted her head slightly. "That's not the same as experience."

"No," he agreed. "But it's the best kind of panic—well-read and under-qualified."

That made her smile, but the worry didn't leave her eyes.

He softened and leaned in. Their shoulders met, the contact quiet but deliberate.

"I'll be careful," he said. "I have no intention of dying in front of your entire family."

"Or at all," she added, quieter now.

He looked at her. Then nodded. "Or at all."

The rest of the market visit blurred pleasantly.

They visited the general goods shop for flint and dried rations. The apothecary for salve "just in case."

Somewhere in the middle of it all, the tension eased. And she let herself forget the past, even for a little while.

The three of them walked through the square—her brother far enough ahead that the space between her and Valen felt almost dangerous. Their fingers brushed once. Twice. Accidental, but unmistakably not.

At one point, Isaac waved toward a small alley near the green. "And that's where Mrs. Haber caught Annabelle with a chicken under her skirt."

Valen stopped walking.

Annabelle groaned. "Please don't."

"She was trying to 'rescue' it from being made into stew," her brother continued, undeterred. "Told Mrs. Haber it was her 'special bird frien d.'"

Valen's expression twisted, an obvious effort to keep his laughter polite.

"I was six," Annabelle muttered, face glowing.

"I've got to make up for lost time," Isaac said cheerfully. "Didn't get to do the whole 'embarrass your sister in front of her very serious suitor' bit last year."

"I'm not—he's not—" She struggled to finish, heat rising in her chest like a flare.

Valen sipped from the small cup of cider they'd picked up from a stall. "You're blushing again."

She glared at both of them. "I should've left you at the blacksmith."

"That's deserved," Valen murmured.

Her brother only grinned, looking far too pleased with himself.

The breeze carried honeyed bread and chestnuts. Laughter from other stalls mingled with a distant fiddle. Town life moved as if none of this were strange.

As if her return, and Valen beside her, were entirely normal.

And for a few stolen moments, it almost felt like it was.

Isaac insisted on stopping at the baker's cart to earn extra favor with his wife. He debated far too long, weighing every pastry like it was a sacred offering.

Eventually, they moved on—Annabelle carrying a small paper bag of sugared almonds—when her brother slowed.

A few paces ahead, a pair of women near the cobbler's stall leaned together, their voices low, eyes flicking in her direction before skimming over Valen. One murmured something that made the other smirk.

The hum of the market carried on, but the prickle at the back of Annabelle's neck stayed.

Isaac's tone dropped. "Don't panic. Straight ahead. It's him."

Annabelle blinked. "Him?"

Isaac didn't answer as he tilted his chin.

She followed his gaze.

Dominic.

He lingered at the far edge of the square, speaking animatedly to a vendor but not really listening. His posture was too casual, his laugh too loud.

Beside him, half-shadowed beneath the awning, stood a woman, younger than Annabelle, heavily pregnant, shoulders hunched as if trying to disappear into the cobblestones.

Annabelle turned quickly, hoping they could slip into the next street unnoticed.

Too late.

"Annabelle!"

His voice cut across the square.

Her grip slipped on the bag, fingers twitching as if her body had decided to flee before she had.

She froze.

Valen tensed beside her.

Dominic strolled toward them, one hand in his coat pocket, the other guiding his wife by the elbow. She moved as if her feet didn't belong to her.

"There you are," he said, voice too bright, too familiar. "I wondered where you'd run off to."

Her mouth opened, but no words followed.

He looked her up and down with a smirk that made her stomach turn.

"I tried to wait for you, my wayward bride," he said, loud enough for everyone to hear, "but I couldn't be bothered."

Isaac took a step forward, but Valen stilled him with a subtle motion.

Dominic turned, gesturing toward the woman beside him. "This is my wife," he said, almost absently. "Much more obedient than you ever were."

The girl kept her gaze low. One hand clutched her belly; the other tugged her sleeve down with a nervous flick, as if unsure what might show.

Annabelle wondered how long it had taken her to stop apologizing for flinching.

Valen's shoulder brushed hers as he stepped forward—a quiet wall of steel.

Dominic blinked and looked him over.

"Well," he said, dragging the word out like it tasted sour. "Hope he was worth the scandal."

Silence did the talking.

Annabelle found her voice, even if it was barely above a whisper. "We should go."

Isaac didn't hesitate, shifting his weight like he'd been waiting for the cue.

Valen fell into stride beside her, body slightly between her and Dominic without making a show of it.

They didn't look back.

Dominic called after them, lazy and amused.

"Don't be a stranger, sweetheart!"

Annabelle's hand shook as she crushed the paper bag in her fist.

She stumbled as her boot snagged in a dip in the road. Valen steadied her, close enough to catch her if she broke.

They were quiet for a while, not speaking again until the bustle of the market had faded behind them and the only sounds were the steady clop of the carriage horses and the snap of reins.

Annabelle sat stiffly, the bag of almonds crushed in her lap, now a mix of sugar and shame.

She stared at the road ahead as if it might split, offering a version where she'd never returned.

The leather seat creaked as she shifted, its groan oddly loud in the hush. A crow called somewhere overhead. A horse's tail flicked once. Nothing else moved.

Isaac finally broke the silence. "Is that really how he treated you?"

She gave a single, slow nod.

He exhaled, more rattled than he probably meant to be. "I had no idea. He always seemed so..."

"Perfect?" she supplied, voice flat.

"Yeah," he said, and looked away.

She let out a small, humorless laugh. "That's what he wanted everyone to think."

Valen didn't speak, but she felt the steady weight of his attention.

Isaac shook his head. "I thought he was—reserved. Maybe a little full of himself, but not..." He trailed off, eyes fixed on the road. "Not like *that*."

Annabelle looked up. "He never raised his voice. Never laid a hand on me. He just broke me down, piece by piece—what to wear, how to laugh, when to shrink."

The silence that followed wasn't uncomfortable, but heavy with things newly seen.

Her brother's grip tightened on the parcel in his lap, paper crinkling softly. "If I'd known..."

She cut in gently. "I didn't want you to know. That was the point. He was good at hiding. And I was good at pretending."

The quiet lingered.

Then her brother said, almost to himself, "That poor girl."

Annabelle didn't say anything. Her hand shifted enough for Valen's to find it.

And when he found it, she didn't let go.

CHAPTER 26

The Departure

Valen knelt by the bed, six items laid out in a neat row: a rolled canvas tent, dried rations, fire starter, extra socks, a shallow tin of salve, his knife still sheathed and resting atop the pack like a silent threat.

He tried unsuccessfully to cram everything into a well-worn rucksack. Definitely too small.

The bag refused to stay shut. He tied it off, checked it, then watched the knot slip loose. A sock escaped like it had second thoughts.

Muttering to himself, he reached to start over—until a gentle voice startled him. "Need some help?"

Annabelle stood in the doorway, hair loose around her shoulders.

"I—" He half-shrugged. "Almost got it. Just can't get the damn thing shut."

She re-rolled the tent, packed it tighter, and cinched it closed. It held without argument.

"Nervous?" she asked.

"What gave it away?"

Her hands lingered on the sack before she turned to him, adjusting her posture.

She cupped his cheek. He leaned into her touch, grounding himself.

"I'm sorry they're making you do this," she said. "I'd honestly forgotten about the whole 'hunting rite of passage' thing. Maybe I hoped they would too."

Valen shook his head. "It's alright. I'd do anything for you."

"Even get eaten by a bear?"

"Especially then. It'd make for a better story." He grinned.

She laughed, but her expression didn't hold it.

"I'll be fine. I've read so many survival books," he said.

"That's not the same as practice."

"No," he said. "But I have the theory. I just need to see if it translates into not dying."

"Ambitious," she murmured.

"I'll come back. I promise."

"I'll be here."

They stayed like that—foreheads resting together—until she tilted toward him. Their noses bumped. He huffed a quiet laugh, and then she kissed him, properly this time.

His hand settled at her waist, anchoring them both as he deepened the kiss.

He stood, shouldered the pack, and headed for the stairs.

Annabelle lingered, just long enough to compose herself, then followed.

Downstairs, boots thudded against floorboards as jackets and bags changed hands with the rhythm of habit. The air carried hints of coffee and worn leather.

Cold crept in through the cracks in the window frame.

The men stood in loose formation: her father checking a compass, Nathan digging through his pack like he'd lost something critical, Peter already making jokes about who'd get the worst blisters.

They did it often. The kind of ease born from shared tradition and mild discomfort, turned annual sport.

Their wives lingered nearby. Offering last-minute reminders, and kisses for luck.

Valen descended into the middle of it all like someone who'd wandered into a ritual with no script and the wrong boots.

Isaac spotted him first. "You ready?"

Valen hesitated, then gave a dry, practiced smile. "As I'm going to be."

That got a few chuckles.

Nathan clapped him on the back and passed him a flask.

Annabelle watched him move to follow, Valen's tall frame silhouetted against the fading light.

He turned and met her eyes one last time.

The door closed with a final, wind-swept thunk. The sound echoed in her chest.

Boots scuffed against the wooden steps. Voices faded into the trees, wagon wheels clattering down the lane.

The children had been wrestled into bed hours ago, dragged off in sleepy protest. Now the house shifted from crowded to quiet.

Annabelle stood in the hallway, arms folded loosely. She stared at the closed door for one long moment.

The wind still whispered through behind the shutters. Silence settled in its place.

She crossed to the kitchen and straightened a few things on the counter that didn't need straightening. Wiped a spotless surface with her sleeve. Something to do with her hands.

The floorboards creaked a second before Eliza padded in, barefoot and smug, wineglass in hand. "I knew I'd find you brooding," she said. "Wine?"

Annabelle blinked. "It's not even dark yet."

"I'll take that as a yes."

A short while later, Annabelle curled deeper into the sofa, legs tucked under her, already two glasses in and deeply regretting it.

Eliza gave her the look, the one that meant she was about to start trouble. "So. How is he in bed?"

Annabelle groaned. "Absolutely not."

Grinning over the rim of her tea, Beatrice said, "That's not a denial."

"I'm refusing to dignify that with an answer," Annabelle said—too fast.

Eliza rolled her eyes. "Oh please. You show up glowing, smiling at thin air—like we're not going to ask?"

"You're impossible," Annabelle said.

"You're *deflecting*," Beatrice chimed in, raising her cup.

A pause stretched before Marian, her sister-in-law, spoke with deceptive gentleness. "And your ears have gone magenta."

Annabelle yanked a pillow into her lap and buried her face with a muffled groan. "I hate all of you."

"So," Eliza mused aloud, "does he make noises? Or is he like... the intense, silent type?"

Beatrice perked up. "Wait. Does he talk in bed?"

Gasping, Eliza said, "What if he reads poetry in that *unreasonably lovely* voice of his right before he—"

"I'm going to scream," Annabelle cut in, her voice smothered by the pillow.

"You're not denying it," Beatrice sing-songed.

"Because if I do," Annabelle said, "you'll twist it into something worse."

"Your fate is sealed," Eliza smirked. "Might as well enjoy the spiral."

Marian sipped her wine, clearly enjoying every second of this.

Annabelle peeked over the pillow, fingers curling tighter around it. "He's... *attentive.*"

Eliza gasped like someone had slapped her. "Well, *that* must be nice."

"I knew it," Beatrice said, clutching her chest.

Annabelle groaned again, sinking deeper. "I thought you missed me."

"We did," Eliza said. "But you don't get to waltz in glowing and expect us to pretend you didn't vanish."

"We're thrilled for you," Marian said. "And we are required to express that by being insufferable."

Eliza flopped sideways, nearly spilling her wine. "Worth it."

They all laughed. Then the energy softened.

Beatrice nudged her drink against Annabelle's.

"No, but really," Beatrice said. "Does he make you happy?"

The question hung in the air.

Annabelle looked at her sisters. Then down at the rim of her glass.

"Yeah," she said quietly. "He does."

Beatrice's fingers toyed with the handle of her mug a moment too long. "Everyone deserves that."

Marian asked, "Do you feel secure with him?"

"Completely," Annabelle said.

Eliza leaned back, letting out a long breath. "Good."

"Security's good," Marian murmured. "But it's not everything."

"We just wanted to make sure," Beatrice said more softly. "You hadn't looked like yourself in a long time."

"But now?" Marian said. "You're back in our lives."

Annabelle blinked, the sting in her eyes catching her off guard. "I missed this."

Eliza grinned. "We missed you."

The wine kept flowing. Teasing gave way to stories and shared memories, laughter slipping between them like it had never left.

Eventually, one by one, they drifted off with murmured goodnights, yawns, and the sound of bare feet on wood floors.

Annabelle stayed a little longer, knowing it wouldn't bring him back. Then, finally, she got up and went to bed.

CHAPTER 27

The Shot

By the time they reached the clearing, the air had cooled and dusk hung blue and heavy over the treetops. The earth was firm but uneven, soft in spots where the last rain hadn't dried.

The others moved with quiet efficiency. Packs hit the ground, tents unfurled, stakes hammered in without discussion. They weren't wasting any time.

Valen picked a spot a little ways off—not far enough to seem antisocial, not quite in the center either. Neutral territory.

He laid out the borrowed canvas, sorted the poles. The rope was tangled, but nothing he couldn't manage.

One of the main supports was missing.

Nobody was watching. Everyone else was busy. Good.

Stepping into the trees, he found a fallen branch long enough to substitute, dragged it back, trimmed it with his knife. Crooked, but it would do.

He braced it and tied it off. The canvas sagged, rope going slack. It held a moment, then collapsed when he let go.

Frustrated, he steadied himself and gave it another try, adjusting the angle.

The knot slid free again, the whole thing folding as if it were a dying animal.

He stood there, jaw tight, shoulders square.

Pressing his thumb and forefinger to the bridge of his nose, he bent down to start over.

A voice called from behind. "Need a hand?"

Valen stared at the mess like it might fix itself out of embarrassment.

He looked back. Peter waited a few paces away, halfway out of his tent, watching with mild amusement.

Valen straightened. "I'm missing a pole."

Peter nodded. "Yeah. That one's always short a piece—been meaning to fix it."

He didn't offer sympathy. Instead, he crouched beside the pile and picked up the crooked branch.

"Creative, though," he added. "I'll give you credit for ingenuity."

"Can I redeem that for a roof over my head?"

Peter grinned. "Only if you ask nicely."

"...Please."

"Better."

Valen stepped aside. Peter took over the knots, done in under two minutes. Annoyingly efficient.

When the canvas finally stood upright, Valen looked at it as though he'd rather kick it back to the ground.

Peter gave him a sideways glance and a crooked smile. "Next time, just shout. No one's trying to watch you fail."

"Noted."

Once the tents were up, Nathan tossed him an axe. "Firewood. There's a downed tree to the east. Should be decent, if it's dry inside."

Valen caught it without thinking. It was heavier than he expected, the handle worn smooth, the edge dulled but serviceable. Still sharp enough to split. It would just take effort.

He nodded and headed into the trees.

The air cooled further under the canopy, thick with the scent of pine and damp leaves. He followed a faint trail to the fallen tree, old and stripped of bark in places, but clean, dry wood beneath.

He found a good spot near the base and scored a rough line. Then set the axe, took a breath, and brought it down.

Working along the trunk, he cut sections as evenly as he could manage.

Once he had a length free, he set it on a flat stone, took another breath, and swung.

The blade lodged instead of splitting true.

He pried it loose, shifted his footing, swung again. And again.

The rhythm was rough, then steadied—muscle over precision, persistence over power.

Sweat gathered at his neck. His breathing turned heavy, but he kept swinging.

That steady cadence pulled him under until his shoulders burned, palms stung, and the pile beside him was more than respectable.

Gathering what he could carry, logs balanced in his arms and the axe slung over one shoulder, he returned to camp.

A splinter wedged under his thumb. He ignored it.

He hadn't carried anything to a fire since childhood. Back then, it had been papers or a coat: always something light.

Isaac looked up from the flames. "Not bad. Didn't think you'd bring back half a tree."

Valen dropped the wood by the pit with a solid thunk and wiped his brow.

He wasn't trying to impress them, but he wouldn't be the weak link either.

The fire crackled high, shadows dancing across the treetops. Smoke curled into the air, tinged with meat and pine.

They made quick work of the meal: cured strips and roast, unwrapped from oilcloth, warmed over the fire and carved into steaming portions.

Nathan poured something strong into tin cups. Valen took one with a nod.

Talk stayed low and lazy. Peter said he'd slipped into a creek a few weeks ago. Isaac claimed he'd screamed like a child. Laughter followed. It was easy.

Valen sat near the edge, not quite in the circle.

He ate in silence, listening.

Isaac asked, "So, Valen—what'd you think? First day out with the pack?"

"Stop calling us that," Nathan said, and threw a twig at him.

Valen took a moment to consider. "Challenging."

"Wait till you see Isaac try to skin something. That's a challenge," said Peter.

"Hey," Isaac called back, "at least I don't try to start a fire with damp moss every year."

Peter grinned. "You all lack foresight."

That earned a groan.

Valen let out a low sound that might've been a laugh.

Nathan caught it. "Look out—he's starting to crack."

Glancing over the rim of his cup, Valen said, "You'll know I'm fully integrated when I start bragging about the size of fish I didn't catch."

That got a real laugh. Even a nod from her father, who'd been mostly silent, nursing his drink near the flames.

It didn't last long. Full of meat, spirits, and cold air, they drifted into tending the fire, stretching out, leaning back into their coats.

Valen returned to his tent, firelight catching faintly on his face as he passed.

He wasn't trying to belong, but for once he didn't feel he had to leave.

By the time he fell asleep, the embers were barely glowing. Somewhere nearby, someone laughed again, but it didn't feel like they were laughing at him.

The world was gray when Valen woke to canvas rustle and the muted clink of metal. Outside his tent, the cold bit his skin as he ducked into the clearing, boots crunching on dewy grass.

Only a ring of crimson char remained where the fire had burned. Ash hung in the air, sharp and dry in his nose.

Isaac crouched beside the remains, stirring the cinders with a stick before scattering dirt over them.

Others moved in slow, familiar rhythms: tightening laces, loading rifles, checking satchel straps. No one spoke above a murmur.

It was a quiet born of routine. Of determination, maybe.

Valen retrieved his borrowed rifle from where it leaned against a nearby stump.

It was well-kept, heavier than it looked. He checked the chamber, then the strap. It felt foreign in his hands, but he gripped it like it mattered.

Nathan passed him a canvas pouch of cartridges. "You'll only need a few. Unless you're a terrible shot."

He nodded in thanks.

Her father stood off to the side, already geared up—coat buttoned, rifle slung with easy familiarity across his shoulder, eyes scanning the edge of the woods like he could see the trail they'd follow.

Peter peered over the group, jerking his chin toward her father. "Valen, you'll go with Edward."

Valen turned to him.

Edward gave a curt nod. "We'll head east, loop down by the ridge."

The others murmured agreement, grabbing their packs and splitting off.

Adjusting the strap, Valen followed. The rifle sat wrong against him, like a coat he hadn't grown into yet.

He knew why he'd been paired with her father.

There was something about the silence between them that felt intentional. He didn't shy away, stepping into the trees after him.

Determined to earn whatever this was meant to be.

The clearing ahead was still and empty. Frost clung to the brush, thin and silver. Their breath hung pale in the air, vanishing before it rose.

Valen crouched a few paces behind Edward, careful to step where he walked. Careful not to fidget.

The silence was heavy.

Edward adjusted his grip on the stock, eyes still on the trees. "You ever hunt before?"

Valen shook his head. "No, sir."

"You're holding steady."

A minute passed.

"What are your intentions with my daughter?"

No shift in tone, no warning—dropped like another observation, same as the weather.

Valen blinked. "Sir?"

"Is this just a passing thing for you? Or are you planning to settle?"

Valen hadn't expected that question, not with the weight of a rifle across the man's lap.

His voice stayed level. "I'd like to be with her. For as long as she wants me."

Edward glanced at him. "You don't sound sure."

"I'm sure of her," Valen said softly. "I'm not always sure I'm what she needs."

Edward was quiet. "Last time she got close to settling down, she ran. You know that?"

"I do."

"And you think she won't run this time?"

"If she does..." Valen paused. "It won't be because I didn't try to make her feel safe."

That earned him a longer look, something close to respect, if not quite approval.

They moved through the trees slowly, in an easy quiet—the kind that comes from knowing where to step and when not to speak. Birds called high and far off. Somewhere in the brush, a squirrel scurried through the undergrowth.

Valen followed Edward's lead with measured footfalls, rifle balanced in his hands. His heartbeat felt too loud, but his breath stayed even.

He could do this. He had to.

Edward raised a hand, stopping them both.

Valen froze, eyes tracking where he pointed.

There.

A low, heavy form lurked just beyond the trees, bristled and broad-backed, its snout rooting quietly near the ferns. A boar.

Valen inhaled and held it, hands dry on the rifle stock, heart pounding.

He looked at Edward. He hadn't moved, rifle at his side, eyes fixed ahead.

Hesitating, Valen whispered, "What do I do?"

Edward didn't mock the question or blink. He gestured toward the boar. "Slow. Steady."

Valen nodded.

Edward shifted beside him, voice quiet and measured. "Line up the shot. Behind the front shoulder, low. You miss high, it runs. You miss wide, it charges."

Valen adjusted his stance and grip.

"Don't hold your breath too long—you'll start to shake. Let the rifle rest against your shoulder, don't fight it. Follow through."

Steadying his aim, Valen exhaled.

"Not yet," Edward said softly.

Valen watched as it lifted its head and sniffed, waited, then dropped again to graze.

"Now."

Valen pulled the trigger. The rifle cracked, echoing clean through the trees.

The boar jolted, stumbled, then collapsed into the brush with a thud.

Valen stood frozen, still halfway through an inhale.

Edward didn't clap him on the back or praise him. He only said, "Good shot."

It landed harder than a hundred congratulations.

Valen exhaled fully, not because he'd hit the mark, but because someone had finally told him he had.

This was what a father was supposed to sound like.

The boar was heavier than it looked, the kind of weight that sank into your arms and settled deep into your shoulders.

Valen mirrored Edward through the field dressing, mimicking what he saw. It was messy, awkward, the smell bitter and heavy, but he kept his hands steady, his expression flat, and only asked questions when needed.

Edward gave quiet, efficient instructions. "Cut here. Keep the blade angled down. Watch your footing—blood makes the ground slick."

Knowledge passed from one man to another, without praise or judgment.

When it was done, they cleaned the worst of it with coarse cloth and river water, then hauled the carcass back—roped and dragged on a rough branch frame Edward rigged for hauling.

Valen returned with Edward, lowering the boar with a quiet grunt.

The others trickled in. Nathan had bagged a boar too, slightly smaller but still decent. Isaac carried a pair of rabbits over his shoulder.

Peter held up a fox with a grim look. "Scared the hell out of me, jumping the trail like that."

Laughter rippled through the group, the tone lighter. Easier.

Peter whistled. "Well, damn. Didn't think you had it in you."

Wiping his hands on a cloth, Valen took the water flask Nathan offered.

Valen stood in the circle now, shoulder to shoulder with the other men, and no one gave it a second thought.

CHAPTER 28

The Homecoming

The house still hummed with clinking dishes and children's chatter, but the spot Annabelle had chosen was quiet.

She'd stepped away for some air. The tea had gone cold in her hand, the porcelain damp where her fingers curled.

Her mother joined her minutes later, the faint smell of bread trailing from the kitchen.

They stood side by side, a distance between them.

Her mother spoke first. "I never thought I'd see you again."

Annabelle stayed silent.

At the window, her mother kept her gaze steady, late afternoon light spilling over the garden.

"You didn't even say goodbye. I knew you weren't happy, but I didn't realize it was that bad." She paused. "You could've come to us."

Something inside Annabelle gave way. "I *did* come to you."

Startled, her mother looked over.

"I tried to tell you what he was like. How he made me act. How he made me feel. I told you he didn't like the way I laughed. The things I wore. The way I spoke."

Annabelle didn't bother to hide the weight in her voice.

"And you and Dad told me I'd get used to it. That it was normal. That I'd settle in."

Her mother opened her mouth, then closed it.

Annabelle pressed on. "He made me feel like I was too much every day. And when I told you that, I was told to try harder."

The expression on her mother's face didn't shift.

"It wasn't that simple," her mother said at last. "We thought he was—"

"Safe?" Annabelle snapped. "You thought he'd take care of me. Make me manageable."

Her mother flinched. "That's not what we—"

"It's exactly what you meant. You didn't want me to be happy. You wanted me to be acceptable."

Another long pause.

Lips pressed, her mother glanced away. She absorbed the blow quietly, like dry earth after a storm.

"I didn't know it felt like that," she said at last.

"You didn't ask." Annabelle turned back to the window.

The silence didn't erupt. It dropped between them like a stone in water.

But her mother stayed beside her, quiet but present. This time... maybe she was listening.

They stood a while longer, watching the garden dip in and out of shadow. Some of the early shoots were showing, possibly asparagus or kale—something stubborn that returned.

Then came the sound of hooves, wagon wheels crunching on gravel, and voices in the distance.

Her mother straightened. They turned together, unspoken agreement drawing them toward the front of the house.

Outside, the hunting party was returning. The rumble grew louder.

Annabelle stepped off the stoop, fingers tightening on her mug. She fumbled with it, nearly sloshing what was left.

The wagon appeared first—canvas streaked with dirt, wood creaking under the weight of game and gear. The men walked back at a relaxed pace, with the kind of tired that comes from coping without comforts.

She scanned the group until she found him: Valen.

He was standing tall, rifle slung over his shoulder, shirt wrinkled, hair wind-tossed.

When he saw her, he held her gaze, a heartbeat too long.

Warmth bloomed in her cheeks, and she had to break eye contact before the air between them felt too thin.

The men veered toward the stable side of the estate, bringing the horses around and guiding the wagon to its usual spot. They were already talking about butchering schedules, meat curing, and cleaning gear.

The women began trickling out, curious and amused, ready with clean rags and remarks about how much mud had made it home this time.

Annabelle skirted the edge of the group, the chatter and laughter muffled under the thrum in her ears.

Valen didn't reach for her, but his eyes found her again when no one else was looking.

A smile threatened; she swallowed it.

Her brother broke the tension. "Look what Valen brought back!" he called, grinning, gesturing toward the wagon where a boar was lashed down. "Dead center. Dropped it clean."

Peter nodded as he passed. "Yeah, he did alright. After the tent incident."

That earned a round of laughter.

Valen gave a tired shrug, adjusting the strap on his shoulder. "It stood eventually."

"You were ready to set it on fire," Peter added.

"I maintain that was a valid tactical option."

They were teasing him—which meant, whether they said it or not, they liked him.

And from the way Valen endured it, brushing a hand across the back of his neck with something closer to amusement, he didn't seem to mind.

They'd nearly finished unloading. The meat was in the cellar, rifles cleaned and stored, gear drying near the shed.

Only Valen and Annabelle's brother remained.

They worked in silence at first, stacking the packs inside. The air smelled of old rope, woodsmoke, and iron, a tired kind of quiet settling between them.

Valen hefted the remaining pack onto the shelf and turned to go.

"You've got a good arm," Isaac said, casual. "Didn't think you'd manage that boar without flinching."

Valen glanced over. "Books teach you more than you'd think. The trick is remembering under pressure."

A faint grin tugged at Isaac's mouth. "Well, they paid off."

He hesitated "She was engaged once. I know you met him."

Valen nodded. "Hard to forget."

Isaac gave a humorless laugh. "Yeah. Always seemed... polished. Controlled. Said everything just the way you were supposed to."

He picked up a coil of rope, winding it to keep his hands busy.

"She changed when they got serious. Got quiet. Started talking like she was measuring every word. Wore dresses she didn't like. Said she was fine. Stopped teasing me—used to be her favorite thing."

He looked up briefly. "We thought she was maturing. Learning how to be... a wife, I guess."

The rope slipped from his hand, rolled onto the ground, and thumped his boot. He swore under his breath.

"But really, she was disappearing."

Valen stayed quiet.

"And then one day she was... gone. She left a note on the counter—'I'm sorry. I can't.'"

Isaac shook his head. "I thought she panicked. Or didn't want the life she was about to have. But now? Now I think she didn't see another way out."

Valen met his eyes. "She didn't."

For a moment, Isaac studied him, then nodded once. "Figured you should know. In case no one ever said it."

"Thank you."

The conversation seemed over, but then Isaac spoke again. "And listen—since we're being honest..."

Valen waited.

"You two arriving together, staying this close—it's not exactly... proper. Not around here. People are starting to talk like it's already settled."

In theory, Valen had known. Knew how it might look. But hearing it aloud landed sharper than he was ready for.

"I'm aware," he said quietly. But it didn't sound quite as certain this time.

Isaac didn't let it hang too long. "People talk."

"I know."

Stepping closer, Isaac's tone stayed firm but not hostile. "I don't care what people say. I care how she gets treated. So I'll say this once. If you're using her, or if you hurt her—even a little."

Something unreadable passed through Valen's expression. "You'll make me regret it."

"That's right."

"I understand." Valen nodded once. "And I won't."

Isaac watched him, then gave a small nod and stepped into the light, the door creaking shut.

A moment later, Valen followed.

The house was louder now: doors opening and closing, boots being shed, voices echoing down the halls. The smell of roasting meat drifted from the kitchen, and somewhere a child shrieked, laughing.

Valen moved into the back hallway, shirt unbuttoned at the collar, sleeves still rolled, smudged with dirt and smoke. He'd meant to wash up, change before dinner, maybe sit in silence for five minutes.

Annabelle leaned against the wall outside the washroom door, arms folded, one foot crossed over the other. Her hair was loose now, her expression unreadable.

"You're back," she said.

"I am."

She looked him over slowly, like she wasn't sure whether to be annoyed or relieved. "You didn't get gored."

"Not for lack of trying."

"You smell like the woods."

He shrugged. "It's where they put me."

She rolled her eyes faintly, but he caught the fondness underneath.

"I missed you," she said, voice low.

His throat tightened. "It was one night."

"That's all it takes."

She brushed a streak of dirt from his cheek. He leaned into the touch without meaning to, more tired than he let on.

"Dinner's almost ready."

"I'll be there."

She nodded, but didn't move.

Neither did he.

When she kissed him, it settled in his chest like a weight and a promise at once.

Then she stepped back and walked away as though she hadn't tilted his world sideways.

Dusk cooled the windows. The house filled again, boots thudding in the hall.

The long table had been reset, candles flickering, the smell of roasted boar rich in the air. Rosemary or juniper added something earthy and sharp to the steam rising from the platters.

Valen took his seat. The others carried on as if his place had always been there.

Annabelle caught his eye, her lips quirking into a look meant only for him.

Conversation flowed easily—stories from the hunt, exaggerated accounts of boars "the size of small wagons," dramatized near-deaths and heroic saves.

"You should've seen Nathan try to bait the trap with his own coat," Peter said, grinning.

"It worked, didn't it?" Nathan replied.

"Only because the boar was probably offended."

The room warmed with laughter.

"You didn't do too badly yourself, Valen," Isaac said, glancing over. "Cleanest shot I've seen in a while."

Valen deflected with a shrug. "Lucky angle."

"Sure," Peter said dryly. "Lucky angle, steady hand, unblinking focus—pure chance."

"You didn't tell me you were impressive," Annabelle said, raising an eyebrow.

Valen tried not to smile as he drank. "Once in a while."

Later, boots echoed down the hall, dishes clinked faintly from the kitchen, and someone put on tea.

The children gathered in the sitting room, curling onto cushions and sofas, tugging at sleeves and pulling books from the shelf like it was ritual.

This time, Annabelle sat in the armchair, legs tucked beneath her, a well-worn book resting on her lap.

Valen settled into the sofa across from her, elbow propped on the armrest, watching as she flipped to the first page.

She read with a warmth that threaded through the quiet like a lullaby. Firelight lit her face, her expression shifting with each character voice. The children leaned closer. One curled up in her lap, fighting sleep.

He couldn't look away.

A moment passed. "You were good with them."

He looked up. Her mother stood nearby, a fresh cup of tea in hand.

"They're easy to like," he said.

She nodded, sipping her tea. "Do you want any of your own?"

His gaze went back to Annabelle, still reading, the child in her lap now dozing against her hip. "I used to."

Her brow lifted. "And now?"

"I think... I stopped letting myself want anything for a while."

She let the quiet settle between them.

Valen looked toward Annabelle again. Her steady voice carried through the room. "I'm starting to remember what it feels like."

A faint, knowing smile curved her mother's lips. Then she left him—alone with the firelight, her daughter's words, and the subtle shift already underway.

CHAPTER 29

The Unraveling

Annabelle sat at the small vanity, hair loose around her shoulders, brush in hand. It caught on a knot near the nape of her neck. She worked through it slowly, undoing the day a tangle at a time.

The room was dim, lit by the amber glow of a single lamp. The hum of the house had quieted: doors shut, fire banked, footsteps muffled.

There hadn't yet been a moment to slip away.

The door creaked open carefully behind her.

She'd come to him before, barefoot and curling close. But this was the first time he crossed the threshold.

Not just into her room, but into the warmth she'd always offered, this time without needing an invitation.

She stopped, the brush frozen, a smile barely curving her lips.

Valen stepped inside, closing the door softly.

He paused a breath away, near enough to catch her scent, to see the lamplight turn her hair to gold.

She met his eyes in the mirror.

"You're not very good at sneaking," she said.

"I was trying not to alert anyone."

"You almost succeeded."

He smiled faintly and leaned against the wall, arms folded.

They were quiet for a moment. The brush moved again, slow and steady.

Finally, he spoke, voice low enough not to carry. "They helped me."

"More than I expected. Your brothers, your father. No one laughed when I messed something up. Not once."

She paused mid-stroke. "No teasing?"

"Well, some. But the kind you can survive."

Her posture shifted to face him more directly.

"They could've left me to figure it out alone," he went on. "But they didn't. Even when I struggled."

"Your father was... patient. He didn't say much. But when he did, it mattered."

Her eyes softened. "He does that."

"I think I needed that more than I realized."

The quiet stretched a beat too long. Then she stood.

They were barely inches apart.

She reached up, grazing his shoulder, smoothing a fold in the fabric.

"You did well," she whispered.

He leaned in, his forehead brushing against hers.

"I missed you," he said quietly.

"I missed you, too."

Neither of them moved to kiss as voices still echoed faintly through the house. But her fingers slid into his, warm and certain.

They stood like that for a while, close and quiet, hearts slowing from the current of the day.

Annabelle exhaled and stepped back. The brush slipped from her hand and clattered on the floor.

"While you were off being useful in the woods," she said, picking it up and setting it on the vanity, "I was being emotionally interrogated."

Valen tilted his head. "Oh?"

"My sisters. Cornered me with wine. Asked too many questions."

He arched a brow, easing out of his boots. "Let me guess. I came up."

She groaned. "Repeatedly. Exhaustively."

The grin that followed was all mischief. "Should I be flattered or afraid?"

"Terrified."

"Oh?" he asked, taking a slow step toward her. "What'd they do?"

"Nothing. It's fine."

"Come on," he teased, crossing the room in unhurried steps. "Tell me."

"Nope."

"Please?"

She shook her head, blushing. "It was nothing."

"So it was something."

He was close now. She bumped into the bed frame.

"Valen—"

"Tell me."

She groaned and grabbed the nearest pillow, burying her face. "They asked how you were in bed."

Silence.

"Oh?" he said, amused and deeply intrigued.

She peeked up enough to see the glint in his eye.

"And what did you tell them?" he asked, one brow raised. "How am I in bed?"

"Stop it."

"No, I want to hear this."

She groaned again, started to turn, but he was already leaning over her, tugging gently at the pillow she was trying to disappear behind.

"I couldn't hear you," he said, feigning ignorance.

"Valen, *please.*"

"Mmm. Not until you tell me."

Lifting her head, she shot him a withering glare. "I'm not telling you."

She moved to hide again, but this time he caught her wrist mid-movement and leaned in.

Close enough that she felt the warmth of him. The smile in his voice.

"Uh uh uh." He gave her a look. "You owe me."

She sighed, long-suffering, and muttered, "Of course I said you were good. Happy?"

His grin deepened. "Almost. What do I do that's good?"

One hand rose, tracing an easy path along her arm to her shoulder.

Her blush bloomed again. "Valen—"

"Mmhmm?" he murmured, amused.

"That is not fair."

"It's perfectly fair," he said, brushing a kiss to her cheek. "I'm just doing research."

"You're the worst."

"Tell me." His voice was gentle, breath warm near her ear.

She stayed silent. Which, frankly, was a mistake.

Because then, his lips trailed to the side of her neck and pressed a kiss just below her jaw.

A gasp tumbled out before she could stop it: a small, helpless sound, like her mouth had betrayed her.

Valen smiled against her skin. "So that's a yes. What about this?"

He kissed lower, beneath the curve of her ear, then slowly down her neck.

A quiet moan followed.

"Valen..." she pleaded.

"Shhh," he murmured. "Still doing research."

His hand drifted to her collarbone, finding the first button of her dress.

He undid it, then another, and another.

Kissing as he went, he let the fabric part beneath his fingers, revealing the flushed warmth of her skin.

"And this?" he asked, slipping the dress off one shoulder, his mouth following the curve.

Her head tilted back, eyes fluttering closed. She didn't need to answer.

He felt it in the way she leaned closer, in the little sigh that escaped her lips.

"Mm," he murmured, tracing his fingers lightly up her ribs. "You're not very good at resisting."

"You're not playing fair," she whispered.

"I'm not playing," he said simply.

Then he slipped the fabric from her other shoulder, fingertips gliding lightly down her arm. His mouth followed with slow kisses along her collarbone and throat.

Each touch bloomed beneath her skin.

He undid the final button and opened the dress, pausing to take her in.

For a moment, she nearly stopped him, the urge to shrink beneath his intentional gaze tightening in her chest.

Her hair was tousled, lips parted, and he hadn't even touched her properly yet.

"Beautiful," he whispered. "Always."

He said it like a vow—something she hadn't known she needed until it landed deep and left her aching.

He didn't rush, kissing her between her breasts, then lower, trailing his lips down her stomach in a lazy path.

His hands moved down her sides, easing her out of her dress, then her underthings, one piece at a time.

He kissed the soft space right above her hip, then down to her thigh, barely brushing the skin.

She twitched, something deep inside tightening. Her hand curled in the bedding beside her.

"Do you like that?" he asked quietly, lips hovering slightly above where she wanted him.

She nodded, struggling for words.

"Say it."

"Yes," she gasped.

Then he gave her what she needed.

His mouth found her, tongue moving in smooth, teasing strokes that made her moan aloud almost instantly. One hand slid under her thigh to anchor her, the other splayed across her stomach, keeping her grounded.

He didn't let her squirm from the tension building with every stroke.

When he slipped a finger inside her, then two, she cried out, hips arching helplessly into him.

"Valen—" she gasped.

"I've got you," he murmured, the vibration of his voice making her shudder.

He kept his rhythm steady, mouth still on her, pushing her higher until she was panting, desperate.

Her body tensed and then broke beneath his touch. She clutched at him, anything to keep from flying apart.

He held her firm until her thighs gave a tiny, involuntary jerk and her breath came in ragged bursts. Then he eased back up, kissing her wherever his mouth landed.

When he reached her lips, she kissed him like she needed air.

"Please," she whispered, voice wrecked. "I need you."

Valen let out a low, guttural sound. He was still fully clothed, but the way she moved against him, how warm and wet she was: he couldn't wait long.

The mattress creaked as he sat back, pulling his shirt over his head and tossing it aside. She watched him, eyes wide.

Her gaze tracked every line of muscle as he unfastened his pants, pushed them down, and bared himself fully to her.

Her leg curled around his waist as he moved over her. She shifted, hips rising in silent invitation.

He entered her in one slow, devastating thrust.

She gasped, head tilting back, lips parting in a soft cry.

His hands planted on either side of her, muscles taut, body shuddering with need as he bottomed out.

Groaning, he dropped his forehead to her shoulder. "You feel—you're—"

He couldn't finish the sentence; could barely think.

She clutched at him, pulling him down, holding him close as he began to move.

Every thrust was deep, rough—like restraint cost more than surrender.

He pressed his lips to hers like he meant to burn it into her bones.

Clinging to him, her hand caught the curve of his shoulder blade, body shifting to meet him.

"Valen..." she gasped, voice breaking against his mouth.

Her spine arched as she chased the edge he was driving her toward.

"Don't hold back. I want to feel all of it," he said against her cheek.

Her legs tightened around him, pulling him deeper as she shattered—her cry caught against his shoulder, every muscle trembling. He felt it ripple through her, the way she held him, and it undid him completely.

He groaned her name, hips stuttering as he drove into her once, twice more, and then came, buried deep.

They stayed entwined, breath and heartbeat slowing in tandem.

When she tried to speak, no words surfaced. Not with her heart still thundering and her thoughts undone.

The air between them felt full of something beyond want or love: the shape of a life they'd both thought was closed to them.

They lay pressed together in the warm stillness. The last of the lamplight flickered and faded.

The room held only heartbeat and heat humming on their skin.

Her leg was looped loosely around his hip, his hand tracing wandering shapes along her waist. Neither rushed to part.

She exhaled, slow, as if her body had only just remembered how to breathe.

Valen's mouth grazed her shoulder. "So…"

She hummed without opening her eyes.

"Would you say you were… thoroughly satisfied this evening?"

She cracked one eye open, glaring. "You're unbelievable."

"Mmm. I was aiming for unforgettable."

"You would."

"And yet, you didn't deny it." His lips brushed her ear.

"You're smug and I hate it."

"And you look very, very satisfied, so yes—I am."

She didn't argue.

"Ask me again in a few minutes," she murmured.

"Oh?"

"I might be able to speak in full sentences by then."

CHAPTER 30

The Slip

Valen stirred, one arm beneath her, the other loose around her back.

Annabelle shifted closer, somewhere between dreaming and waking, her nose brushing his throat.

Barely more than a whisper, she said, "I love you…"

It slipped out like it belonged there, like she'd said it a hundred times, like her heart was tired of waiting for her mouth.

Valen went still, his breath slowing.

For one sharp second, he thought she was awake.

But her breathing stayed steady.

Relief washed through him—the moment didn't demand a reply.

He pressed a kiss to her forehead.

She didn't stir. She might not have realized she'd said it.

But he did.

He carried it low in his chest.

He dressed and looked at her once more before slipping out. Her brothers were outside, halfway through repairing the fence. He joined them without fanfare, claiming he could be useful.

Or maybe for the company.

The morning drifted by, unspoken words lingering in the quiet.

By the time Annabelle sat at the kitchen table, her hands were curled around a mug long since cold. The house held a rare hush, as if even the walls were listening.

The children were outside. The sisters had gone to town for something "necessary" and, according to them, absolutely not gossip-fueled. Light pooled in the stillness, warm with the scent of whatever had been simmering on the stove earlier.

Her father sat across from her, flipping through the newspaper, pretending not to listen. Her mother, at the sink, dried her hands and watched her daughter's reflection in the window.

"You seem... settled," her mother said at last, voice low but sincere.

"Is that a good thing?"

Her mother's smile was soft. "It is."

Her father stayed on the same page.

"You just look different," her mother went on. "Lighter."

"I feel different."

Her mother came to sit beside her, not too close. "Are you sure about him?"

It was concern in the gentle, maternal way: never good with emotion, but meaning it when it showed.

"Yeah. I am."

Her mother watched her for a long moment, then brushed a stray curl behind her ear like she had when Annabelle was little.

"You're always welcome here. You don't have to disappear again if things get hard."

Annabelle blinked, something tightening in her chest.

Her father cleared his throat, started to speak, stopped. The newspaper crinkled in his grip.

And then he spoke without looking up. "We should've noticed. With Dominic."

The words landed heavier than the room seemed built to hold.

Annabelle turned.

He set the paper down, folded it, and looked straight at her. "We thought you were just being difficult. Or impulsive. You've always had a mind of your own—we figured you'd come around."

Her mother reached for her hand. "But that wasn't fair."

He went on, pacing his words like he had to push each one past pride and regret. "We thought we were doing what was best for you. That you'd grow into it. And when you left, we didn't understand. But we should've asked. We should've listened."

He paused.

"We're sorry," her father said. A little stiff, but sincere.

Annabelle stared at her mug, then gave a small, watery smile.

"Thank you," she said. "It wasn't just you. I didn't know how to say what I needed then either."

Her mother squeezed her hand. "Well. You're saying it now."

Annabelle smiled.

Her mother studied her, then tilted her head. "So... do you think he might be it for you?"

Annabelle's smile flickered, shy but steady. She looked down at the mug's rim, then nodded once.

"Yeah," she said. "I do."

The silence that followed was warm, like something unspoken had slid into place.

Her mother exhaled through her nose, like she'd been holding the question in for days.

Her father shifted in his chair.

"I've seen the way he looks at you," he said, voice calm. "Doesn't seem like he's faking anything."

Annabelle glanced over, surprised by the softness in his tone.

"He's quiet. Keeps to himself. But he listens." He paused. "Seems like a good man."

Coming from him, it might as well have been a standing ovation.

Annabelle's eyes burned, but she blinked it back.

"He is," she said. "He really is."

This time, the quiet around them wasn't waiting for anything. It was content.

By midday, that stillness had given way to movement again.

The house had been busy—children underfoot, footsteps everywhere. The smell of bread, smoke, and something sweet drifted through the halls. Conversations wove through rooms like thread.

Annabelle moved through it easily, helping where she could, smiling often. At one point she sat in the sun with her niece curled against her side, humming low and tuneless while shelling peas into a bowl.

All the while, her words from that morning stayed with Valen.

He had helped with small things: fixed a loose shutter, chopped kindling, made himself useful. But if anyone had looked too closely, they might have noticed the way he kept glancing over his shoulder, the way his hand stilled whenever she laughed.

What her brother said echoed in his mind, about honor and appearances.

He hadn't thought any of that would matter to Annabelle, but now every smile felt a little out of reach.

Maybe it wasn't enough to love her quietly. Maybe she needed something to hold onto.

He'd carried it all day, like a root beneath his ribs he hadn't decided to keep close or let bloom.

Late afternoon brought them a moment alone, tucked in the old garden shed behind the house. Light filtered through a warped window; the air was thick with herbs and earth. The door was half-closed, the household a distant murmur.

Reaching for the curtain, she knocked a jar off the shelf. It hit the floor with a soft thunk. She only laughed.

The smell of dried sage rose up as the jar rolled into a patch of dust. She kicked it with her toe.

"Do you remember what you said this morning?" he asked.

She blinked, a wrinkle of confusion passing over her features. "This morning...?"

"You said...'I love you.'"

Her eyes widened; color bloomed in her cheeks. "I—did I really?" she breathed. "I didn't mean—I mean, I didn't know I said—"

He stepped forward, catching her hand before she could fumble further.

"I—" He paused, like the words caught somewhere in his chest. "You did. Say it."

"Well, just so we're clear," she said, voice hushed but sure, "...I do."

He blinked, half-smiling. "You do?"

She nodded. "I love you, Valen."

Squeezing her hand unintentionally, Valen took a breath. "I... love you too, Annabelle."

That stopped her. Her breath came too fast, like the moment was too full to hold.

Reaching up, Annabelle cupped his face and kissed him.

Somewhere unseen, a mirror clicked in its frame—like it had been listening.

No one noticed, but something had shifted.

The hours slipped by in a hush that didn't need filling.

By evening, the quiet had deepened into calm.

Inside, the house stilled, the faint echo of voices down the hall, the creak of old wood as the day settled into night.

They were alone again, finally.

Near the parlor window, they stood together, stars beginning to flicker in the dusky blue outside. A gentle breeze stirred the curtain; the fire's warmth lingered low in the hearth.

Valen's hand stayed twined in hers. He hadn't let go since she said it.

I love you, Valen.

It still echoed in his chest, hours later.

She smoothed a loose strand of hair back, lost in thought.

He'd thought about waiting—about asking her first, properly, if she even wanted marriage, if she believed in it anymore. But some part of him, shaped by duty and instinct, pushed forward anyway.

"There's something I've been meaning to ask you," he said quietly.

"Oh? What is it?" She turned toward him fully, eyes bright with expectation.

Valen took a slow breath.

"I've been thinking about... everything," he said. "The trip. Your family. Something your brother said to me."

Annabelle's expression shifted. "Okay..."

He pressed on, voice steady.

"I don't want people thinking you gave yourself to someone who wouldn't stand beside you. Someone who'd let you carry that shame alone."

She only stared at him, thumb rubbing her knuckle, an old nervous habit. The air changed.

"I want to do right by you," he said. "To be the kind of man you could lean on. Without shame."

His fingers hovered, then reached for hers.

"Annabelle…" He took a deep breath. "Will you marry me?"

He tried to smile, but it didn't reach his eyes. He was already bracing for her answer.

Silence.

His heartbeat was loud. He almost said her name again. Almost apologized.

Her smile faded. He watched stillness settle in her shoulders, the way her breath barely moved.

Fingers twitching, she started to lift them toward him, then stopped.

Finally, she said, "It's not that I don't want to."

He blinked.

"It's that we haven't even talked about it, Valen."

He opened his mouth, then shut it.

Her gaze dropped, then shifted to his eyes.

"After everything I've been through—you at least owed me that."

His brow furrowed. "Annabelle—" He moved to take her hand, but she was already pulling back.

"I'm not saying no forever," she said quickly. "Just… no for now. No to being asked for the wrong reasons."

She drew a breath. "Because this? The way you did it?" Her voice cracked, but she held her ground. "It feels like a step backward. Like something someone else decided for me."

Looking away, her eyes stung, but her spine stayed straight.

"And I can't—" she faltered, caught herself. "No. I *won't* go back there."

Valen didn't know what to say. He'd expected relief, maybe tears, but the calm hurt worse.

He hadn't meant to break anything. Even so, maybe he had.

In the silence, with all that softness coming apart at his feet, Annabelle stepped toward the door.

She closed it gently, leaving the fire to burn alone.

The house emptied into its nighttime stillness.

It was dark—the kind that settles deep after the fire's gone out, after the last creak of floorboards, after the last whispered goodnight.

Valen lay in bed staring at the ceiling. He unbuttoned his collar and sat for what felt like hours before lying back.

The room felt too quiet. Too sharp around the edges.

He told himself not to read into it.

But the proposal kept replaying: what he'd said, and how she'd looked when he said it, like a door clicking shut behind her eyes.

Perhaps this was where the end began.

So when the door eased open past midnight, he thought he was imagining it.

Then came soft footsteps, a familiar silhouette in the doorway.

He sat up, confused.

"Annabelle?"

She didn't answer as she stepped inside.

For a moment she stood there, undecided whether to reach for him or retreat.

Her voice was faint but steady. "Just because I'm angry doesn't mean the love's gone."

Valen froze, a shaky breath escaping.

She crossed to the bed without hesitation and slid under the covers like it was the most natural thing in the world.

He turned to look at her, eyes searching. "You came back."

"I never left," she said simply.

He found her hand beneath the blanket. This silence didn't hurt; it held them.

———————◆———————

Elsewhere, the room of glass and ego had changed. Across the chamber, the mirrors began to fog.

She hadn't touched them. No one had.

Mist crept over the glass like breath released. She was still holding hers.

The counter had been falling all day. It was 637 that morning.

Now:
217
194
168

Tick. Tick. Tick.

She'd tried to stop it: spoke their names, smiled at the mirror. Even begged. They kept disappearing.

Barefoot now, with broken heels long discarded, she stood as if still waiting to be chosen. Her red dress sagged at one shoulder, slipping like it wanted to leave first.

Trembling fingers smoothed a curl at her temple that refused to stay.

Once, her lips had worn a red that dared anyone to question it. Now, the color was so smeared that only ruin remained.

The mirror couldn't fix her. Not this time.

Voices echoed from beyond the mirrors. Men, unmistakably.

"Was she always that desperate?"

"She used to be charming."

"Ugh, no. I never liked her."

Her mouth trembled.

113
87
56

The mirrors rippled. Cracks widened.

One flickered: a girl with perfect ribbons, clutching a lollipop, watching a boy walk away, wiping tears on his sleeve.

Behind her, her parents whispered promises: *You can have anything you want, our sweet Seraphine.*

And she believed them.

39
27
15

She screamed, shrill, like glass dragging across stone.

Nothing stopped it.

9
3
0

Silence fell. The chamber dulled completely.

The mirrors warped inward. Reflections vanished. Fragments rained down in slow collapse.

One shard remained, trembling in place. She went to touch it. Her hand cast no shadow.

She reached for her name—and found nothing left.

CHAPTER 31

The Belonging

The table buzzed with chatter and cinnamon. The children were half-dressed, sticky with jam. The women were already planning future visits.

"You're not allowed to vanish for a year again," Eliza said, pointing her fork at Annabelle. "You have to write. Regularly. I want details."

Marian grinned. "Especially the scandalous ones."

"I'll write," Annabelle promised. "No disappearing acts."

"You're coming back for the birth," Beatrice said.

"And birthdays. And harvest," her mother added.

Annabelle laughed. "So... every other week?"

"Exactly." Her mother smiled, giving her hand a final squeeze. "We're just glad you came back."

Outside, the farewell was less sentimental but no less genuine.

"Next time we hunt," Isaac said, clapping Valen's shoulder, "you're baiting the traps."

"Only if Peter doesn't cook again," Valen said.

"Hey!" Peter protested. "That stew could've fed a battalion."

"Of boars, maybe," Nathan muttered.

Her father stepped forward, quiet as ever, and looked at Valen for a long moment. "Take care of her."

"I will," Valen said with a nod.

The door opened behind him. Annabelle stepped out, cloak wrapped tight, bag in hand.

"Ready?" he asked.

She nodded, and they crossed to the carriage together.

Standing a few steps away, she watched as Valen fastened the last strap.

Her parents joined them at the end of the drive. Her mother came to Valen first, offering a smile that wasn't just polite but genuine—the kind that took time to earn.

"Thank you," she said. "For loving her the way she needs."

Valen gave a soft laugh. "Honestly, she makes it easy."

Her father nodded once. "You're welcome back anytime."

He wasn't prepared for how much that meant. He only managed a nod in return.

Then her mother turned to Annabelle, reaching without hesitation, arms open.

"It was so good to see you again," she whispered. "Even if it was just for a while."

Annabelle held her tighter. "It won't be the last time."

Her father kissed the top of her head, awkwardly, like he wasn't used to it but had decided now was the right moment to start.

Behind her, Valen had already stepped into the carriage, waiting quietly as she climbed in to join him.

As the wheels began to turn, she watched her family shrink, eyes fixed on the glass.

"You're quiet," he said after a while.

"I didn't think it would hurt to leave again," she said softly. "But this time... it hurts in the right way."

The carriage rocked into the hush of trees and gravel.

Neither spoke for a long while. Annabelle tucked herself into his side, eyes half-closed, one hand resting lightly on his chest.

The leather creaked beneath them. Somewhere in the sky, a hawk called. Annabelle's fingers curled in the fabric of his coat, like she didn't quite know what to do with stillness yet.

He hadn't moved since, one arm draped around her back.

She broke the silence first.

"So. What did you think? Be honest."

"About?"

"My family. The chaos. The mud. The unsolicited baked goods."

He sighed, then smirked. "It's clear where you get it from."

"Get what from?"

His smile softened. "Your warmth. Your vibrancy. Your nurturing. Your patience."

Her expression shifted, playfulness giving way to something quieter.

"All of it," he said.

She nestled close again, resting against his shoulder.

"Good answer," she whispered.

The carriage kept rolling.

At last, the wheels crunched to a stop outside the estate, the last light of evening brushing the treetops gold.

Annabelle stirred first, blinking awake. He followed, slower to return. Neither moved for a moment.

They stretched in near silence, limbs stiff from the ride.

Valen murmured something wordless as he stepped out for their bags.

Annabelle found the key—familiar brass against her palm. She crossed the porch and turned it in the lock, the sound quiet but certain.

Inside, the space felt still. She held the door as Valen returned with the last of their bags, the thud of luggage settling just past the threshold.

Then she closed it behind him.

The latch clicked home.

Outside, the carriage rumbled away, fading into the night.

Annabelle leaned against the wood, tension easing from her shoulders.

They'd barely set down their bags when Valen's stomach growled.

He grimaced, trying to ignore it.

"Hungry?" she asked, amused.

He turned his palm out, like he was expecting something to appear.

Frowning, he did it again.

"What are you doing?" she asked.

"It's not working."

"What's not?"

"I usually just…" He shrugged. "Think about food, and it shows up."

She arched a brow.

"I don't know how to explain it," he said. "It's just what I do. Or used to."

"When did it start?"

"After Seraphine left me, I guess. I just couldn't be bothered. With anything."

He looked down. "Seemed like the less I needed, the less I could lose."

"She hurt you that badly?"

"No, I mean... she did. But I don't think it started with her."

He rubbed the back of his neck. "I've kind of always been... closed off, I guess. Ever since I was young. I think I'd gotten so used to it, that I stopped noticing."

She was quiet a moment, then reached out, fingers brushing his.

"I get that," she said softly. "It was similar with Dominic. Shrinking was easier, for a while. Until I realized how small I'd gotten."

Her voice dipped. "There was hardly anything of me left."

They stood there a moment longer.

Then she smiled. "Well, come on. Let's see if this still works by hand."

In the kitchen, they didn't make anything fancy: root vegetables not yet soft, a handful of dried herbs, half a loaf of bread still mostly good if you trimmed the edges. He found a jar of beans in the cupboard and eyed it like it might bite him.

Annabelle did most of the work.

She handed him a spoon; he splashed broth onto the stove. Close enough. He tried to look offended when she snorted, but it didn't last. He couldn't remember the last time he'd done something badly and been allowed to laugh at it.

They moved around each other like they'd done it a hundred times before.

By the time the bread was sliced and the soup smelled edible, the house felt warmer.

She ladled it into bowls. He set the table badly.

When they finally sat down, neither said much. They simply ate. Together.

They finished eating and stacked the dishes in the sink. The last warmth from the kitchen lingered on their skin.

They'd been gone nearly a week.

Days spent apart. Nights curled into borrowed time. Only once had they truly touched—and it had felt like breaking something open.

Now there was no one to hide from. No doors between them.

Annabelle stepped into their room without pause. He followed carefully, like the floor might give out beneath him.

The familiar creak of the hinges, the scent of linen, the weight of all they'd been holding in: it all rushed in at once.

He shut the door behind them.

Annabelle turned to face him. They stood in the dim light, shadows curling along the walls, dust catching in the air.

He moved toward her. His palms found her hips, steady and familiar, and she melted into him with a quiet exhale. Her cheek rested against his chest. Her arms circled him.

"I missed this," she murmured.

"I... I missed you," he said at last.

Her hands threaded into his hair. He kissed her like he didn't know how much he'd needed it.

Clothes came away between kisses. She pushed his shirt from his shoulders. She traced down his chest, finding old scars and new tension. His touch slid along her waist, her back, the curve of her spine.

When he laid her down against the bed, he hesitated. A flicker of doubt. She caught it.

Her hand found his, fingers lacing. "You okay?"

His gaze searched hers, uncertain. "I keep thinking about how close I came to ruining it."

"You didn't." Her voice was soft, certain. She cupped his cheek, thumb brushing beneath his eye.

"One mistake doesn't erase everything else. You've been kind. Patient. Steady. You've shown up—for me, for all of this. That counts too."

He started to respond but stopped, the words catching.

"Shhh," she murmured. "I love you. And I'm not going anywhere."

Something loosened in him. He pulled her close, breathing her in.

A few moments later, when he entered her, they moved together in the slow, rhythmic letting go of everything they'd held back.

Sheets tangled as they shifted. Her fingers gripping him like he was the only steady thing left.

His mouth found the hollow of her throat, then her collarbone, then her lips again.

Their eyes met often, lingering each time.

Care gave way to need. Hands gripped instead of grazing. Kisses deepened, tasting of hunger.

She whispered his name against his jaw. He said hers like it was a secret he couldn't keep.

Outside, the wind rattled the window panes.

Their rhythm stuttered.

He came first, pressing his face into the curve of her neck, muscles tightening before giving way.

Her release followed, her whole body softening shortly after, like something long-held finally let go.

She stayed curled against him, waiting for her heartbeat to settle.

The ache in her chest was softer now, less jagged—but it hadn't gone. It shifted, restless, asking to be put somewhere her hands could reach.

ACT IV

ROOTED

CHAPTER 32

The Desire

Valen reached for her in his sleep. His hand met only blankets.

He blinked awake. Sunrise pushed pale light past the curtains. He stayed there, half-buried in the sheets, listening.

Then he heard it: the scrape of furniture legs on wood.

A pause. A slow drag. A grunt. A soft thud, then a dissatisfied sigh.

He sat up, rubbed his face, swung his legs over the bed. The sound came again: downstairs.

Too early for anything to be this loud.

The library door was open. He stopped in the threshold, eyebrows lifting.

Annabelle stood in the middle of the room, hair tousled.

The rug was askew. The sofa shoved partway to the opposite wall. The chess table turned crooked. A chair was stuck between the window and a bookshelf, angled like it had tried to escape and given up halfway.

She frowned at the chaos as if it were being difficult on purpose.

He watched her. "Need a hand?"

She turned with a jolt. Her expression was pure frustration.

"I was trying to get this chair by the window," she said, gesturing vaguely, "but it looked weird with the sofa, so I moved that, but then the chess table was in the way—"

She broke off. "Now everything looks stupid and I hate it."

Valen blinked, glanced around. "I think I see your problem."

"You're not allowed to laugh."

"I wasn't going to." He stepped into the room, eyeing the tilted chair. "But what did the chessboard do to deserve this?"

"It existed."

"A fatal flaw," he said with a solemn nod.

She sighed and nudged the sofa. It didn't budge.

"Let's try it this way." He moved to the far end.

They lifted it and dragged it back near the hearth.

She shifted back and clipped the chess table with her leg. "Ow," she muttered, rubbing the spot. Then squinted at the sofa. "Still not centered."

"Better than mid-room exile."

"Barely."

They stood there, breathing a little heavier than either wanted to admit.

Valen studied her. "Why now?"

She'd changed. The room hadn't. That felt wrong now.

"I wanted the chair by the window," she said, quieter.

He waited.

Adjusting her stance, she scanned the library for an answer.

"I just needed to change it. I don't know." The words came out smaller than she meant. "I wanted it all in place before you saw."

Her fingers toyed with the hem of her sleeve. "I didn't want you to think I was making a mess."

Valen chuckled and crossed toward her. "It's alright."

His voice was calm, steady. Reassuring without judgment.

Annabelle smiled.

They tried again together, shifting angles, sliding the rug, adjusting the sofa to center it on the hearth without blocking the flow.

He matched her pace without trying to lead. They disagreed once—he thought the armchair blocked the fireplace, she insisted it anchored the room—but they reached a compromise.

The chessboard was placed in the lounge, making space. The reading chair finally found its home beside the window, angled to catch the morning light.

As they eased the last piece into place, he watched her. How easily they moved together now. Out of step sometimes, but never clashing.

He didn't correct her when she adjusted the rug a little too far left. He let it be. Something had shifted.

Annabelle stepped back and took it in.

"There," she said. "Perfect. The chair's where I wanted it. The rest looks cozy by the fire."

"I'm happy with it. Are you?" she asked, turning to him.

Valen looked at the room, then at her. "If you're happy, I'm happy."

She narrowed her eyes, half-teasing. "That's not an answer."

"It's all I've got," he said, deadpan. "Looks better than before."

She smiled, more easily this time. "Thanks for helping."

He shrugged. "You were fine on your own. I only made it quieter."

Later, Annabelle curled into the new chair by the window, feet propped on the sill, a book on her knee. Sunlight poured in, warming the space, catching in her hair. It was where she'd wanted it. Where she needed it.

She tore a piece of bread from the breakfast Valen had brought—uneven, slightly burnt—and didn't seem to mind.

He sat by the fire, one arm over the back of the sofa. A small pile of mending rested beside him: a glove with a worn seam, a button worked loose. He threaded the needle slowly, working with steady focus.

They didn't speak much, but the stillness felt settled.

Annabelle closed her book, thumb trailing the spine.

"I was thinking," she said.

Valen glanced over.

"I want to see about getting an easel. I think I want to start doing larger paintings."

"I might have one upstairs you can use—or keep."

"Oh? Did you paint?"

"Not since I was a child. My mother did."

He set the thread aside and they headed up the stairs.

Past the guest room she'd stayed in was another door. He opened it and stepped inside.

The walls were pale blue, dusty wainscoting lining the bottom.

Near the window stood an easel. A half-finished oil painting rested on it: a vase of flowers. The real ones still sat on the sill.

Along the far wall, an ornate crib waited untouched, a few pillows and a stuffed bear arranged thoughtfully inside.

"Is this...?"

"Yeah, this is the nursery. Obviously didn't get much use after I outgrew it, though. Not sure why they kept the crib."

She crossed the room and picked up a pair of small shoes tucked in the corner, leather, worn soft with age, laces still neatly tied.

"I love baby shoes," she murmured, thumbing the laces. "Anything tiny, really."

Valen watched her, something in his chest pulling taut. Quiet, and a little too close.

She set them down, then looked at the crib. "Why did *you* keep it?"

He blinked, caught off guard. "I—uh... it's a nice piece. Solid wood."

"Mm. Shame to let it go to waste..."

"What are you implying?"

She only smiled, brushing past him into the hall. "You're clever. You'll figure it out."

It took him a few seconds. By the time it clicked, she was nearly to their room.

She was halfway out of her dress already, one shoulder bare.

He blinked. "Are you... are we—?"

"Let's just see what happens." She let the rest of it fall.

She crossed to him, hands cupping his face as she kissed him.

He held her there for a moment, just looking at her. "You're sure?"

Her smile softened. "I've never been more sure of anything."

Drawing her close, he wrapped his arms around her waist and guided them toward the bed.

His shirt was barely open before she pushed him back, climbing on top of him, fingers tracing down his chest.

When she shifted her weight, tension rippled through him.

She went still.

A breath escaped him, eyes flicking away. "Sorry. It's not you. I'm just... scared of how much this means."

Her voice softened. "It's alright. I am too."

She leaned in, forehead to his. "But—we're in this together."

That landed deep. His hand slid to her back, steadier now.

Her mouth met his again, slower this time.

Beneath her, he relaxed, the tension giving way to something warmer. Something open.

His hands came to her hips, rocking her against him. The friction sent a jolt through both of them.

Reaching between them, she undid the button of his trousers. He sucked in a breath.

She pushed them low enough to free him, fingers brushing the length of him. He groaned, forehead pressing to her collarbone.

A quiet sound left her as she climbed into his lap, straddling him fully. His palms slid up her thighs.

He sat up, mouth trailing down her throat until her pulse stuttered.

She shifted again, lining herself up, and sank down onto him with a gasp.

His hands gripped her hips, breath shaking as he filled her. She paused, giving them both a moment.

When she began to move, he met her rhythm, fingers sliding up her back to anchor her close.

A stray feather poked his shoulder through the pillow—he swatted it aside without breaking pace.

She moaned softly each time she rocked forward, tension curling low in her belly. His mouth found hers again, swallowing the sound as pleasure climbed.

"I love you," she whispered into him.

He shuddered. "I love you, too."

The words tipped him over. His grip tightened. A moan broke from him as he came.

She followed seconds later, collapsing against him, breathless and trembling in his arms.

For a long moment, neither of them moved. Just the hush of breath, skin cooling against skin.

Eventually, they rose and began to redress.

"So. About that easel..." she said, smoothing her skirt.

"Huh? Oh—right. What about it?"

"I'm not sure it'll fit in here."

"You could keep it in the nursery."

"I think I'd like my own painting space," she said. "A proper one. Good light, if possible. It doesn't have to be huge."

Her tone was casual, but the uncertainty was there.

He straightened. "You want your own studio?"

"If there's room. Just a corner, maybe. Near a window. I can make it work."

Valen tugged the last button into place, already moving toward the hall. "I have the perfect spot."

She blinked. "You do?"

He held out a hand. "Come see."

They made their way downstairs, past the sunny dining room where light spilled across the table. He stopped at the narrow staircase to the tower, beside a door she hadn't noticed before.

It creaked as he pushed it open. It caught on something. He gave it a firmer shove and knocked over a box inside.

Annabelle peered around him.

The room was small but not cramped, boxes and old furniture stacked in quiet disarray. Light poured through a tall window overlooking the back garden, washing the space in pale gold.

She stepped in carefully, the floor creaking beneath her. Dust hung in the air, catching the glow.

"It's perfect," she said.

Valen leaned against the doorframe, watching her. "It's yours. I'll bring the easel down later."

"Are you sure? What about all this?"

He glanced at the boxes. "We'll find another spot. I've been meaning to go through it anyway."

Her gaze drifted back to the window, expression soft and full.

"Thank you," she said. "Really."

She lingered a moment more. "I might need help getting the furniture in."

"I suspected as much," he chuckled.

In her mind, the space was already rearranged, and she couldn't wait to make it hers.

CHAPTER 33

The Keepsake

They spent most of the morning clearing space.

It wasn't just heavy lifting, though Valen did most of that, but more like peeling back layers. Boxes marked in faded ink. Dusty drapes. A lamp with no shade. They moved slowly, letting the work fill the quiet.

Most of it was harmless: old linens, broken furniture, unused frames. But in the corner, behind a warped dresser, was a smaller collection of boxes, deliberately placed.

Valen paused, studying the stack. "Let's go through these in the library."

She nodded.

They carried them out one at a time. He set the first on the table and just... stared at it.

She went back to the studio for another.

When she returned, he'd opened the box. She hesitated in the doorway.

He was hunched forward, elbows on his knees, shoulders drawn in. In his hands, cradled like it might fall apart, was a small tintype photo, faded but intact.

A boy, six or seven. Tousled hair, a look on the verge of mischief—lips pressed as if he were holding back a grin, trying to behave.

Beside him, a man with stern, tired eyes, one hand on the boy's shoulder like he didn't know what else to do with it.

And a woman, seated in front. Composed but not cold. The faintest curve to her mouth, more suggestion than smile. She looked like someone keeping everything together without letting it show.

Valen's fingers traced the edge. He nearly dropped it, catching it awkwardly in his palm.

She set the second box on the table, then sank onto the sofa beside him, resting a hand on his knee.

Silence felt safer than words. She stayed close.

"Tell me about her," she said softly.

"Her name was Rosalind."

He paused, the name tasting unfamiliar in his mouth, as if he hadn't said it aloud in years.

"She smelled like rosewater and something warm—fresh bread or sun on cotton."

Another pause. Longer this time.

"Her laugh was quiet. You had to earn it. But when you did, it felt like you'd done something right with the world."

His fingers tensed slightly against the frame.

"She was the only one who let me be a kid," he said. "Everyone else had expectations. Tutors. Staff. My father. Always watching. Always correcting. But she just... let me play."

Annabelle stayed still.

"I liked when my father was out of town," he said. "She and I would build tents in the sitting room. Drape blankets over the chairs. Bring books and snacks inside. We'd stay up giggling for hours."

A faint smile tugged at his mouth, then slipped away. "Father never would've allowed such 'tomfoolery.'"

Annabelle's hand stayed on his leg, her body angled toward him.

"She left with my father one night," he said. "Promised me she'd be back soon."

His voice held, thin and fragile, like speaking too loud might crack it.

"I cried. Begged her not to go. Clung to her cloak, not understanding why she couldn't stay."

He swallowed.

"I stayed in that chair all night, facing the door, wide awake."

"When it finally opened in the morning, I thought she'd have pastries or something silly. But it was just my father."

"His eyes were red. I'd never seen him like that."

A second passed. And then, quieter, "He said she wasn't coming back."

Annabelle's fingers curled at his knee.

"I didn't understand. They never told me she was sick. It all happened so fast."

His thumb brushed the tintype again, slower now, as if he didn't want to put it down.

She watched his face, the light catching at his jaw, his mouth set. As if too much might spill out if he loosened it.

"My father tried to hide as much of her as he could after she was gone," he said. "Told me there were no pictures, and to stop asking."

His fingers stilled on the photo.

"I used to think I imagined her face. That I made it up."

"Maybe it was more than he could handle. I don't know. He never spoke about her. Hardly talked about anything, really."

"I've never had anyone to talk to about this," he said. "My father was gone a lot after she died. And I just... shut down."

Still, she kept her hand on his knee, steady and grounding. He looked at her, eyes tired but open.

He set the photo aside and reached for her.

Pulled her into his side, then closer, until his face found the curve of her neck. His breath was shaky at first, then deeper.

Her arms came around him, drawing loops between his shoulder blades.

Eventually, Valen sat back.

He wiped the corner of his eye with his thumb, like it was nothing. But he didn't meet her gaze.

"Thank you," he said softly.

"Of course. I'm glad you at least have one picture of her."

"Yeah. Me too," he murmured. "...I don't think I'm ready to go through the rest of the boxes today."

"They're not going anywhere," Annabelle said. "They can wait."

He exhaled, long and low.

"I'll just stack them here," she said, nodding to the corner.

He picked up the photo and paused at the doorway. "I'll be right back."

A few minutes later, he returned empty-handed.

"I put it on my dresser," he said. "I think it'll be nice to see her every day."

The rest of the afternoon passed.

Annabelle cooked something warm: roasted vegetables, a bit of stew, bread toasted with herbs.

When the quiet stretched, she asked, "You doing alright? I'm sure today's been... a lot."

Valen rubbed his neck. "I think I just need some time to let the dust settle."

She nodded and reached for his hand.

They sat that way a while, fingers loosely twined. Her touch drew soft arcs across his skin.

Later, as the sink filled with soapy water, Annabelle hummed while she worked.

Valen appeared in the doorway. "I'm going to go sit with her for a while."

She gave a small smile. "Take your time."

He stepped out into the evening air. Shadows stretched down the garden path.

She finished the dishes, wiped down the counter, and let things settle back into stillness.

Upstairs, she stood at her dresser, fingers working through her hair in the lamplight.

She didn't notice him at first—just the quiet creak of the floorboard behind her.

"Thank you," he said.

She glanced at his reflection. "Hmm? For what?"

"Just... for being here."

His hand brushed past hers as he reached for the hairbrush on the dresser. He started at the ends, slow and careful, like he was afraid to hurt her.

She closed her eyes.

He hit a knot and winced. "Sorry."

She hadn't realized how tense she still was until now.

When he finished, he set the brush down.

"I love you so much," he whispered.

"I love you, too."

She kissed him, then drew him into her arms.

He leaned in, face tucked against her shoulder. Like something broken learning how to be held again.

CHAPTER 34

The Studio

Annabelle turned toward him, limbs tangled, sheets kicked down. Foreheads pressed together, neither ready to let the day in.

"Sleep well?" she asked.

Valen cracked one eye open. "I did. But I dreamt someone kept putting cold stones on my legs."

She blinked innocently. "Stones?"

"Heavy ones. They woke me up every time."

"Weird," she said. "Anyway, I think I'll get up."

She started to pull back, lifting the sheet.

He caught her before she could slip away. "Oh no you don't."

She squeaked a laugh as he dragged her into bed.

"You thought you'd escape that easily?"

"Valen—"

But whatever protest she'd been planning dissolved as he leaned in and kissed her.

She resisted, more out of habit than defiance, but it melted quickly.

Her cold feet slid along his calves. He grumbled theatrically.

They stayed like that, tucked beneath the blankets in the hush of the morning.

Yesterday cracked them open.

Today was for rebuilding.

Annabelle nudged him with her knee. "Come on. I want to see how the light falls in the studio before it gets too late."

He groaned into the pillow. "Ruthless."

She grinned and climbed out of bed. "You'll live."

Shadows slipped across the floor as the day stretched. They moved slowly, but together.

After breakfast—and one more of Valen's failed attempts to slice the bread without crushing it—they started moving furniture.

Annabelle wiped every surface, opened the window to air it out, and tucked a small blanket under the dresser's crooked leg.

The whole room seemed to exhale, brushed in warmth.

They found a sturdy desk and chair in a lesser-used parlor, dusty and buried beneath a heap of forgotten books. It wasn't fancy. The drawer stuck, enough to test a person's patience.

"Just tilt it like this," Annabelle said, breathless as they angled it through the narrow hallway.

"It won't fit like that."

"Then this way?"

Valen paused, recalculated, and finally wedged himself into a better angle, pushing from the far side.

With a satisfying thunk and a shared grunt, it cleared the threshold.

She leaned against the doorframe, flushed and triumphant.

They set the desk by the window, angled to catch the same glow she'd once seen through the panes in the library. The chair went next.

He carried the easel in, setting it up in the far corner of the room.

With her arms full, she brought in what few supplies she had: brushes, pigments, a cloth stained with old color, and a pile of curled papers.

She placed everything carefully. It wasn't perfect, but it was hers.

Then she sat, shoulders dropping as the quiet settled in.

"This is exactly what I needed," she said. "Thank you. For the room. And for helping me set it up."

She turned to him, warmth in her voice. "It feels like it's... mine."

He lingered in the doorway, then left her with her thoughts.

It used to feel dangerous, taking up this much space. But the room didn't shrink. Neither did she.

The same old phrase still crept in: *You don't deserve this*. But it didn't hold the same weight anymore.

The days settled into a rhythm.

Annabelle painted often—sometimes for hours, sometimes in short bursts between meals, walks, or shared cups of tea.

The desk gathered the kind of clutter that meant something was being made: mismatched jars of brushes, half-used palettes, smudged rags, stacked pages in varying states of done.

She no longer had to pretend there was a right way to paint. Now, it could be whatever she needed it to be.

Now and then, she hummed while she worked. Other times, she let the stillness fill the room.

Valen had started working again too, filling the library with loose pages, frayed covers, scraps of leather, and ceramic pots of paste and dye.

He spent hours bent over the desk, the room faint with the scent of glue and parchment, smoothing brittle edges and pressing seams flat.

They didn't speak much while they worked, whether in separate rooms or sharing the same quiet space, but the calm between them had never been more full.

Over dinner one evening, Annabelle spoke animatedly—half to herself, half to him—between bites of roasted vegetables and fresh bread.

"—I think I finally figured out the shadows in a garden sketch I've been working on. But I want to start it over—the paper's too textured. I'm almost out of green. Definitely low on yellow too."

She took another bite, already mid-thought.

"And if I do the landscape I've been planning, I'll need pastels. I'll have to check how much money I've got left, but—"

She paused, suddenly aware of how he was looking at her.

"I'm rambling, aren't I?"

Valen hid a grin behind his wine. "I like you like this."

"...Rambling?"

He took another sip. "It suits you. That light in your voice."

"Thank you... I think."

They fell quiet as they ate.

"I think I might need to try to earn a little." Her hand drifted to her napkin. "Wait, where are you—?"

"One moment," he said, already gone.

He returned with a heavy pouch and set it on the table. "Here."

"What is—?" She loosened the tie and peeked inside. The weight made sense now: coins. "Wait. I can't accept this."

She pushed it toward him. "This is your money."

He sat back down and picked up his fork. "Why not?"

"Because it's yours. I still have some," she said, brushing a crumb from her lap. "But if I wanted more... I don't even know where I'd start."

Valen set down his fork. "Alright then. You were a natural with your nieces and nephews. What about a governess?"

"No, I'd probably need references. And a reputation slightly less... complicated."

"Fine. Seamstress?"

"I was never very good at sewing. My hems were always crooked. I once sewed a sleeve shut."

"Tutor? Maybe art?"

"Oh! Yeah, I could do that. It's what I know best. I could teach younger girls—do little workshops or something."

Her voice faltered. "But what if they wanted to do it here?"

She sighed. "Ugh. That wouldn't work either. Not with the way people talk. I mean, I live with you. I'm unmarried. That's already a story."

Valen pushed his chair back. "Then what *do* you want to do, Annabelle?"

Her words didn't come right away.

"I'm not trying to push," he said. "But I offered money. You didn't want it. I gave you ideas. You shot them all down."

Her jaw tensed.

"It's not my fault," she snapped. Then winced. "I didn't mean it like that. I *am* glad I'm here, but it's just..."

He waited.

"I'm trying," she said, softer. "I... don't want to owe anyone."

"I understand. But I'm not sure how to help when every answer's a dead end."

She was silent for a long moment. "I'm sorry."

"I'm not asking for an apology. Just let me stand with you in this—even if you're not sure what comes next." He slid the pouch back across the table.

"I want to share it with you. I'm already sharing everything else. And besides..." He nodded toward the bag. "This way, you can get whatever you want."

She looked from the pouch to him. Her smile flickered. Reaching for her glass, her sleeve caught the spoon. It clinked sharply against the plate.

"I—I still don't like that I'm not contributing." She didn't look up. "But thank you."

She tied the bag and set it beside her. "I mean it."

It was generous. And terrifying. Like forever pretending to be a favor.

"...I think I'll get a few things tomorrow," she said. "Nothing extravagant. Just... what I need."

Her thumb skimmed the pouch seam. "Maybe even something I don't."

She wasn't sure if she felt giddy or ashamed.

Valen nodded. "Good. I hope you enjoy yourself."

"I'd... actually like you to come with me."

"You mean I won't slow you down this time?"

"Oh, you will," she said. "But that's a risk I'm willing to take."

CHAPTER 35

The Outing

"Coin purse," Annabelle said, checking her satchel.

She pulled a folded, well-worn paper from the side pocket.

Valen squinted. "Is that what I think it is?"

She unfolded it, smoothing the edges. "Of course. I kept it."

His brow arched. "You've only gone once."

"So? It's a limited edition." She grinned. "And besides, it's beautiful. I couldn't throw it out."

The map had always felt like permission—to go, to stay, to wander. She didn't need it today, but it still felt right to carry.

He huffed a soft laugh and shook his head as she tucked it away and slipped her key into her cloak. Together, they stepped out into the morning air.

The walk was quiet: boots crunching on the dirt path, wind threading through the leaves, birdsong and the distant hum of town life riding the breeze.

Valen reached for her hand.

Annabelle hesitated; her fingers hovered, then pulled back.

He looked at her calmly.

She sighed. "Sorry. I just... don't know what people will think."

"I haven't been out of my house in years," he said with a wry smile. "I'm sure they'll have plenty to say already."

She laughed softly, but tension lingered in her shoulders.

They walked a few more steps before she spoke, voice low. "Just so you know... I may have told some people in town that I was widowed."

Valen's step slowed. "Oh?"

Nodding, her eyes stayed on the path. "It started when I fled to Creswell. I didn't have a chaperone, and living alone would've raised too many questions. Saying I was widowed just... made things easier."

He was quiet for a moment. "Makes sense."

She looked over, surprised by how simple that was.

He met her gaze. "You let me know what you're comfortable with. Let everyone else worry about their own comfort."

She reached for his hand.

Some part of her whispered this was too much. She ignored it.

Their fingers laced easily, and they walked on.

When they reached the market, the town was already in full swing.

Voices rose over carts and counters—fresh vegetables, warm bread, polished buttons, handspun cloth. The air was thick with yeast, cinnamon, and roasting meat. Louder than Annabelle remembered. Busier. But the energy was infectious.

Heads turned. A hush followed them past a busy stall. Near the flower stand, someone whispered, loud enough to hear, "Is that Gideon's boy? From the Eldcroft place?"

"I thought no one lived out there anymore."

"He hasn't been seen in years."

"Is that his wife?"

Annabelle's fingers tightened around Valen's.

A breeze stirred her cloak. Too warm for the season, or maybe just her nerves.

He gave her a small smile and leaned in. "Where to first?"

She looked about, then pointed at a narrow storefront glowing with golden light.

"Let's save the art shop for last. First…" She breathed in, smiling. "The bakery. That smell is divine."

"Lead the way."

Inside, cases gleamed with fruit spirals, flaky custards, sugar-dusted braids. Annabelle moved down the case like she was studying fine art.

She leaned in, nose nearly to the glass. "One of those… and two of those. Ooh, and one of each of those in the back."

Behind the counter stood a girl, perhaps a year younger, all curls and a smile just a bit too wide. She wrapped them with quiet efficiency.

Annabelle placed a few coins on the polished wood counter.

"That's quite the haul," the girl said. She turned to Valen. "I assume this is your wife?"

"No," Valen said. "But I fail to see how that's—"

"Well," the girl interrupted, lips curving. "Let me know if you're ever looking."

There was a pause.

Annabelle reached for the parcel, voice a little too sweet. "Thanks. We will."

The shopgirl blinked. "Oh—I didn't mean—"

Valen rested a hand at her back. "Let's go."

Outside, she shot him a grin. "Clearly, you're in high demand."

"Apparently."

"Should I be worried?"

"You? Never." He smiled. "Why—jealous?"

"No." She scoffed. "...Maybe a little."

"That definitely won't go to my head."

She rolled her eyes and took his hand.

After the bakery, the town relaxed. Fewer glances, or at least easier to ignore.

Annabelle led them through the square, pausing to squeeze his fingers or point out whatever caught her attention.

They stopped at a stationery shop, windows crowded with journals, ink bottles, and parchment.

She browsed slowly, thumb brushing over envelopes and wax seals. "I think I want to write to my family. In between visits."

Valen watched as she selected mint green paper and deep emerald ink.

At the soap stall, Annabelle paused as lavender, orange blossom, and something darker—clove or amber—lingered in the air. She picked up a bar, breathed in, smiled.

Then frowned, the price catching her eye.

"They're beautiful," she murmured, setting it back down. "But much too expensive."

Before she moved on, warm light caught her eye across the path.

"Ooh, candles," she said, already halfway there.

Valen stayed behind. Watched her lean over a shelf, half-obscured by candlelight.

Picking the three she seemed drawn to, he had them wrapped and paid quickly, tucking them into his coat.

He rejoined her just as she sniffed another candle.

"They have beeswax," she said. "Real beeswax."

"I believe you," he said with a soft laugh.

She turned, glanced at the sun. "Art shop?"

"Art shop."

The bell above Sable & Thread chimed as they entered.

It smelled the same: linseed oil, sawdust, paper, pigment. Shelves lined the walls, tidy and familiar.

The same shopkeeper manned the counter, glasses perched, ink on his cuff.

He looked up and froze.

His gaze flicked to Annabelle. Then Valen. Then back again.

"Pardon me, but..." the man said, cautious. "Haven't I seen you before? You were... weren't you—?"

He hesitated. Then, more delicately, asked, "A *widow*?"

She paused.

"Yes," she said simply. "Turns out he was just asleep."

She moved past the counter into the aisles like nothing had happened.

The shopkeeper blinked at Valen.

Valen shrugged.

He scratched his head. "Well, I'll be..." Then went back to re-labeling a jar.

Annabelle took her time, starting with watercolors, then oils, gouache, and a pastel set in muted tones. Larger brushes. Two canvas rolls she'd stretch herself. Heavyweight paper.

Smaller things too: charcoal, a mixing knife, pigments she hadn't tried before.

Valen lingered nearby, quietly holding the growing stack.

"Too much?" she asked, eyeing the stack.

"No such thing."

At the counter, the shopkeeper tallied slowly, sneaking glances between them like he wasn't entirely convinced he was awake.

She handed over the coins without hesitation.

Valen stacked the items as they were wrapped: brushes first, then pigment tins, paper, canvas. He tucked them into a neat bundle and nodded.

She smiled. "We should do this more often."

He raised an eyebrow, adjusting the package. "Shopping for half the store?"

"Exploring town," she said, nudging his elbow. "You, out in daylight. It's kind of charming."

He grunted, smiling. "Let's not make a habit of it."

She laughed.

The square had quieted. Stalls shuttered for midday meals, carts rolled into side streets. Sunlight warmed the cobblestones, softened by a breeze.

They passed a small cart under a striped awning, glass jars and paper parcels catching the light. Annabelle slowed.

"Ooh," she said, reaching for a paper-wrapped roll near the back. "I haven't seen these in ages."

Valen peered over her shoulder. "What are they?"

"Candy wafers." She fished out a coin. "I loved them as a child."

She tucked the sleeve into her cloak pocket like she meant to save them.

But then, a few steps later, she opened it and crunched one between her teeth before he could speak.

Pastel discs filled her palm: pinks, greens, off-white, dusty purple. She popped a green one in.

He stared as if she'd just licked the side of a building. "You're actually eating that."

"Mmhmm."

"What does it taste like?"

She held one out. "Try it."

He did. Chewed once. Then frowned as though he was on the losing end of a bet.

Annabelle burst out laughing.

"This is drywall," he muttered. "Maybe if someone spilled perfume on it first."

She grinned. "I always liked them."

"I can tell. You've inhaled half the sleeve."

"I'm pacing myself."

He pointed at the little stack in her palm. "Why are you separating them?"

"I save the chocolate ones for last," she said, nudging the browns into a separate pile. "They're my favorite."

He gave her a flat look. "You know there are entire cakes with real chocolate in them."

"Not the same." She popped another wafer into her mouth. "Drywall with nostalgia. Nothing better."

She was still smiling when a voice called out, "Excuse me—are you Mr. Eldcroft?"

Valen stopped and turned.

A man and woman stood a few steps off the path—middle-aged, dressed for comfort more than wealth. She held a parasol. He leaned on a cane he clearly didn't need.

Valen blinked at them. "Yes?"

"Oh, my goodness," the woman said. "I thought so. You're Gideon's boy, aren't you? From the estate east of town?"

He nodded slowly. "That's right."

"Goodness, no one's seen you in years," the man said, smiling too broadly. "We all thought the house had been left empty."

Valen gave a polite half-smile. "No. Still there."

They both looked at Annabelle, clearly dying to ask.

"So this must be...?"

Annabelle returned the gaze calmly, but didn't offer anything.

The woman leaned in. "We hadn't heard you were married. Or engaged. You know how small towns are—we like to keep up."

Valen's smile didn't waver, but the light behind it dimmed.

"She's a friend," he said simply. "A very dear one."

"Oh! Of course," the man said quickly. "We didn't mean to intrude, it's just—well, people are curious, and it's so rare to see—"

"Excuse us," Valen said, calm but unmistakably firm. "We've got a bit of a walk ahead of us."

He nodded once, not unkindly, and turned.

Annabelle followed, her hand sliding easily into his.

They didn't speak for a few paces.

Then Valen exhaled through his nose. "That was exhausting."

Annabelle huffed a quiet laugh. "Could've been worse. They could have asked for a wedding date."

He made a face. "I should've said it already happened. We eloped. In the garden. Two chickens in attendance."

"A goat played the violin."

He gave her a sideways look, clearly amused.

She leaned in, brushing their arms together.

"They're just curious," she said gently. "But to ruin your debut—your grand reentry into society as an eligible bachelorette—like this? Unacceptable."

"Absolutely. Now I'll never find a proper suitor." He gave a mock sigh, then softened. "But really. I knew this would happen the second I stepped outside."

He glanced at her, voice lower. "Doesn't mean I regret it though."

By the time they reached the estate, the sun was skimming the treetops with afternoon gold. The walk back had been quiet and companionable, broken only by the occasional teasing remark or gentle squeeze of hands.

At the door, Annabelle reached into her pocket and pulled out the key.

She headed inside first, and the familiar creak of the floorboards greeted them.

Valen passed her the parcel, and she clutched it to her chest with glee.

"Thanks again," she said, smiling up at him. "For all of this."

And then she was off, half-skipping down the hall toward her studio, curls bouncing, boots thudding lightly against the floor.

He stood there a moment longer, watching her go. A quiet smile tugged at his mouth.

Then he moved into the kitchen, set the package of pastries gently on the counter, and slipped out of the room and up the stairs.

Crossing through the master bedroom, he entered the bathing chamber. Dim, cool, the scent of lavender already lingering faintly in the air.

He placed the wrapped soaps one by one on the small wooden stool beside the tub, neatly arranged, like an offering.

CHAPTER 36

The Offering

Annabelle had all but vanished into her studio, the sound of brushes tapping glass and water pouring faintly through the hall.

Valen brought her food at some point: bread, fruit, something she barely registered beyond the fact that it tasted good.

She painted for hours, losing track of time.

Later, they curled up in the library, her legs draped over his lap as they read by firelight. He'd pulled a few volumes she hadn't seen before—old texts, delicately flourished, their margins filled with hand-inked notes.

Eventually, she closed her book with a soft thud and stretched.

"I'm going to take a bath," she said, rising. "Join me, if you'd like."

She tossed the invitation over her shoulder with a wink.

Valen looked up, mouth twitching like he'd had a thought he shouldn't say aloud. "In a few. Let me put these books away."

She left him there and padded back to their room, pleasantly sore from hours hunched over her easel.

In the bathing chamber, she brushed out her hair and undressed—loosening the fastenings at her back. She stepped out of her clothes, folding them neatly on the bench, her skin bare in the candlelight.

She crossed to the tub to draw the water, then froze with a quiet gasp.

Three soaps sat on the bathside stool, each wrapped in soft paper and tied with twine. A trio of scents rose: lavender, citrus, and clove.

The bedroom door clicked behind her.

She turned, still entirely unclothed, and stepped into the room.

"Valen!" she said, eyes wide, smiling. "The soaps—you didn't have to."

He looked up—and completely lost the ability to speak.

His eyes swept over her, lingering on every curve. Then he caught himself and smiled. "I wanted to."

"They were too much," she said, stepping toward him.

"What?" His voice dropped. "I'm not allowed to spoil you sometimes?"

He moved closer, touch light as he traced his thumb along her cheekbone.

She hesitated, overwhelmed by the sudden rush of want.

Then she met his eyes, tilting her head slightly, a curl of mischief at her smile.

"How can I show you my appreciation?" she asked, voice low and honey-sweet.

He opened his mouth—probably to say she didn't have to—but her hands were already at his buttons, and the words disappeared.

The first button slipped free. She kissed the skin beneath it.

Then the next. Another kiss.

She worked her way down his chest, kissing as she went.

He drew a breath.

"I can think of a... few things," he muttered, voice rougher now, his attention fully shifted away from any lingering thoughts of bathwater or soap.

Her hands moved to his waistband.

She felt him growing harder against the fabric, the heat of him bleeding through even before she undid the button and tugged at the ties.

Kissing lower, she followed the line of bare skin above his trousers, then looked up at him.

"You keep finding new ways to undo me," he murmured.

"I think of it as... gratitude."

Her hand slipped beneath the fabric, confident in the way he tensed at her touch.

A low breath escaped him as his palm found her shoulder, grounding himself.

She sank to her knees.

Took her time.

Soft and steady at first, her mouth teased him just enough to tighten his muscles, to draw his hips closer.

She tested the rhythm—long strokes, then short flicks—learning what made him tense, what made his fingers curl in her hair.

Heat flickered behind his eyes. His jaw clenched.

"You keep that up," he said, voice hoarse, "and we're not making it to the bath."

She rose slowly, skin flushed in the candlelight.

"Who said anything about bathing?" she whispered.

He stepped in, hands at her hips, walking her back to the bed with a hard kiss.

She sank onto the sheets, pulling him with her, legs wrapping around him, one hand catching his belt as he stripped off the rest.

Then he was over her, on her, in her—slow to start, then deeper, guided by the heat she'd already lit.

She met him with a gasp, lips at his jaw, fingers dragging down his back. Her toes curled in the blankets.

He came first, with a quiet curse, his head buried against her neck.

She followed, legs tightening, breath stuttering, held together by his weight and the warmth between them.

Finally, he rolled onto his side and drew her with him, her leg sliding over his as his hand traced a slow line down her spine.

"You realize," he murmured, still breathless, "now I'll have to buy you fancy soap more often."

She smiled against his skin.

Later, when quiet surrounded them, the bath was warm and slow.

The only sounds were their laughter and the shifting of water.

He sat behind her, arms loose around her waist, her back resting against him. She reached for the clove-scented bar, lathering it before turning in his embrace.

"Hold still," she said, grinning.

His eyebrow raised, but he let her drag it across his collarbone and down his arm.

She sat back to wet the soap again, imagining how she'd paint him: the curve of his shoulder, light skimming water on his chest. Just for her.

Lost in thought, she dropped the bar. It thudded against the tub and slipped beneath his knee.

She scooped it up, nudging him as she did, and resumed washing him.

"You're going to rinse that off, right?" he asked, eyes half-lidded.

"Eventually."

He took it from her fingers. "My turn."

She tilted her chin, lips parted, as he brought the lather to her chest. His touch was slow, thumbs gliding from collarbone to ribs.

"This isn't very thorough," she whispered.

"Last time I was too thorough, you complained."

She elbowed him, water sloshing as she laughed.

Eventually, the water cooled, and they had no choice but to rinse, dry off, and put on warm clothes.

"Looks like a clear night. Want to do dessert outside?"

"You mean I wasn't sweet enough for you?"

She swatted lightly at his arm.

"I'm dying to eat those pastries," she said, already heading downstairs. He followed, grabbing a tray while she unwrapped them.

At the garden doors, she peeked out, then slipped into the kitchen and rifled through the cupboards.

"What are you looking for?" he asked.

"You'll see—perfect!" She returned holding an old preserves jar, its label faded and curling.

"What's that for?"

"Fireflies." She rinsed it, tapping the water out before drying it with the threadbare towel near the sink. "Ready?"

On their way out, she scooped up the picnic quilt from beside the door. The last bloom of sky was nearly gone.

Spreading the blanket out on the grass, she sat cross-legged and took the tray from Valen.

They ate in silence, warm air snug around them. Crickets perked up between laughs as Annabelle got powdered sugar on her nose.

"Oh, look—there's a bunch now. Ever caught one?" She grabbed the jar, heading for a corner of the yard.

"Maybe when I was young."

Darting forward, she snatched a firefly from the sky.

She opened her fist over the jar, letting the bug slip inside. "I forgot how much they tickle."

Valen stood across the lawn, making vague grabs at the air.

"Watch one closely," she said. "It'll come to you—if you're patient. But you have to be ready."

"Good thing I've got enough patience for the both of us," he said, grinning.

He waited for a firefly to flash, then reached.

"Did you catch it?"

His hand was empty. "Who knew this required actual skill?"

She added another firefly to the jar. "You'll get it."

"Not yet. Keep watching." She stood beside him, tracking one with her finger. "Almost... and... now."

The firefly lit up. He cupped his hands around it.

He peeked in, its light still glowing. "I got it!"

"I knew you could do it. Want to add him to the jar?"

The bug crawled up his finger and flew. Valen reached up and caught it again.

She held the jar out.

Pushing the firefly inside, he covered the opening with his hand. "What do we do with them now?"

"We enjoy them for a bit. Then we let them go."

He watched them climb over each other, one flying to the top of the jar before settling on the glass. Their lights flickered in turns.

"I think I'm ready. If you are."

She nodded.

Lifting his hand, one flew out immediately. Another crawled onto his fingers, lit up once, then took off.

The last firefly clung to the surface.

"I wonder if it knows it can leave," he said.

"It'll figure it out. Give it time."

The bug glowed again—once, twice—then rose and vanished into the dark.

He kept staring into the grass until he couldn't tell which ones they'd caught.

Annabelle lay back on the quilt. "I always forget how many stars there are."

He crossed the yard and joined her, setting the jar on the tray. They lay in silence for a few moments.

Then he pointed at the sky. "See the bright orange star? Arcturus. And over there—the blue one—that's Spica."

"I never knew they had names. Aren't there pictures too?"

Chuckling, he lifted a hand. "Yes—constellations. That bright cluster up there? Ursa Major. The Great Bear."

"That's supposed to be a bear? I just see random dots."

Valen shifted closer until their heads touched, grass crinkling beneath them.

"Start with the brightest one," he said, tracing an invisible line. "Now follow it, star to star."

"Still doesn't look like a bear. Maybe a horse."

"Or somebody that fell over." She giggled. "A canoe with legs. No—two people carrying a door."

She turned to him. "You're quiet."

His fingers were laced tight over his stomach. "Just thinking."

"You don't have to keep it all in." She rested her head on his shoulder.

"I know." He paused, lips pressed thin. "I don't have the words yet. Just feel... different. But I'm alright."

"Don't forget—you can wish on the moon. Maybe it'll come true."

"Are you going to make one?"

"Yep, the same one I always do."

"...To be happy?" He didn't flinch, but the hollow feeling swelled anyway.

"No, I'm already happy." She leaned up, kissing him on the cheek.

"I wish I could stop hearing imaginary people's thoughts." Her thumb grazed her sleeve's hem.

"What does that mean?"

"Just... like pretending I know what other people are going to say. Before they even show up."

"Darn, that was going to be mine." He smiled. "Guess I'll come up with a new one."

He closed his eyes. The crease between his brows faded as he pulled her closer.

"What did you wish for?" she asked.

"To stop worrying about how long good things will last. To just enjoy them while they're here."

"A noble goal." She gave him a squeeze. "And I'm here to help however I can."

"Thank you." He was quiet for a moment. "I think you're learning to tune them out. At least a little."

Her shoulders tensed. "Maybe. Some days more than others."

He pressed a gentle kiss to her forehead, arms tightening around her. The fireflies were gone. Only the moonlight remained. Somewhere in the trees, an owl hooted.

She looked up at the stars, her thoughts too quick to name.

Whatever stirred inside her—it wasn't finished yet.

CHAPTER 37

The Line

Days blurred together. The weather held—warm mornings, soft evenings, the scent of blooming things drifting through open windows.

Annabelle painted. Often.

Some days, she sketched in the garden, curled on sun-warmed stone or stretched in the grass, watching the light shift across the sky.

Other days, she vanished into the studio for hours: apron streaked, fingers stained, curls falling loose.

Today was one of those days.

In the library, Valen bent over a page so delicate he barely breathed. A pot of fresh paste to his right. A fine-bristled brush to the left. He was midway through realigning a torn margin, adjusting it until the faded ink lined up just so, when the floorboards creaked across the room.

He glanced up.

Annabelle stood in the doorway, barefoot, sketchbook pressed to her chest like it might run off without her.

"Hey."

He straightened. "Everything alright?"

"Mmhmm. ...I wasn't going to show you. But I think I need to."

He set the brush aside and left the book open to dry. "Alright."

She crossed the room, then held the sketchbook out, gaze lowered. He took it carefully, eyes falling to the open page.

An unfinished painting, but striking. The paper had warped where the pigment ran thick; a thumbprint smudged one side.

The edges bled, blurring into light: a girl beneath a tree, her face indistinct, as if she hadn't decided whether to stay or fade. Light pooled around her like water.

"This is... stunning."

She searched his expression. "You're not just saying that?"

"No." He shook his head. "I mean it. There's so much *you* in this."

Annabelle gave a small smile. "I wasn't sure about sharing it," she said. "But I couldn't stop thinking about it. The thought just got too loud."

Valen handed it back, fingers grazing hers. "Then I'm honored."

She smiled, crossing to one of the armchairs, sketchbook in hand, glancing up now and then as he returned to his work.

They sat like that for a while: him dabbing paste into a tear with slow precision, her flipping to a new page, sketching something small and abstract, just to keep her hands moving.

"Haven't you been working on that same book all week?" Her tone was light. Teasing, maybe. "It's not like you need the money. Why bother?"

Valen's hand stilled. The brush hovered a breath above the page.

"What do you mean?"

She shrugged. "I just mean... you could be doing anything. But you're fixing old books for fun? I don't get it. You could be doing something bigger. Something more important."

He set the brush down—carefully—and left the room.

"Valen?" she called. "What's wrong?"

His voice carried from the hall. "I'm going for a walk."

Blinking, she sat there with her mouth half-open, heart starting to thud.

She hadn't meant anything by it. At least, she thought she hadn't.

The library felt too still.

She waited. Ten minutes. Fifteen. Long enough for guilt to bloom and curl tight in her chest.

When he finally returned, she started, "Valen—"

He raised a steady hand, drew a breath. "Sorry for walking out. I needed to find my words."

She said nothing.

"I do not appreciate being patronized for how I spend my time," he said, voice measured. "Book restoration is a noble effort. A calling, even."

"I taught myself young, after the spine cracked on a book my mother gave me. I wasn't ready to let it go. This"—he gestured to the library, the tools, the book on his desk—"lets me focus. Gives me purpose. Fills me with immense satisfaction."

He let the words hang.

"For you to treat it as beneath me..." His jaw flexed. "That stings."

Annabelle froze mid-breath. "Valen... I—"

"I'm not finished."

She went quiet.

"What I'm saying is this, it would be no different than me calling your paintings a waste of time. You're not making money. So what's the point?" He paused. "But I wouldn't. Because I see the joy they bring you."

His voice softened. "And it's only fair that I find my own joy, too."

He hesitated, then let his shoulders ease. "Now, I'm finished."

She stayed silent, heat rising in her face.

"I'm so sorry," she said at last, barely above a whisper.

"That's not—I didn't mean—" She shook her head. "I'm an idiot. I never should have said that."

Her eyes dropped. "I didn't realize it meant so much. And you're right—even if it hadn't. You get to choose. It wasn't fair of me to judge."

She sat still, hands knotted in her lap.

After a long pause, she glanced up.

Her voice was softer, uncertain. "Can you... forgive me?"

"I can," Valen said. "And I will."

He paused, tension still flickered faintly in his eyes. "I need a little more time to calm down."

She nodded. "I understand. Let me know if you want to talk more. Or if there's anything else I can do."

"I will," he said.

Returning to his desk, he settled back into the delicate work of aligning the torn margin.

Annabelle stayed in the room. She crossed to the shelves, pulled down a slim book with worn corners, and curled up on the sofa. The velvet cushion sank under her weight, quieter than she expected.

The minutes passed slow. An hour, maybe more.

Pages turned as the fire crackled. A single pop broke the silence.

She kept her eyes on the page, resisting the urge to look, until a flicker of movement drew her. The edge of his mouth eased before he looked back down.

Eventually, he set the brush down, sealed the jar of paste, and joined her on the sofa. The light through the window had turned amber.

Resting a hand on her thigh, he rubbed his thumb gently over the fabric of her skirt.

She glanced toward him. His expression had softened, the line between his brows gone.

Then he pressed a slow kiss to her forehead.

Her fingers stopped worrying at the rough spot on her wrist.

They stayed in the library a while longer, both reading.

Annabelle stretched, setting her book aside, and said, "Come on. Let's figure out dinner."

They took their time cooking, moving easily around each other at the counter.

He chopped vegetables, practicing his precision, while she stirred at the stove, steam curling the ends of her hair. Their hands brushed occasionally as they passed each other.

Once, she leaned over to steal a slice of carrot, hesitated, nose wrinkling faintly, then took it anyway. He raised an eyebrow and kept cutting.

By the time they sat down to eat, the sky had softened into blue-gray, the windows catching the fading evening light. Forks clinked against plates, punctuated by the occasional low murmur or passing smile.

Near the end of the meal, Annabelle pushed the last bite around her plate and glanced up.

"Hey. I'm sorry again. About earlier." She hesitated. "I think I said it because I didn't understand how something so... quiet could matter. Which is probably more about me than you."

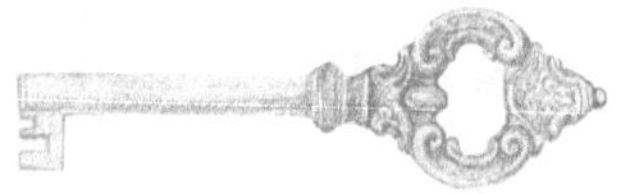

CHAPTER 38

The Invitation

"Want to play?" Annabelle gestured toward the chessboard by the hearth. The pieces caught the light as the fire flickered behind them.

Valen crossed the lounge. "Are you ready to lose again?"

She scoffed. "You conceded. That means I won."

"You got lucky."

"Lucky?" she said. "Please. You were clearly intimidated by my overwhelming brilliance."

"I was being generous."

"We'll see how generous you feel when I'm holding your king."

Valen's brow twitched, a smirk tugging at his mouth. Then he sat, pushing up his sleeves. "Bold words for someone who once opened with a pawn and a nervous breakdown."

She laughed. "You remembered that?"

"Of course. I study my opponents."

"You were studying me?"

"Still am."

She smiled, flushed, and adjusted her black knight without looking away.

He made the first move.

They played in silence, the fire's soft crackle and the clink of glass the only things keeping time.

"This feels different," she said, still watching the board.

"You're not bracing anymore."

"I'm still trying to win."

"But you're not playing like you're proving something."

She looked up, met his gaze, then moved her bishop without flinching. "Remember when you said I don't see what's right in front of me?"

"I do. Took you long enough."

She gasped, hand to her chest like he'd wounded her. "Rude."

They kept playing, more evenly matched this time, with laughter, feints, and muttered curses.

Eventually, the game wound down: pieces scattered, strategies spent.

Neither of them won.

He sat back, studying her. "You've changed. Since that first night."

"For better or worse?"

"You don't flinch when I look at you."

"You don't hide in riddles anymore."

"Sharp as ever."

She smiled. "Rematch tomorrow?"

"Wouldn't miss it."

They sat a little longer after that.

The board stayed as it was—an unfinished game in a room finally warm.

Later, the fire dwindled to a low glow, and the quiet of afternoon settled over the house.

Annabelle sat cross-legged on the sofa in the library, sketchbook balanced on one knee, her pencil moving in slow, thoughtful strokes.

The midday light filtered through the tall windows, catching the edges of her curls and the curve of her page. Across the room, a stack of paper and a half-empty teacup waited untouched.

She was refining the line of a shoulder, debating the angle of a window-pane, when a sharp knock sounded at the front door.

Valen was already crossing the hall.

"I've got it," he said.

She nodded, but her pencil stayed poised above the page.

Muted conversation followed: several voices, low and polite. Then footsteps.

"Apologies for dropping in unannounced," a man said. "We were nearby, and I thought I'd save you the trouble of sending a courier."

"Of course," Valen replied. "It's ready."

Valen reappeared, leading a well-dressed older couple into the library.

The man was slightly stooped, with silver hair and a sharp, intelligent gaze. He carried himself like someone who'd once held authority, and was only just beginning to lay it down.

His wife, by contrast, moved with practiced grace, her expression warm, gloved hands folded neatly in front of her.

"Mr. and Mrs. Trell," Valen said. "He commissioned a restoration a few weeks ago."

"Annabelle. It's lovely to meet you both," she said, returning to her sketch.

Valen turned toward the cabinet near the far wall and began unlocking the case. Mr. Trell followed.

Mrs. Trell lingered.

Her gaze drifted to the sketchbook in Annabelle's lap. "Oh," she said. "That's lovely."

Annabelle looked up. "Thank you."

"Do you work in charcoals often?"

"Sometimes," she said, tracing the edge of the page. "It helps me think."

Mrs. Trell stepped closer, studying the sketch. "You have a very natural line. Quite confident."

"You're kind to say so." Annabelle's cheeks warmed.

"It's not generosity," Mrs. Trell said, smiling. "It's curiosity. And perhaps a bit of selfishness."

"Selfishness?"

"I meet with a handful of women in town," she said. "A casual gathering every Thursday. You'd be just in time if you came tomorrow. Some bring knitting, some embroidery, some... unresolved opinions about everything."

"There's always tea. And laughter. And space to exhale, without anyone breathing down your neck." She winked.

Annabelle smiled, but her grip on the sketchbook tightened. "That sounds lovely. I'm just not sure I'd be much of a contributor."

"Nonsense," Mrs. Trell said. "But you don't have to decide now."

She reached into her bag and drew out a calling card, ivory and delicately printed, and extended it. "If you ever feel like joining us."

Annabelle took it carefully, brushing her thumb over the embossed lettering. "Thank you. I'll think about it."

"That's all I ask."

Valen had retrieved the book from the cabinet, its spine now clean and whole, gilt lettering gleaming like new.

Mr. Trell accepted it graciously.

"You brought it back to life," he said, turning it over. "Exactly as I remember it. Thank you."

"It was my pleasure," Valen said.

Mr. Trell nodded. "I'll have more for you. A couple friends of mine—collectors, mostly—have been watching your work from a distance. You may hear from them."

Valen's mouth tugged toward a smile before he caught it. "I'd be amenable to that."

There were a few more pleasantries and quiet goodbyes. The couple made their way back through the hall, Valen escorting them out.

Once the door closed, Annabelle exhaled and pressed her hand to her forehead. A brief dizziness passed, maybe from the stuffy room—or skipping lunch.

She looked down at the card in her lap: simple, elegant, embossed with the name Mrs. Gregory Trell.

Before Valen returned, she tucked it into the back of her sketchbook.

Later, the dining room had settled into its usual quiet. The plates were mostly cleared, the last of the roasted vegetables pushed aside. Her wine glass sat mostly full, marked only by a faint smudge from an earlier sip.

The candles had burned low, softening the edges of the space.

Annabelle ran a finger along the stem of her glass, then glanced up. "I think I want to go."

"Go where?"

"Oh—right. Sorry." She tucked a loose strand of hair behind her ear. "Mrs. Trell hosts gatherings in town. On Thursdays. Just a few women, tea, and probably too many opinions. That sort of thing. I don't know, I just thought—"

His brow lifted, followed by a quiet smile. "You should go."

She studied his face. "You really think so?"

"I do. You've been in this house with me every day for weeks. I think it'd be good for you to be around people who aren't me."

Annabelle exhaled softly, tension easing from her shoulders. She gave a small laugh.

"Not that I'm tired of your company," she said, glancing up. "But it might be nice to meet a few new faces. Friendly ones."

His smile deepened. "I think that sounds perfect."

They lingered over what remained of the meal, the quiet between them easy.

When the final candle guttered low, Annabelle rose first, gathering their plates. Valen followed her into the kitchen, brushing her fingers lightly as he took the tray from her hands.

They moved through the familiar rhythm of the evening—checking locks, dimming lamps, their footsteps soft against the old wood floors.

At the hearth, she unpinned her hair, loosening the twist at her neck as Valen stirred the coals back to a steady glow.

She let her clothes slip to the floor. Then she crossed to the bed and turned down the covers, fingertips brushing the linen.

When he looked up, she was watching him.

"You're staring," he said quietly. "And naked."

She stepped toward him. "Perhaps."

"What's the occasion?"

"Do I need one?" She tugged at the hem of his shirt where it had bunched, fingers slipping beneath the fabric.

"I suppose not."

Slowly, she pushed it over his shoulders, then kissed the place it had been.

"This wasn't what I expected tonight," he murmured, voice rougher now.

"I just... I could use the distraction. Before tomorrow. If that's okay."

"You don't need a reason." He pulled her into a hug.

At the bed, she eased back first, nudging the blanket into place with her feet. He undressed the rest of the way, then joined her.

A pillow shifted with a soft puff of air. The sheets were cool, but their bodies warmed them quickly.

His hand skimmed her waist, pausing where the curve deepened, as if memorizing her all over again.

He kissed her slowly, lips brushing hers, then trailing to her jaw. His breath warmed her collarbone before his tongue followed.

Annabelle's fingers threaded into his hair. Her back arched as his mouth closed gently over one breast, then the other. He took his time.

She sighed, reaching between them, curling around him. He groaned, hips twitching as she stroked him in slow rhythm.

He slid his hand between her thighs. She tensed, then shifted toward him, chasing more as he moved with certainty.

Kissing her again, he eased her onto her back and positioned himself between her legs. He pushed into her slowly, watching her face, waiting for the little exhale that meant she'd gone under.

Their hips rocked together steadily.

She drew him deeper, moaning into his shoulder. His mouth found her throat, her pulse, then her lips again.

At some point, her hand caught the back of his neck and held him there. His thrusts deepened, drawing a gasp from her, then another.

"Right there," she whispered. "Keep going."

She didn't last long. A few moments more, and she came with a long, slow shudder—arms tight around him, her body arched as if the moment had lifted her beyond control.

He followed a minute later, hips faltering as he pressed deeper, lost in her and nothing else.

Silence stretched between them. His head rested against her chest, her fingers tracing absent patterns along his back.

Eventually, he murmured, "Feeling any better?"

"Yeah," she said. "That helped. Thank you."

He huffed a tired laugh against her skin. "I aim to please."

"We should do that before every social event." She nestled in closer, cheek brushing his shoulder. "I'm not saying I'll be glowing at tea tomorrow, but I might float in."

CHAPTER 39

The Step

By the time the sunlight turned sharp, Annabelle was pacing. Two dresses lay on the bed.

One was soft, familiar, worn without thought. The other was newer, nicer—more than she was used to.

She frowned at both, as if they'd said something rude.

"Why is this so difficult?" she muttered.

She changed her earrings. Changed them back. Adjusted her hair a third time.

Valen leaned in the doorway, barefoot. "Do you always interrogate your clothing before social gatherings?"

"Only the important ones," she said.

He stepped in, eyes on the bed. "Which one's losing?"

"This one says 'harmless recluse with decent taste.' That one says 'I'm pretending to be normal.' I can't decide which is worse."

"You'll look fine in either. But the second makes your eyes look lethal, so I vote that."

She stared. "Not helpful."

"It's helpful. You just hate that I'm right."

She rolled her eyes, picked up the second dress, and finished getting ready.

Downstairs, she nibbled at fruit and half a roll, too nervous for tea. He handed her the sketchbook she'd nearly forgotten and walked her to the door.

She hesitated, hand on the knob.

"You'll be fine," he said.

"I want to hate it."

"You might. But you won't hate yourself for going," he said.

He kissed her, his hand warm at her neck.

Stepping outside, she exhaled, only then realizing how tight her chest had felt.

The path into town was quiet, midday sun pleasant on her shoulders as she made her way toward the cottage. The satchel tugged at her arm with each step, sketchbook tucked safely inside, nerves keeping pace beneath her ribs.

Mrs. Trell's cottage wasn't large, but it had charm. Stone walls covered in ivy, lace curtains drawn back from the windows, and the faint smell of cinnamon and polish lingering in the air.

Annabelle stood on the stoop a breath longer than she meant to, fingers curled around the satchel strap.

She could hear voices inside: laughter and the clink of china. Her feet didn't move.

Then the door opened.

"You came," Mrs. Trell said. She stepped aside. "Come in, come in. Don't worry—we've only just started."

Annabelle entered. The warmth was immediate.

The front room was cozy, women settled in mismatched chairs around a low table crowded with teacups, half-eaten scones, and a small mountain of embroidery hoops and knitting needles.

Scissors clinked softly. The tang of lemon polish turned her stomach, just a little. She blamed the nerves.

The conversation dipped. A few eyes flicked her way. Then Mrs. Trell said, "This is Annabelle."

A ripple of greetings followed: nods, smiles. Someone made room on the settee.

"I brought my sketchbook," Annabelle said. "I wasn't sure…"

"Perfect," said Mrs. Trell, waving her toward a chair by the window. "Just don't catch anyone's bad side."

That earned a soft laugh.

The woman on the settee said nothing.

Annabelle sat, smoothing her skirt and opening the sketchbook in her lap. Her fingers itched to draw. It gave her somewhere to look. Something to do.

Tea came her way without ceremony: jasmine. She took one small sip, attempting to keep a polite face, then left it to cool. A plate of scones followed.

Conversation resumed, and she remained at the edges of it.

"Where did you say you were from?" one woman asked, not looking up from her knitting.

"Dunbridge," Annabelle said, setting her teacup down. "Originally."

"Ah. And you're with Mr. Eldcroft now, is that right?" Another voice, sharper. "Living at the estate?"

Annabelle's stomach twisted, but she kept her tone even. "Yes."

Brows lifted. The silence stretched.

"I imagine that's... unconventional," someone murmured.

Annabelle's smile didn't slip. "So is Valen."

That got a few polite chuckles. One woman bit into her scone without comment, which somehow felt like the strongest endorsement yet.

"I always assumed he lived alone," another said, laying her knitting needles down. "People say he doesn't even come into town."

"Not often," Annabelle said. "But he's worth knowing."

The women eased back into their rhythms. A few leaned over to see what Annabelle was sketching. One of them commented on her shading. Another offered a slice of almond cake, along with the story of how she painstakingly made it that morning.

She hadn't won them over. But she'd made space for herself.

When the gathering began to wind down, Mrs. Trell walked Annabelle to the door.

"You did well," she said softly, looping her arm through Annabelle's for just a moment. "They're cautious with new people. But they liked you. I could tell."

"I wasn't sure they would."

"They're used to stories. Not real people walking into the room."

Annabelle lingered on the stoop, sunlight warm across her back. "Thank you."

"Come again," Mrs. Trell replied. "Next time, it'll be easier. It always is."

The sun was lower now, the breeze softer. With each step, Annabelle's shoulders eased a little more.

She'd survived it. Maybe even enjoyed it.

Valen met her at the door, as if he'd been listening for her steps. He took her satchel and kissed her temple. She smelled like charcoal and jasmine.

She leaned into it a moment longer than intended. The day had been good, but her body felt off, like she'd run farther than she had.

At the sitting room threshold, she paused, just for a second, then stepped forward.

"Well?" he asked once they were inside. "Was it awful?"

She laughed, too fast to feel like relief. "Only a little. But I think they liked me. At least... some of them did."

"That's a good start."

She exhaled, settling into the arm of the sofa and leaning her head back.

He raised a brow. "And you went anyway."

She managed a half-smile. "Yeah. I did."

Valen sat on the sofa with a book open in his lap, watching Annabelle draw nearby.

Her brow was furrowed, fingers smudged with charcoal, paper half-filled with rough lines.

"I stopped by the gallery in town," he said.

She didn't look up. "Oh?"

"They host rotating exhibits," he said. "Feature a few local artists. I thought—well, I mentioned your name."

She froze, fingers halting mid-curve. "You showed them something?"

Valen blinked. "No—of course not. I wouldn't do that without your permission. I just asked if they'd be open to seeing your work sometime. If you were interested."

She sat back, eyes flicking toward the fireplace. "So now they're waiting for something I haven't even decided I want to give."

"They're not waiting," he said. "It's just an open invitation."

"What if I can't do it again?" Her voice rose. "What if it was a fluke? What if it's not even good? You're the only one who's seen it, and you love me—of course you'll say it's good."

Valen opened his mouth, then stopped.

"And if they hate it?" she said, too fast. "Or worse—they don't care. They just nod and move on, and it disappears into a wall no one looks at again."

Her hands were fists in her lap, shoulders tight, breath quick.

"And then it's out there," she whispered. "And I can't get it back."

"Annabelle," he said, low and steady. "You don't have to share it. Not if you don't want to."

She looked down.

"I just thought..." He took a breath. "You paint the way people feel when they don't have words. That matters. And yes—I love it because I love you. But even if I didn't... I'd still stop in front of every one of your pieces."

Her throat tightened.

"I know it's terrifying," he said. "But what if—somewhere out there—someone needs to see it? Maybe to feel a little less alone."

She blinked quickly, but didn't speak.

"The important thing," he said, quieter now, "is that you like it. That it means something to you. And if it does—maybe it's alright to let someone else see it too."

Her shoulders sagged a little.

"I just wanted you to have the choice. That's all," he said.

She fussed with her sleeve. "I'm scared."

"I know."

Her eyes found his. His expression held no expectations.

"You don't have to decide tonight," he said. "Or ever. But your work is worth something. Even if no one else sees it but you."

Her gaze dropped. "You make it sound simple."

"It will be. When you're ready."

Her breath escaped in a slow exhale, and she nodded.

She wasn't sure she'd be brave. But she wanted to be.

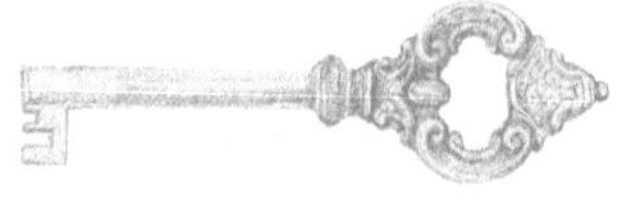

CHAPTER 40

The Unveiling

By the end of the week, Annabelle was disappearing into the studio each morning and reemerging only when the sky turned pink, if at all.

Her tea sat forgotten on windowsills. The brush rarely made it back to the jar. Her dresses bore streaks of ochre and cerulean.

Each time Valen entered, she shifted enough to block the easel. He stopped asking after day three.

So he brought her meals, left them on the side table, and waited—time passing in brushstrokes and silence.

One evening, she stepped out of the studio, hands clean, shoulders settled.

"...I want to show you something," she said.

Valen looked up from the book he wasn't reading.

"Are you sure?"

She nodded. "I think so."

He followed her inside. She crossed to the easel and removed the cloth.

It was color and movement, tangled lines and smears.

There was tension in it. An ache, perhaps. But also a pull, as if the whole piece was bracing for breath. Almost ready to let go.

Valen came closer and studied the curves, the knots of dark and light, the shapes that seemed to fight and flow at once. "This is what you've been feeling. All twisted up."

Annabelle crossed her arms. She didn't trust her hands to behave.

"But it doesn't feel stuck. It feels like it's about to loosen," he said. "Is that what it is?"

"It's... what I can't say out loud."

Valen turned back to the piece. "You don't have to. Not if this says it for you."

He stood there a while, eyes tracing every thread of color, as though the tension might lead him to the place she'd finally set it down.

Annabelle watched him, caught between pride and fear.

"I want to share it."

"Are you sure? Only if you want—"

"I want to." She cut him off. "No—I need to."

"What you said before... about someone else needing to see it." She hesitated. "It's something I wish I'd had. Back when I was still running from myself. When I didn't know if anyone else ever felt this tangled inside."

Her voice dropped. "Maybe it won't matter to most people. But maybe it'll mean everything to one."

She finally looked up. He was already smiling at her.

"Are you thinking the gallery in town or somewhere else?" he asked.

"I think the gallery. It's a starting point, at least. See how it goes."

"That's a great idea."

"And if they don't like it, maybe it's just not the right place."

Valen slipped an arm around her shoulders, pulling her gently against his side. "Then we'll find the place that is."

He pressed his lips to her temple and stayed there for a few moments.

They headed to bed shortly after, the painting left uncovered, still drying in the corner.

She curled into him beneath the blankets. No more tension in her spine or tightness in her jaw.

Sunlight crept in through the windows as the house below stirred—the low clink of crockery, the thud of wood into the stove.

Annabelle stretched slowly, her limbs warm under the covers.

When she came down, the table was already set.

"Morning," he said. "You look rested."

"I feel it."

They ate quietly, their feet brushing beneath the table every so often.

Afterward, she lingered while he finished rinsing the dishes, folding a dish cloth idly. "Do you have any frames? I want to see it fully. Like it's meant to be."

"I should."

He led her to a small storeroom tucked past the dining room. A few frames hung above a low workbench.

Annabelle considered each of them, stepping back and squinting.

Nothing felt right. The ornate ones tried too hard. The simple ones weren't enough.

"What are you looking for?" he asked as she turned another frame.

"I'll know it when I see it."

Valen took the frame from her, and set it with the others. "Then let's go find the right one."

They left the house a few minutes later, Annabelle cradling the painting in her arms, cloth drawn over it like something fragile but breathing.

She shifted her grip, almost dropping it. Her hands were too dry.

The walk to the market was quiet, their footsteps soft on the packed dirt path.

Town bustled just ahead—carts trundling past, vendors calling out from shaded stalls—but Annabelle barely registered it. Her focus tunneled in on the weight in her arms, the painting wrapped and fragile against her chest.

The frame shop sat just off the square, tucked between a tailor and a restaurant, its windows dusty but welcoming. Painted in curling gold letters on the glass was *The Gilded Edge: Frames of Distinction*.

A bell chimed softly overhead as they entered.

Inside, the air smelled of sawdust and shellac. Long planks leaned in corners beside drying frames. A set of chisels lay across a padded workbench, their handles smudged with varnish.

An older gentleman stood near the counter, busy regilding an ornate frame. He gave them a polite nod. "If you need assistance, you know where to find me," he said, before returning to his work.

A handful of finished frames leaned against the far wall, waiting for portraits that never arrived, or maybe once held them.

Valen held the painting while Annabelle ran her fingers over gilded corners, lacquered finishes, carved scrollwork.

She lingered on the boldest frames, hovering over each flourish.

Then she saw it.

A frame near the back—its woodgrain polished, the knots left visible.

"This one," she said. The wood pricked her thumb as she lifted it.

"Is this the one?"

"It's not perfect. But I like it."

"Sounds familiar."

She smiled.

They carried the frame to a quiet corner of the shop. Annabelle nestled the painting inside, admiring it for a moment. Her fingers rested lightly on the edge, where wood met canvas.

Together, they brought it to the front.

The shopkeeper set down his tools. "Find what you were after?"

"We did. Could you secure it?" she asked, passing it over.

He took it behind the counter and fitted the frame with a sure hand, tapping in a few small nails to keep the canvas steady.

"Interesting piece you've got," he said, inspecting it.

Annabelle handed over the coins and picked up the painting. "Thank you."

The shopkeeper nodded, already returning to his work.

She paused before stepping outside to re-cover it with the cloth. It was thin, but enough to keep it hidden from the world.

For now.

Valen stood beside her as they headed back out. "Did you want to take it there now?"

"Might as well. I think I'm as ready as I'll ever be," she said—though her voice sounded steadier than she felt.

The walk to The Penumbra Gallery wasn't far, but her nerves crept in. Her breath shortened, pulse skittering faster with every step.

She'd walked past it. Peered through the glass. But never crossed the threshold.

Valen held the door for her, and she headed in.

The space stretched wide: open ceilings, tall windows, pale wood floors that echoed with each footfall. Sunlight poured through the skylights, catching on glass, paint, and the occasional shimmer of gilt.

There were landscapes and portraits, abstract smears and perfectly rendered still lifes. Some pieces were sharp and precise. Others looser, wilder. But none of them looked like hers.

It hit all at once: the noise of silence, the echo of her boots, the gallery smell of dust and oil. She froze just inside the door.

He glanced down at her and caught it. The flicker of uncertainty, the too-wide eyes, the breath held a little too long.

She met his eyes.

He gave her a barely-there nod, the kind meant only for her, then approached the desk.

The woman there—middle-aged, bespectacled, with a small mole near her cheekbone that disappeared into a smile—looked up, her smile polite but soft.

"Mr. Eldcroft," she said. "Good to see you again."

"Likewise, Ms. Voss," he replied. "When we spoke last week, you mentioned there might be a guest spot opening soon."

"One opened up earlier this week." She glanced at Annabelle. "This must be the artist?"

"Yes, she is," Valen said, stepping aside.

Ms. Voss adjusted her glasses, then smiled at Annabelle. "A pleasure to meet you. I'm the gallery manager. I'd love to see it."

Annabelle's fingers stayed locked around the frame, her weight balanced too tightly on the balls of her feet, like bracing for flight.

Then she nodded. And slowly pulled the cloth away.

She held it out, unsure whether to turn it upright or let her take it. But Ms. Voss came forward, hands clasped behind her back, and simply looked.

She studied it for a full minute, gaze roaming the curves and color, the depth and stillness, the tension humming just beneath the painted surface.

"This is lovely," she said.

"Oh." Annabelle blinked. That was all she could manage.

"Come on," Ms. Voss added, already rounding the desk. "Let's find it a home."

She beckoned with a motion that was casual and practiced. As if this happened every day.

People brought pieces of themselves here all the time. They bared something raw, and the world didn't collapse. It simply... made room.

Ms. Voss led them to the far side, where a small space waited between two existing pieces—a tightly rendered still life of a woman with a severe expression, and a loose, almost dreamlike field of flowers that seemed to float in and out of itself.

"Here," Ms. Voss said. "This spot should give it some air."

She turned to Annabelle, hand extended gently.

Annabelle looked down at the painting, let out a breath, and passed it over.

Ms. Voss accepted it like it was glass. Carrying it to the wall, she hung it without a fuss.

She wanted to look away. She didn't.

It fit.

Its tension hummed between the flower field and the still life, as if the wall had been waiting for something to balance them.

"Now," Ms. Voss said, stepping back, "we just need the card for it. One moment—I'll be right back."

She disappeared toward the desk.

Annabelle stayed where she was, staring at her painting. It was out there now. Visible. And still standing.

And so was she.

Out in the open, under natural light, surrounded by strangers' brush-strokes: it didn't look out of place.

Valen stepped beside her and gave her hand a quiet squeeze. "I'm so proud of you."

"I'm proud of me too." She said it quietly, as if she was testing the sound of it.

They stood that way for a long while, fingers intertwined, taking it in—not just the painting, but everything it had taken to get it on that wall.

The gallery manager returned with the small cardstock placard and a pencil already in hand. "And the artist's name?"

"Anna..." She corrected herself. "Annabelle Greenwick."

She wasn't going to shrink for anyone anymore. Not even herself.

Ms. Voss nodded, wrote it down. "And the name of the piece?"

Annabelle looked up at the canvas.

"Unraveled," she said.

"Perfect," Ms. Voss said, finishing the card in a neat hand. She slid it into the small slot beneath the frame, where the others were labeled, then stepped back for a final glance.

"We're having an open house Thursday evening," she added, almost offhandedly. "Nothing fancy. Just a few regulars and a little wine. People love meeting the artists."

Annabelle blinked. "I—thank you. I'll consider it."

"No pressure," Ms. Voss said with a small smile. "But we'd love to have you."

They walked home slower this time. The canvas was no longer in her hands, but it still weighed on her. Heavier now, but in a different way.

Annabelle kept her eyes on the road, her arm tucked into the crook of Valen's arm.

"That was... less daunting than I'd imagined," she said eventually. "But it also feels real now. Like someone might actually see it."

"They will. And that's a good thing. You already did the brave part."

She gave a small, uneven smile. "Maybe. Or maybe they'll hate it."

"Then they'll move on to the next frame and forget," he said simply. "But if even a single person lingers and feels something—that's enough."

CHAPTER 41

The Promise

Sunlight had just begun to warm the windows when they stepped into the garden, boots brushing the grass before the heat could settle in.

They followed the curve of the stream, the splash of water on stone marking their pace.

Annabelle slowed, eyes on the stream, fingers trailing a nearby leaf. "...I think I want to do the open house. Will you... come with me? Just in case?"

"Of course. But just in case what?"

"I don't know... What if they hate it? What if they laugh?"

"Yes, the terrifying world of wine, critique, and polite nods," he said dryly.

"Exactly. I'll need backup."

"Well, I've got sharp elbows and a mean glare. You'll be safe." Valen nudged her.

She laughed, and he smiled like it was something he'd been waiting to hear all day.

By midday, they spread a blanket in the far corner of the garden, where the hedge opened just enough to let the breeze in.

Valen brought out fruit, cheese, and a still-warm loaf from the kitchen. She painted in her sketchbook between bites. He read aloud from a book he barely pretended to be serious about.

The day stretched long and slow.

"Come with me." He led her inside, the fading sun casting long streaks of light behind them.

They climbed the narrow stairs to the tower room, steps echoing gently underfoot.

Annabelle crossed the room and opened the balcony doors. The air that met them was cool and sweet: sun-warmed stone, summer air, the faint scent of something blooming below.

As she stepped out into the warmth, the breeze caught her hair—like the tail end of a breath held too long.

Valen stood behind her, watching the sunset turn her skin to gold, her dress stirring in the wind.

"You've undone me," he said quietly.

She turned, searching his face.

"Annabelle, I've watched you grow into yourself. I've seen you angry. Afraid. Brave. Brilliant. I've never respected anyone more."

"You're everything I never knew I needed—and nothing I expected," he continued. "You are fire, and kindness, and stubbornness, and grace."

"I love the way you fight for what matters. The way you paint when you're overwhelmed. The way you laugh like you don't care who hears it." He drew a shallow, shaky breath.

"You don't complete me, Annabelle. You make me want more—for myself, for the world. I'd be honored to spend the rest of my life beside you."

He reached into his waistcoat pocket, and there it was: small, silver, and perfectly understated. "Will you marry me?"

Her heart raced ahead of her thoughts. "Valen—I—"

"Yes," she said, breathless. "Yes. Of course."

Not because she was ready to be chosen, but because, for once, she had chosen herself first.

She flung herself into his arms, laughter catching in her throat. He held her close, cradling the back of her neck as he kissed her.

When they finally pulled apart, she rested her forehead against his. "You're the first place I've ever felt safe enough to stay. And I don't want to go anywhere else."

He lifted her fingers the way he had once before—when she wasn't ready. When neither of them were.

"May I?"

She nodded, blinking a little too much, lip caught in a smile that was absolutely not hiding tears.

He slid the ring onto her finger as if the motion itself meant something sacred. And maybe it did.

The weight of it settled in as she stared down at her hand.

His arms wrapped around her waist, backing her into the stone wall. Her fingers threaded through his hair.

"Tell me again," he whispered.

"Yes. Of course I'll marry you," she said, drawing him into another kiss.

The air had gotten cooler, but they didn't notice. He tugged at her dress, she fumbled open his waistcoat.

Somehow her knee bumped the wall mid-shift. She winced, laughed, but didn't let him go.

A gasp slipped from her as his touch found her thigh, hot against her chilled skin, the contrast dizzying.

"I love you," he said, voice low against her throat. "You have no idea how long I've wanted you. Just like this."

"Then come get me," she whispered, pulling him down into the shadows, "before the sun lets us go."

They stumbled to the chaise by the window, old cushions sighing beneath them as they collapsed together in a tangle of half-removed clothes.

Valen laid her back, cupping her face like he still couldn't believe she'd said yes.

She touched his cheek, thumb brushing the stubble along his jaw.

He eased her dress higher, baring skin he already knew by heart.

With careful fingers, she unfastened the last buttons of his shirt and pushed it off his shoulders, her palms skimming over warm skin and muscle.

Her touch slid down, until she found him—hard, already aching for her.

He groaned low in his throat, pressing his mouth to her collarbone. "I don't want to rush this."

"Then don't," she murmured, brushing her lips along his ear. "Just don't stop."

He reached between them, slipping her underthings down and off. Then undressed himself with quiet urgency.

She shifted, welcoming him between her legs. Her arms slid around his shoulders, one leg hooking at his waist.

He slid into her with a slow, shuddering groan. She gasped, her grip tightening on his back.

His rhythm was deep and steady, pulling quiet sounds from her throat with every thrust.

She moaned in answer, tilting her hips to meet him.

The tension built between them like a storm. She was close: he could feel it in the way she clung to him, the stutter in her breathing, gasps slipping from her lips like surrender.

She came with a breathless cry, her whole body tensing beneath him, clutching at his arms.

He followed with a broken groan, mouth hot at her shoulder, hips jolting forward as he came undone.

They stayed there: bodies pressed close, hearts thundering, their exhales mingling between them.

Annabelle brushed a kiss to his cheek. "I think we're in trouble."

"Oh?"

"Once we're married, the townsfolk won't have anything to gossip about."

He gasped. "A tragedy. Doomed to a quiet, scandal-free life."

"Dreadful. I'll miss the attention."

"Don't worry, I'll give you all you could ever want."

She leaned in. "You already have."

Eventually, they got up, gathering their clothes from the floor, bumping into each other and laughing in the dim light.

They hurried through the halls back to their bedroom.

Under the covers, they huddled close. Before long, he was softly snoring beside her.

She shifted, restlessness prickling at the edge of her calm. He pulled her closer, pressing a kiss to her shoulder blade.

Curling into his warmth, she let the worry go slowly.

Her gaze drifted to the ring on her finger, moonlight catching on silver and promise.

Then she let her eyes close.

CHAPTER 42

The Becoming

Annabelle stepped into the gallery, her breath tight in her chest. Evening light caught on the necklace Valen once called *dangerous in the best way*.

She'd chosen the dress days ago. Practiced her hair twice before getting it just right.

Tonight wasn't just a debut. It was a door opening.

The gallery buzzed: glasses clinking, music threading through the walls, conversation floating in the air.

Patrons, artists, and the simply curious wandered from piece to piece, wine in hand.

Annabelle paused in the doorway, steadying her breath.

She wasn't the only one stepping forward—Valen walked beside her, his touch warm at her back.

"There you are," said Ms. Voss, the gallery manager, weaving through a cluster of guests. "Your piece has been the talk of the evening."

Annabelle's surprise flickered, then vanished beneath a smile.

They picked up glasses of wine and moved toward her painting. Valen stayed close, letting her lead.

Four older patrons clustered around it, murmuring in low, fascinated tones.

One woman gestured at the center, tracing an invisible shape in the air. "The colors—vibrant, but not garish. That's hard to pull off."

"Yes, but the turmoil," said a man. "Something's churning under it. You can feel it."

Annabelle stood nearby, heart caught high, listening.

One of them asked, "Do you know where the artist is from? Local, I assume?"

Ms. Voss stepped up and smiled. "Actually, the artist is right here."

"You?" the woman said. "Oh—that's wonderful."

"It's absolutely arresting," said another. "Do you have more?"

"Were you trained?"

"How did you plan the movement?"

The wineglass stem was cool against her fingertips, grounding her as praise washed over her like light.

She waited for the catch—for the tone to shift, the questions to edge toward condescension.

But it didn't. They were genuinely curious.

For a breath, she almost turned away. Then the words found her.

She spoke softly at first, then clearer. Talking about brushes. Color theory. About emotion in abstraction. About knowing when a piece was done, and when to leave it raw.

More guests gathered around her.

Valen stood a few feet off to the side. He met her eyes with a quiet smile, like he'd expected this all along.

She turned back to the growing circle, glowing.

One asked if her work would join the gallery rotation, another invited her to a small exhibition next month.

A second glass found her hand, barely touched before she abandoned it, like the first. Even the idea of wine turned her stomach lately.

A familiar voice reeled her back.

"Well, if it isn't our debut artist," said Mrs. Trell, approaching with a pleased expression and a woman Annabelle half-recognized from the gathering.

"You've made quite the impression," Mrs. Trell added with a knowing smile.

The other woman leaned in, conspiratorial. "So... are congratulations in order yet?"

"Actually, yes. We're engaged." Annabelle beamed.

Mrs. Trell lit up.

The other woman actually gasped. "Truly? Oh, well, that *does* change things, doesn't it?"

"Congratulations, dear. How lovely," Mrs. Trell said, and she meant it.

"Yes, I imagine he must be thrilled," the other added. "You were dazzling tonight."

"Thank you," Annabelle said simply.

Across the gallery, Valen's gaze met hers. She winked—and gave the faintest shrug toward the door.

Outside, the night air hit her like a second wind: cool and bracing, sharp against the thrill of everything still crackling through her limbs.

Annabelle all but bounced down the steps.

"Did you hear them?" she asked, slipping her hand into his. "They were asking if I take commissions. One of them said my work looked like movement and emotion collided. Valen—can you believe that?"

He smiled to himself, the warmth settling in his eyes.

"And Mrs. Trell—did you see her face when I said we were engaged? I thought she might spill her wine."

She laughed again, too loud and too happy to care. As if, for once, the world had stopped asking her to apologize.

"I've never felt so—" She paused, searching for the word. She blinked up at the stars, the night air sharp against her cheek. It didn't feel like dreaming; it felt real.

"So whole. So seen. Like I didn't have to pretend. Like I was finally allowed to just be myself."

He squeezed her hand.

The walk back from the open house was slower than it needed to be.

His fingers slipped beneath her cloak, resting just above her waist. She toyed with the lapels of his jacket, knuckles grazing the bare skin above his collar.

He pressed her into the garden gate and kissed her like it had been weeks since they'd touched.

They barely made it to the side door.

Behind them, the laughter and firelight of the open house faded into memory.

Valen's mouth brushed her ear as he fumbled for the key.

"You should have seen yourself in there."

"Valen—"

"Radiant. Confident. Like you owned the room."

The key turned—she stepped through—and he was already reaching for her.

He kissed her the moment they crossed the threshold, hands at her hips, then sliding lower.

Her fingers tangled in his hair as she kissed him back, like she still hadn't gotten enough of him.

They stumbled down the hall.

Boots kicked off. His coat landed with a thud on the floor. She tossed her gloves toward the table and missed.

She gasped as he lifted her, her legs wrapping instinctively around his waist.

"You don't know what you do to me," he murmured into her neck. "Watching you tonight—I could barely think straight."

She moaned, fingers digging into his arms. "Then stop trying."

He carried her up the stairs like she weighed nothing. He stumbled once on the last step, laughing against her mouth.

Kissing his throat, she undid the first few buttons of his shirt, pulling the fabric off his shoulders. He didn't bother taking it all the way off.

They reached the bedroom. He set her down, hands already undoing the fastenings of her dress.

"You stood in front of all of them," he said, breath ragged. "Let them see you. And you never flinched."

She turned, a shiver sliding down her spine as he undid the last clasp with unsteady precision.

"I wanted you all night," he whispered, kissing the curve of her shoulder, where all those eyes had lingered. "Every time someone looked at you, I wanted to pull you away and take you right there."

She spun to face him, her gaze deepening. "Then take me now."

He didn't need to be asked twice.

They crashed into each other, mouths hot and desperate.

She shoved his shirt off. He slipped her dress down, kissing every inch of skin he revealed.

They were a mess of limbs and breath: backs hitting walls, her laughter breaking against his lips as he caught her mid-step and lifted her again, his trousers already half-undone.

She held his gaze a moment too long—long enough for doubt to creep in. So she kissed him before it could catch up.

He laid her down, mouth tracing her skin, lingering until she squirmed.

Then he slid into her, one hand gripping her thigh, the other braced above her head.

A gasp escaped her, fingers grasping at the sheets.

For a breath, he stayed still, buried deep, forehead pressed to hers. Then he began to move faster, like he was trying to make the night impossible to forget.

She met him every time, her nails dragging down his back, her moans turning breathless and broken.

Release took her with a sudden cry, body clenching around him, head thrown back, lost in sensation.

He followed moments later, groaning her name as he sank into her, nuzzling into her neck. His breath warm and ragged on her skin.

The haze of want faded, leaving them flushed and quiet, minds slowly catching up to their bodies.

"I love you," she whispered after a while.

"I know," he said, kissing her forehead. "I love you, too."

"You were right, by the way," she murmured. "This necklace is dangerous."

"What do you mean?"

"You couldn't keep your hands off me tonight."

"I couldn't keep my eyes off you either."

She kissed his chest. "Clearly I should wear this more often."

"You should. Confidence looks radiant on you."

She curled closer, smiling into his skin.

Outside, the sky had deepened, like the world was finally catching its breath.

It hadn't always been easy; growth never is.

But together—choosing themselves, and each other—that was enough.

EPILOGUE

✦

WHOLE

The Home

The sun dipped behind the treetops, painting the garden gold.

On the porch swing, Annabelle balanced a sketchbook on her belly, a tin of watercolors open beside her. Her brush moved in lazy lines—gesture and memory both.

The children scattered across the yard, elbows flying, laughter rising like smoke.

Near the hedge, Aurelia shrieked with delight as Vincent and Graham tried to ambush her from behind a barrel.

Cecelia toddled past them both, a ribbon clutched in her hand like treasure. Celeste, cross-legged on the ground, attempted to braid a daisy chain and shush the wind.

In the middle of it all, arms wide and roaring dramatically, was Valen.

"Uncle dragon's coming!" he bellowed, lunging in slow, theatrical menace.

The children squealed and scattered.

Annabelle smiled, brush pausing mid-stroke. Grass in his hair, dirt across one cheek. His shirt—white earlier, she was pretty sure—was now stained, crumpled, half-untucked. A mess of effort and joy.

Her husband was nothing like the brooding man who once haunted his own estate. He looked like someone who belonged.

Her mother rocked beside her, tea in hand, eyes on the chaos beyond the hedges.

"He wears them out more than your father ever could," her mother said, smiling into her tea.

Annabelle chuckled. "He loves it."

Her mother reached over and rested a hand on her belly. "And you?"

"I think I finally feel settled."

"Good," her mother said. "You deserve that."

Brushing her palms on her skirt, she stood and raised her voice across the yard. "Children, supper!"

Then, her mother stepped inside as a chorus of groans rose up. One tried to bargain. Another claimed not to be hungry at all.

Valen stood, brushing grass from his trousers with mock exhaustion.

"No dragon ever gets a moment's peace," he muttered, herding the children up the porch steps. His grin tugged sideways, crooked with effort.

Annabelle set her sketchbook aside and pushed to her feet.

"Looks like you had a good time," she said, eyeing his disheveled state.

"I always do."

"You really commit to being the favorite uncle."

"I have a reputation to uphold," he said, brushing dirt from his sleeve. "Even on borrowed ground." His hand found her belly.

Everything took more effort now: sitting, standing, even sleeping. But she didn't mind. Not with him here. Not with this life.

He traced a slow arc beneath her navel. "I can't wait till ours gets here."

His touch lingered.

She leaned into him, letting his arm anchor her, steadier than the porch's creak. "Me neither."

He kissed her, soft at first, then deeper.

Annabelle glanced at him. "I've been thinking about what to name her."

He looked over, curious. "Oh?"

She drew in a slow breath, like it might hold her steady. "Rosalind."

He froze.

She watched him, unblinking. "After your mother."

He stared, stunned, like the name had knocked something loose in him. "Are you... *really*?"

"Of course," she murmured. "You loved her. She meant so much to you."

Her fingers threaded through his. "It would be a beautiful way to keep her with us."

His mouth parted, but no words came. Just the quiet blink of someone whose eyes had started to sting.

After a pause, he swallowed hard. "She would've loved this," he said softly. "Loved you."

He pulled her close, burying his face in her hair.

Arms tight around him, she rested her cheek to his chest, steady with the beat beneath.

Then Valen eased back, one hand guiding her chin up until their foreheads met. His lips brushed hers. "Oh, wait. I felt her kick."

Annabelle leaned in closer. "That's Rosalind for you. She's been kicking all day."

He smiled, a quiet thing, like a man who'd finally found where he belonged.

She felt full—not the grand, sweeping kind, but something small and steady. Like warm hands over a child's kick. Like dinner in the oven.

They stayed like that for a while, the sounds of the family drifting from inside, the scent of bread and herbs winding its way through the open windows.

From the kitchen, Cecilia shrieked; Aurelia giggled close at her heels. Baby Everett let out a triumphant shout at nothing in particular.

"Come on," Annabelle said. "Let's go in before they eat all the rolls."

Valen groaned. "Not the rolls."

She deadpanned, "Unforgivable."

He held the door as they stepped into the warmth: the glow, the clatter, the noise of family.

Outside, the sky deepened, colors softening from gold to violet to blue, wrapping the porch in dusk. On the swing, her sketchbook waited open: page wet, lines unfinished, holding the last light like breath.

Sneak Peek: The Threadbound Order

COMING 2026

If you enjoyed the tension, longing, and emotional stakes in *Never Just Enough*, you might like where I'm headed next.

---◆---

The Threadbound Order

She sees what others can't. She pulls what no one should.

And she's the only one who hasn't vanished—yet.

Emeline Vellace sees shimmering threads of possibility winding through every choice. She thought everyone could. That she was just bad at using them. That her failures in a world of magical precision—crafted, shaped, fractured—were hers alone.

Until someone finally notices.

When a charming stranger with too many questions enters her life, Emeline thinks she's being seen. Understood. Maybe even wanted. The pull between them is immediate—and impossible to trust.

But interest is rarely innocent—and not all threads lead where you hope. Some even burn.

The Threadbound Order begins with a tale of quiet power, dangerous longing, and the people we cling to—especially when we know it will ruin us.

Spice Guide

This novel includes scenes of emotional and physical intimacy as part of the characters' growth. These moments are woven into the story with care and intention.

These chapters contain on-page, primarily open-door sexual content:

- Chapter 8: The Embers
- Chapter 9: The Crescendo
- Chapter 10: The Steam
- Chapter 12: The Chase
- Chapter 17: The Mend
- Chapter 18: The Warmth
- Chapter 20: The Edge
- Chapter 29: The Unraveling
- Chapter 31: The Belonging
- Chapter 32: The Desire
- Chapter 36: The Offering
- Chapter 38: The Invitation
- Chapter 41: The Promise
- Chapter 42: The Becoming

Acknowledgments

This story came out of nowhere—or maybe it had been waiting all along. I didn't know what I was writing until it was already on the page. Only afterward did I realize how personal it was, and how much I'd needed to tell it.

To my husband: thank you for years of quiet encouragement, for giving me the kind of steady love I once thought only existed in fiction, and for never once making me feel like I had to earn your belief in me.

To the friends and early readers: thank you for your openness, your curiosity, and your kindness. You helped me feel safe enough to share this part of me.

To anyone reading now: my greatest hope is that you found something you needed in these pages. Maybe comfort. Maybe a nudge. Maybe the reminder that peace and steady love are real—and that you are enough, exactly as you are.

—E.V. Thorne

E. V. Thorne

Author's Note

I didn't set out to write something personal—but it turns out I did.

Somewhere between the first words and the last, this story revealed itself as something I needed to write. I only recognized how much of myself had landed on the page when I reached the end.

Annabelle's art gallery arc, in particular, hit closer than I expected. The fear of being seen, of putting something vulnerable into the world—that wasn't just hers. That was mine.

If this book gave you a sense of safety, softness, or simply the feeling that you are enough—I'm so glad. That's all I ever wanted.

About the Author

E. V. Thorne writes emotionally rich romance about safe, stable relationships—the kind she once doubted existed, but now writes from the other side.

With a background in psychology and a soft spot for how people heal, she builds stories shaped by intuition and vulnerability—then refines them until only what matters is left.

When she's not writing, she's usually chasing the whim of a new hobby, tugging on creative threads to see where they lead.

Stay Connected

If you enjoyed this story, I'd be so grateful if you left a review on Amazon or Goodreads.

You can find updates, bonus content, and more at evthorne.com.

www.ingramcontent.com/pod-product-compliance
Lightning Source LLC
Chambersburg PA
CBHW032031120726

47901CB00001BA/167